Dylan Coleman is a Kokatha Aboriginal–Greek woman from the far west coast of South Australia. She has a PhD in creative writing from the University of Adelaide, where she lectures in Indigenous health at the Yaitya Purruna Indigenous Health Unit. Dylan has worked for over twenty years across a range of areas in Aboriginal education, health, land rights, and the arts, with a focus on community engagement and social justice. She lives in Adelaide with her son and they enjoy training together in Brazilian ju jitsu. *Mazin Grace* is her first book. It was shortlisted for the Commonwealth Book Prize and longlisted for the Stella Prize.

T0094924

Mazin Grace

DYLAN COLEMAN

UQP

First published 2012 by University of Queensland Press
PO Box 6042, St Lucia, Queensland 4067 Australia
Reprinted 2012, 2013, 2014, 2016, 2018, 2019

www.uqp.com.au

Cover design by Kirby Armstrong
Cover photographs © Getty Images; Shutterstock; Lutheran Church of Australia
    Archives: the author's mother, Mercy ('Grace' in *Mazin Grace*), stands at the
    front; Mercy's mother, Pearl ('Ada'), holds daughter Margaret ('Sarah');
    Pearl's younger sister, Millie Starri (nee Coleman), stands on Pearl's right.
Typeset in 11.25/14 pt Bembo by Post Pre-press group, Brisbane
Printed in Australia by McPherson's Printing Group

National Library of Australia cataloguing-in-publication data
is available at http://catalogue.nla.gov.au/

Mazin Grace / Dylan Coleman
ISBN: 978 0 7022 4934 1 (pbk)
             978 0 7022 4868 9 (pdf)
             978 0 7022 4869 6 (epub)
             978 0 7022 4870 2 (kindle)

University of Queensland Press uses papers that are natural, renewable
and recyclable products made from wood grown in well-managed forests.
The logging and manufacturing processes conform to the environmental
regulations of the country of origin.

I dedicate this book to truth, justice, love and freedom.
To my mum, Mercy, for your guidance.
To my nana Pearl, for your strength of spirit.
To Aaron for his support. To my son Wunna for all things of substance in my life.
And to Fub, for your courage.

Contents

Glossary

These Kokatha language words are based on Mercy Glaston-bury's pronunciation at the time of recording and writing her story. Mercy Glastonbury is the author's mother.

biggy ngunchu	pig
bilgi	dirty
blanketie	blanket
boi	expression for a word similar to 'show off'
booba	dog
boogardi	shoes
boongada	bad smell/bad smelling
boonie	horse
boonri	boss
boonri boonri	very bossy person
boonu	edible paste made of flour and water
boorar	wild peach
bugadee	filthy dirty
bullocky cow/bull	a white man who gives things, often alcohol, to an Aboriginal woman
bultha	clothes
bulya	good

bunda	money or stone/rock
bunna	goanna
burru	meat
buyu	cigarette
diggled	burnt to a crisp
djita	bird
djuda	stomach
djudayulbi	someone who eats too much
djuding	men's heavy hitting stick
djugu	pants
dudbin	down/going down
duthu	underpants
garnga	crow
gibara	wild turkey
gidja	child
gidjida mooga	children (gidjida = child, mooga = plural, more than one)
goojarb	'serves yourself right'
goola goola	sexual/interested in sex
gooloo	head lice
goomboo	urine
goomboo minyi	someone who urinates a lot
goomboo wally	toilet
goona	faeces
goona mumpun	bum
goonanyigidi	naked/naked bum
goona oona	dirty bum
gorn	expression: 'go on'
gu	to belong to/belonging to
gubarlie	old woman
gubby	water or an alcoholic drink
gubbydja	drunk
gubbyngarl	to drink
gudadee	teeth
guddadu	heart
gudji	wooden spear
gudle	hole
gugga	head
gugga bunda	bald head
gugga uru	hair on head

gujgi	spear
gulda	sleepy lizard
gulda marra	crabs
guldi	ghost
guling	baby
gumberdy	awry, ugly or unsightly
gunja	beard
guru	eye
guru mooga	eyes
guru wada	glasses (eye things)
imbarda	shame
imin	tabu
indie	isn't it so?/yes it is
ingan	play
jibin	stick
jidla	daggy
jinardoo	Nyunga person who can perform magic
jinditji	a bush found on the far west coast of South Australia
jindu	sun
jindu duthbin	sun going down
jinga	death, die, died
jinjie	backside
jinjie wongera	arse about face (back to front or mixed up)
jinka	cart
jinna	feet
jinna nigardi	bare feet
joobardi	silly, stupid or idiot
jooju	song
jooju ingin	playing, song or singing
jookie jookie	chook/chicken
joongu joongu	yams
joonie thuda	pregnant
jubu	side of the hip
jumoo	grandfather
kuka	meat
mai	food
malu	kangaroo

manardu	big
mimmi	breast
minga	sick/sickness
minya	small
minyardu	cold
moodigee	car
mooga	plural, more than one
moogada	angry
moolya	nose
moolya bilgy	dirty nose
moona	hat
mudgie	boyfriend or girlfriend
mudgie mudgie	to act interested in someone as a girlfriend or boyfriend
muggah	no
mummatja	father
mumoo	bad spirit
munda	ground
munyadi	throat
murdi	back
muroo	black
murra	hand
murra bidi	fingernail
ngoonji	lie
ngoonji bula	that's a lie
ngoonyin	sweet edible berry
ngudgie	covetous, envious
nguggil	armpit odour
ngulu	scared
ngulya	forehead
nigardi	naked
nunkerie	healer/medicine person
nyarni	sheep
nyindi	know
nyimi	lips
nyumu mai	mussels
Nyunga	Aboriginal person
Nyunga mooga	Aboriginal people
oorlah	boy
rabbity	rabbit

tharldu-bula	true as true
Tjidpa	name given to Superintendent
tjilbi	old man
tjilga	prickle
tjunu	snake
ungu	sleep
wada	thing
wada mooga	things
wadi	initiated man
wadu	wombat
wah	face
walaba	white (woman)
walaba goona muroo	white woman with a black arse
walbiya	white (man)
walbiya gu gidjida mooga	white man's children
walbiya gu minga	white man's sickness
walbiya mooga	white people
walga	wild tomato
wanna	ocean
wanna mai	sea food
weena	woman
weena mooga	women
wiyardtha	mother
womoo	fluffy white edible substance found on mallee tree leaves
wonga	talk/language
wongan	talk
wonganyi	speaking
wultja	eagle or policeman
wunyi	girl
wurly wurly	whirlwind
wuthoo	makeshift shelter
yudda	mouth
yudoo	good
yumbra	blowfly
yuree	ears
yuree bamba	no ears/not listening
yureeminga	earache

1

Minya wunyi wonganyi

My name is Grace. Grace Dawn. That's 'cause I was born just as the jindu came up over our Kokatha country on Koonibba Mission. Papa Neddy gave me my name. Said if it's good enough for Superintendent to call 'is girls Charity and Hope, it was good enough for me to 'ave a Bible name too. Mumma Jenna said she brought me into the world a year before that big war finished, just over a year after my sister Eva was born.

Ada, my mother, was my sister 'til I was about five years old. For Eva it was a bit older, before we knew the truth. Still call 'er Ada now, outa habit I s'pose. Can't say when I first knew that Papa Neddy and Mumma Jenna weren't really my parents but my grandparents, and that my big sisters were really my mothers, or 'aunties', as whitefellas call 'em. It was more of a slow thing, like a ringworm. A minya faint circle on your skin, then itchin'. Could be mozzie bite, but before you know it, it's full grown and there's no mistakin'. It was kinda like that.

We got a big family, though, lotsa mothers and fathers, sisters and brothers. We all live in a little cottage on the Mission. There's lotsa cottages just like ours that other Nyunga families live in too. But not the Mission workers – Superintendent, Pastor, Nurse, Teacher. All them mob, they live in flash houses or nice rooms, not like ours. They different from us. They look at things different-way, funny-way. I reckon they see things mixed-up-way, sometimes. They don't understand our ways.

Big mob of family live in our cottage. There's Ada, me and my sisters – Eva, Sarah and Lily. Eva's my big sister, we always fightin' but we really close, too. Sarah was born when I was minya wunyi, only three. She the quiet one. I always look out for 'er 'cause she a softie and gets hurt sometimes. Lily, come next, she 'The Lily of the Valley', like in the song, or most of the time we call 'er Lil-Lil, like minya, 'cause she little girl. We sleep together on one big bed in our bedroom that's at the back part of our cottage. Then, there's Uncle Murdi, 'is other name, Malcolm.

Sometimes, us Nyunga mooga got couple of names – our Nyunga name, and the name we christened with in the church on the Mission. Not everyone has Nyunga names, depends if you given one or not, mostly by the old fellas or family. Nyunga-way, Uncle Murdi's Ada's brother. All my uncles are my fathers and all my aunties are my mothers. Uncle Murdi's wife Soossy, 'er other name Suzie. They got a baby, Matthew. Yudu, that's Uncle Murdi's dog, a blue heeler, real clever dog. 'Is name mean 'real nice lookin'' in our language, 'cause he's a nice lookin' booba. All them mob sleep in the kitchen in our minya cottage. Then, there's Uncle Jerry, 'is other name Jeremiah. He Ada's other brother. He's married to Aunty Ruthie. Their kids, Harry, Mona and baby Jeremiah. They had 'nother minya baby that passed away. She's in heaven with God and 'is son Jesus, now. That baby's jinga, so we don't say 'er name no more, so we don't call 'er spirit back to us. That's Nyunga-way. Uncle Jerry's family sleep in the bedroom at the front with Uncle Wadu's family. 'Is other name Wallace, 'nother brother of Ada's. 'Is family, Aunty Nora and their kids Polly, Sandy, and Joshua or Joshy. They my sisters and brother too. All them kids my sisters and brothers Nyunga-way, they what whitefellas call 'cousins'.

Ada's got other sisters too, Margaret or Maggie, and Rose, but they don't live on the Mission, they live at Mount Faith. Aunty Maggie kids, Andy, Hope, Julie, Marie and baby Joan. Aunty Rose's got a minya daughter Dee-Dee Doe, and Aunty Dorrie looks after 'er here on the Mission sometimes. Dee-Dee's my bestest friend. We the same age and stick together like yumbra mooga stuck in honey. Mumma Jenna say, 'Real sweet how they play together, like minya twins.'

Ada's sister, Ester or Essie, she with Uncle Adrian or Ardi, and their kids, Adrian and baby Julianne or Jilly. They sleep in one room with one big double bed, one single bed, and a cot. Sometimes, they share that room with Ada's other sisters, Dorrie (Dorothy), Mim (Magda), Wendy (Gwendalyn) and Molly (May). They're not married, got no mudgie mooga, so they sleep in the single bed, there. Or they just squeeze in anywhere, wherever there's room to sleep. But sometimes they away working for whitefellas, walbiya mob, doin' cleaning, milkin' cows, things like that. Only sometimes they come to stay, except for Molly. She always here, she's big girl, like teenager. I wish she go and work away sometimes too 'cause she always teasin' us kids but she's Mumma Jenna's big baby. She tease us all the time, especially when Mumma's not 'round to growl 'er to stop. All them mob used to share that one room with Papa Neddy and Mumma Jenna, too. They like them minya sardines squashed in there before, us too in our double bed.

But now, Papa Neddy's built 'nother lean-to out the back for 'im and Mumma Jenna. He clever 'cause he a builder. He can build houses and big buildings with bunda mooga. He even built some houses and shops in Ceduna for walbiya mob. He reckons that when he's a young boy he got sent away to learn to build them places. Them walbiya mooga were real cruel to 'im and strict too but now he knows how to build houses 'cause they showed 'im. Papa Neddy's strict too but he's deadly, he takes care of us, all 'is minya granny mooga. If us kids play up, he growl us, might even give us a beltin'. Worst of all, sometimes he crack that whip of 'is if we actin' up naughty-way, 'specially if we dawdlin' to church or runnin' in the rain gettin' wet, 'cause we might get minga. We cut it flat-out-way then, 'cause that whip hurt like hell if it hit us.

We got another name too, it's Oldman. That's our last name. Papa says it came from way over the wanna on a big ship, from Ireland. Two twin brothers, one named Nat gave us 'is name through Granny Dianna, my Kokatha great grandmother, long time ago, when them walbiya mooga started comin' to our country. Granny Dianna had a big strong brother, and he was a very special man Nyunga-way, 'is name mean the same as light from the moon. He taught Papa lotsa things. Papa always told us we 'ave a strong Kokatha bloodline that we must never forget and even though Mumma Jenna is Mirning and that blood runs through us too, we must hold strong to our Kokatha side, Papa's Mumma, Granny Dianna's side and 'er brother, that special one. That's how I've always known, proud-way, that I'm Kokatha. That's what Papa taught us, that's what Granny Dianna and 'er brother Jumoo taught 'im. They always tell us this our munda here and all the way 'round this way, where them rockholes are out that way, then back this way over to them other rockholes, and over that way to the Gawler Ranges, too. Big lot of Kokatha country and we gotta look after it, make sure it stays strong. Granny Dianna even got one rockhole same name as her, 'cause that's our country and she boss woman for all that place.

Even though them cheeky kids at school call us other names, we know we're right Nyunga-way because of Granny Dianna and 'er brother and Papa and Papa's sisters and brothers. Sometimes those kids call us other names like 'Williams' pigs', and 'whitefella kids', walbiya gu gid-jida mooga, and sometimes filthy names too like walaba goona muroo, that mean, white person with a black arse. Those kids got no shame, hey?

But Mumma and Ada and our other mothers tell us, 'Don't take no notice of them. They just snotty-nosed little pigs themselves with no respect, talking like that.'

It's real hard to look at your mother as your mother, when you've never bin sure who she is to you, 'cause you've always called 'er Ada. She even smell different when I lay near 'er in our big old bed and she givin' mimmi milk to Lil-Lil. It's a different smell from when I was minya. That's 'cause I sucked old Mrs Lizzy Dempsey's mimmi when I was a guliny, when Ada run outa milk. That's what Mumma Jenna told me, she say that I had to go to other weena 'cause Ada never had any milk. But I nyindi that old Mrs Dempsey smells right to me, she the one who fed me and help me grow up strong-way. Babies are smart, you know, they don't forget things like that. Even when they grow up to big adult and forget, the baby in them still knows. I nyindi, 'cause when old Mrs Dempsey says, 'Come 'ere girl,' and pulls me into 'er mimmi and gives me big hug, she smells right to me. I know 'er smell and I just want to stay there like that for a long time breathin' 'er in, that same smell from when I was growin' up strong-way from a minya guling. That's one of the best smells ever. That, and malu tail cooking in the campfire after the men come 'ome from huntin', and Mumma bakin' damper in the ashes, and bakin' bread, and cookin' boorar pie in our old wood oven. They the best smells in the whole wide world.

I still go and see old Mrs Dempsey all the time. She live close-way to us on the Mission. She got soft spot for me. Sometimes, I help 'er husband, old Mr Arthur Dempsey, pullin' out the weeds on the paths. That's 'is job. We don't talk much. Don't need to. We just kind of understand what each other thinkin'. That's how it is with me and old Mr Dempsey. That's how it is with a lotta the old fellas. They don't need to talk much with their mouth, 'cause they talkin' other ways. Not like them walbiya mob, they make my yuree hurt the way they go on and on sometimes, 'specially Teacher. There only so much I can put up with in class with Teacher jabberin' on all the time. When I had enough, I just look out the window and think about playin' outside. That's when she slam the ruler on the table and tell me to look at her, look at 'er in the guru, while she talkin' to me. She don't even know that's not right Nyunga-way. You don't go starin' like that, that's shamejob. They might think you want to be mudgie mudgie with them, or that you cheeky, or lookin' for trouble. For someone who meant to know a lot, Teacher sure is dumb sometimes.

But Mr Dempsey, he respectful old man, he talk deadlyway. 'Is smile say the most. With a nod, it says, 'Hello there, girl. Good to see you,' or, 'You done a good job today,' and, 'Well done.' 'Is last smile of the day says, 'I'll see you tomorrow, then,' and it's always real wide and warm and grateful-like. That's my favourite.

But you know, that one old, bushy, grey eyebrow says a lot too. When it goes straight up like that on 'is ngulya, it's askin' me, 'So, you 'ave decided to turn up today, 'ave you?' or 'What you got there, girl?' And sometimes it says, 'Can I help you pull out that big weed?'

When 'is eyebrows squish together and go down over 'is guru, they usually sayin', 'What you diggin' a big hole in the munda like that for? That weed's not a damn mallee root, girl.' And when both them eyebrows go up together and he sticks 'is lips out, this way or that way, he pointin' with them. He wants me to pick somethin' up for 'im here, or he showin' me somethin' over there. 'There's more weeds over that way,' he says by pointin' 'is lips.

Sometimes, if I help old Mr Dempsey all day, every day, he gives me five shillings from 'is pay. That's when I give 'im a big smile and he know what I'm sayin' even though I 'aven't opened my mouth to wongan. He just knows, he nods and smiles back at me with 'is end-of-the-day smile.

I cut it then, flat-out-way, to the shop to buy cake with minya sultanas in them and eat 'em real slow-way, real sly-way, 'cause if my sisters or brothers see me I'll 'ave to give them some and my minya djuda's just too hungry to share. Besides, I bin workin' real hard-way with old Mr Dempsey all week for my minya treat. Sometimes, I force myself to stop eatin' it all at once and hide some cake up inside our fireplace, on the ledge there, for when my djuda's aching for food and sendin' me real joobardi. I 'ave to do it real sly-way, though.

'What you lookin' for up there?' Eva ask.

I jump out from under the fireplace, put my murra up and turn it over as I walk past 'er and cut it, quick-way, out the door. I don't need to tell 'er with my mouth 'cause she knows what I say with my murra. I say, 'Nothin', I'm not lookin' for nothin.' Just as well I didn't 'ave to open my mouth 'cause all them crumbs would fall out, and she'd 'ave known then. Instead, she follow me out the door, and my minya mai stash safe for another day.

Us Nyunga mooga use our hands to talk like that a lot too, you know. We make lotta signs with our murra mooga, our eyes, our lips and the way we turn our head, that all says lotta things. When I move my murra like this, I say, 'Where you goin'?' or 'You 'right?' Papa reckon's usin' 'is murra to talk to the other men when they out huntin' help them catch malu. If they yelled out to each other it frighten the malu away. So if they come 'ome and turn their murra that way, they sayin', 'We got nothin'. We got no malu out huntin' today.' And I always think that's probably 'cause someone couldn't keep their big mouth shut. But when we turn our murra this other way, we're sayin', 'You got food?' or 'You got money?' We can say, 'Someone's comin'', like this, or 'Leave it now,' or 'Later,' like that. But most important thing we do with our murra, most respectful thing, is shake murra with family when someone dies, when they jinga. That's real important. The most respectful thing you can do with your murra. And if you don't, it's very, very, disrespectful. Real cheeky. We taught that when we real young. We taught how to be respectful like that. That's Nyunga-way.

That's another way how we different from walbiya mooga, we talk in other ways. We don't 'ave to 'ave talk goin' on, and on, wonganyi non-stop. Sometimes, we say lotta things quiet-way to each other without opening our mouth and they don't know what we sayin'. We gotta talk like that sometimes, 'cause them walbiya mooga on the Mission won't even let us use Kokatha wonga either. We gotta talk English. We talk our Kokatha wonga loud-way at 'ome but not when they around. At school, if Teacher hears us, she growl and sometimes hit us on the murra with the ruler. So we talk it in whisper. 'Joobardi weena, boonri boonri.' That mean, 'Silly woman, bossy boots.' That's what Teacher is sometimes, that's what us kids call 'er, anyway. Imagine if I said that loud-way in English. Teacher would give me good hidin'. So when we can't talk or even whisper in lingo, 'cause they listenin', we use our murra, and other parts of our body, to talk safe-way.

Sometimes, it's real important to talk to each other without wonganyi, 'specially when welfare mob come. That's when we gotta talk real quiet-way or they might grab us fair-skinned gidjida mooga and we'll never see our family again.

2

If welfare get us, we finished

They got silly ways sometimes, them walbiya mooga, real silly ways. That Sister McFlarety, she's always sniffin' 'round, lookin' to grab us, and sometimes welfare mob from town come snoopin' with her too. When Mission walbiya mooga come and tell everyone to clean up their houses, then we know trouble's comin'. Sometimes, Nyunga wonga goes real fast. The grown-ups call it the West Coast Sentinel, like the newspaper, 'cause it goes round real quick-way and everyone know everyone's business, tharldu-bula! Or we call it the Nyunga Grapevine. It's not a proper grapevine, with grapes, we just call it that when news spreads fast. Sometimes we might hear from other Nyunga mooga on the Mission that welfare's comin' from town. Most the time, our Nyunga Grapevine's faster than that big black car that drives 'round flat-out-way. If we lookin' we can tell when it's comin' from miles 'way. We see them big clouds of dust blowin' up over the mallee trees, over there. We nyindi they comin'.

That's when Mumma Jenna round up us kids quick-way and tell us she takin' us out to get mai, to get joongu joongu, boorar and walga, if they in season, or gulda or rabbity. She take us out the back of Mission, long-way into the scrub. If we lucky we get lotsa proper bush mai then, and our minya djuda mooga real full and content. Sometimes when she take us out like that, we might get back late-way to Mission, when it's startin' to get dark and the welfare mob gone. Sometimes when we come back we hear 'bout kids being put in the Children's 'Ome or taken away and we never see 'em again. It makes everyone real sad. Some Nyunga families never the same again when their minya ones go. They just mope 'round real sad-way.

Mumma Jenna says, 'Losin' ya minya ones leaves a big heavy hole in your guddadu.' That's what it feels like. Then she say, 'As long as the Good Lord gives me breath in my lungs, I'll fight for my kids an' minya grannies not to get taken 'way.'

She reckons we lucky we 'ave the Children's 'Ome here on the Mission or more kids would be taken long-way, and that we lucky again, for bein' able to stay with our own family. We stay at 'ome in our minya cottage with Mumma and Papa and Ada and all our other mothers and fathers and sisters and brothers. Not like them other poor kids who get put in the Children's 'Ome or even worse, get taken long-way away and don't ever get to see their own mob again. One minute you playin' with 'em, and next minute they gone. It makes us kids real sad and angry. Some grown-ups even fight them welfare mob, but welfare always win. Once they got us, that's it, we're finished. We just gotta be real clever and sly to beat them at their own game. That's why we run and hide before they come and steal us.

'Why they want to take us for, Mumma?' I ask one night when we walkin' 'ome through the scrub, jindu duthbin, with all my minya sisters and brothers runnin' 'round Mumma tryin' to keep up, lookin' 'round scared-way, real ngulu, that mumoo or jinardoo might get 'em. Mumoo, them bad spirits. Or jinardoo, that Nyunga who knows magic. Whitefella's name 'boogie-man' but Nyunga-way they real and can hurt you.

'Some of them walbiya mob got funny ways,' Mumma says, Lil-Lil on 'er jubu. 'They must think you kids better off somewhere else.'

'Why?' I ask her. ''Cause we whiter?'

She growl me, tell me to stop askin' 'er questions, she gotta make sure all of us kids get 'ome safely. She yell out loud-way then, check they all there, that mumoo or jinardoo hasn't grabbed one of 'em when she's not lookin', I s'pose.

I just hang my gugga down and walk along quiet-way after that, thinkin', 'Why Mumma growlin' me?'

I can't help what I look like. I can't help it if them welfare mob want to take me away. Welfare mob like mumoo but I'm not scared of no mumoo, not in the dark, not our mumoo anyway.

When Mumma say, 'I thank the Good Lord that he looks over us and protects us, and Jesus keeps us safe,' I look up at the sky and see the moon. I reckon like our old Jumoo, it shine down and protect us at night like God, keepin' us safe from welfare.

Mumma scoop up my hand in 'ers then, and she says, 'You kids safe for 'nother day, girl. That's the main thing.' And I can see 'er teeth shinin' through the moonlight and I know she smilin' 'cause we all together and safe. 'Er smile's all warm, like it's holdin' all us kids in tight, pullin' us into 'er mimmi, like it sayin', 'I will never let them welfare mob grab you. Never in a million years.'

But sometimes we don't always know when welfare comin'.

Like that time, Molly, Mumma's youngest daughter lookin' out the kitchen window and laughin', 'Hey, Grace, your mumma comin' 'ere.'

'Who you talkin' 'bout?' I ask, 'cause I nyindi Ada's 'way all day workin', and Mumma Jenna's out the back.

Molly laughin' real loud-way now. 'Look, your mumma comin' for you, she gonna take you away.'

'Who?' I run to the window and push 'er out the way.

'You know your mumma, Sister McFlarety.' She laughin' at me, teasin' me.

I get real moogada then. 'That old bag, she not my mumma,' I yell at her. 'Welfare,' I scream out warnin' my sisters and brothers, 'welfare comin'.'

Then, I run flat-out-way and slide under the bed in the kitchen. I hear the other kids jinna scatterin' in all directions, just like hide-and-seek but real scared-way. If we get found we lost for good. Then there's a knock at the door. I squash myself up close to the wall. Molly sits in

14

the middle of the bed and the mattress goes right down 'cause it's got broken springs and she's squashin' me. It's lucky I'm only minya six year old and real skinny but it still 'urt. 'Bloody, Molly,' I hiss at her, real moogada-way. My breath real hot and I start sweatin'.

I can hear Mumma walkin' from the back room. She unlatch the front door.

'Hello, Jenna. Is everything all right here?'

She got funny-sounding voice. She talk like she in charge of us like Pastor and Superintendent. I can tell she's lookin' Mumma Jenna right in the eye. This weena's like a mumoo in our house, but a worst kind of mumoo, worse than our Nyunga one. I can see my murra shakin' in front of my face. She could grab us right now and we'd never see Mumma or Papa or Ada or any of our family again. I put my murra mooga over my face 'cause I don't wanna think about it. Why don't she just go away and leave us mob alone? Don't she know she's not welcome 'ere? We wanna stay with our family. She should go steal 'er own mob's kids. What for she want with us minya Nyunga gidjida mooga, anyway? Hasn't she got kids of 'er own?

'Where are the children?' she askin' Mumma.

'They must be out playin', Sister.' Mumma's voice so quiet I can hardly hear her.

'Make sure they are here next time I come.' 'Er voice sounds like Teacher growlin' us to listen.

I feel sick, my djuda's all squirmy. 'Go away, go away,' I'm startin' to scream in my head now.

I think she's walkin' towards the bed, so I peek out from behind my fingers. At least if 'er murra comes down to grab me I can bite 'er real hard-way and make a run for it. I don't know what this weena looks like, properly 'cause I only seen her from long-way or 'er jinna and two fat legs close up, in all the years she bin lookin' for us. But she must be real fat and 'ave jinna minga, 'cause I never seen so much jinna squished into a weena's boogardi like that before. No wonder she's grumpy. 'Er feet probably hurt like hell. She's gettin' close now. I hold my breath. 'Snoopin' old cow. Get outa here.'

Soon the door closes, Molly gets up, and I squeeze out from under the bed and go straight for 'er and give 'er a good kick in the shins, hard as I can. She's screamin' and trying to catch me, but I cut it out the back door, real quick-way.

'That not my mumma,' I yell at her. 'That fat old battle-axe not my mumma.' My eyes stingin' now 'cause my tears real angry ones. Molly's always teasin' us when Mumma not around and she'll give me floggin' if she catches me so I keep runnin' out the back until I know I'm safe. I turn 'round. 'Hey, Molly.' I wait till she listenin' good-way. 'That big fat gubarlie not my mumma. She your mumma, indie? You fat and ugly like 'er. She must be your mumma.' I put my murra on my hip, lean back and let out big loud laughs. 'Ha. Ha. Ha.'

Now the kids come out from hidin' and they laughin' too. I can see Eva shakin' 'er 'ead, big smile on 'er face, and Adrian, Polly and Sandy with murra mooga on mouth, tryin' to stop laughin'.

Next minute, I'm layin' flat-out on the munda with minya stars whirlin' round my gugga. I see Molly's shoe layin' next to me and I 'ear 'er screamin.' 'Don't you be cheeky to me, you little cow.'

All the kids laughin' now. They tryin' to cover their laughin' but minya Sarah's burst out cryin'.

I get up and dust dirt off my dress. My head's hurtin' real bad but I don't want Molly or the other kids to know, so I flick my 'air back over my shoulders, stick my nose in the air, snooty-way, stick my tongue out and walk off. Huffin' under my breath, 'You might be a king-hot-shot with your boogardi, Molly, but you still real ugly.'

'What you say to me, you cheeky little runt? What you say?' She start runnin' for me, then.

'What, you not only ugly, you deaf too?' I yell out with my murra in front of me.

I cut it quick-way round the house before she can catch me. My sisters and brothers runnin' behind me now. They in trouble with Molly too for laughin'. I know I was cheeky to Molly but she shouldn't tease like that. Welfare could grab us kids and take us away for good. Who would Molly 'ave to tease then?

3

Where I belong?

One thing I know for sure, that old Sister McFlarety not my mumma. She too ugly and she got big fat barrel legs and mine real skinny. Molly just goona stirrin' me. But it's hard to look at your mother as your mother when you always called your grandmother 'Mumma'. Even though I kind of knew that Mumma Jenna and Papa Neddy's my grandparents, it's still real confusin' thinkin' about why they say your grandmother your mumma. Ada my real mumma? What about my mummatja?

Eva says it happen that way 'cause of that Commandment Pastor talks 'bout in church on Sundays: 'Thou shalt not commit adultery.'

'What's that mean?' I ask 'er one day. 'You not allowed to grow up to a adult? You 'ave to stay a kid all your life, or what?'

'Don't be stupid,' she says to me, 'er face all screwed up. 'It means you can't be mudgie mudgie with someone else's man or you'll go to hell, with fire and brimstone.' Eva always thinks she know everythin' 'cause she's older, but she's not always right. Anyways, I'm only minya six year old, how I meant to know all these big fancy words?

One day, our mob go over to Williams' farm, near Nelson's Tank, bit further on from Mission, for Papa and the uncles to 'elp Old Rod with 'is fencing – he's walbiya farmer and he real good to us mob. Come reapin' or shearin' time, lotta Nyunga mob go out and 'elp farmers with their crops and sheep. Papa says we should thank the Good Lord and Old Rod for giving our family work on the farm so that we 'ave food in our djuda. Papa and Old Rod, they both tjilbi mooga, one Nyunga, one walbiya. When we campin' at the farm we stay in a minya tin hut near the pigsty, with nice soft sand to sleep on, and a fire in the middle to cook our mai and keep us warm when it gets real minyardu.

Me and Eva there playin' 'round the pigsty, pokin' the big mumma sow with a stick. She squealin' and getting real moogada tryin' to bite us, but we on the other side of the fence and jump back when she go for us. Mumma Jenna yell out for us to leave that biggy ngunchu alone. We sneakin' past the tin hut 'cause Mumma in there with the minya gidjida mooga cookin' stew, and she might tell us off again, and we wanna go play other side of the big farm'ouse.

'Stay 'way from that farm'ouse and leave them walaba weena mooga 'lone,' Mumma always growl us wunyi mooga.

'What's in there, that big 'ouse?' I ask Eva, wipin' my moolya bilgi on my bultha as we get closer to the big shady veranda. 'What's behind that door and them windows with them flash lacy wada mooga hanging up there, so we can't peek inside to see?'

'I don't know,' Eva say, kickin' a minya pebble on the munda then lookin' up again through 'er 'air.

We stand there, lookin', wonderin'. Old Rod live there with Mrs Williams and their two kids. Then, we see a gubarlie stick 'er 'ead 'round the corner of the 'ouse and stare at us. Me and Eva jump back and look at each other. She real scary with 'er minya guru wada mooga on the end of 'er moolya, wah all screwed up like she's lookin' real cross-way at us. 'Er skin's wrinkled like dried out walga. But she don't say nothin', she just starin' at us like she tryin' to work us out.

'She's that scary old lady who comes to stay at the farm sometimes,' I whisper to Eva under my breath.

'Yeah, that's Old Rod's wiyardtha, indie? But she real creepy lookin',' Eva tell me through her closed gudadee.

I grab Eva's murra. We both shakin' but we just stand there frozen-way, too ngulu to move. Don't she know it's shame to stare like that? But she walaba, she don't know much 'bout Nyunga ways. She wearin' a black dress that go down to the munda. She look like that witch Teacher read to us 'bout in them fairy stories at school. Eva musta bin thinkin' the same thing as me, 'cause we both turn 'round same time and cut it, flat-out-way down the track past the trees.

'What that gubarlie lookin' at us like that for?' I ask Eva puffin', leanin' over with my murra mooga on my knees, catchin' my breath.

'She probably lookin' for Old Rod.'

'What she blind or joobardi or somethin'. Can't she see we just minya wunyi mooga, she wanna go over to the back paddock there, if she lookin' for 'im.' I screw up my wah and scratch my gugga, thinkin'. 'What you reckon she wanna boil us up in a big kitchen pot, or roast us in the oven?' I stare at Eva real ngulu-way, my guru mooga nearly poppin' outa my gugga.

'Oh, you real simple,' Eva says shakin' her gugga.

We walk back to the shed, where Mumma's cookin' a stew on the fire, all the minya ones playing 'round 'er in the dirt. Lil-Lil sees us and puts her murra mooga out to be picked up. I grab 'er and give 'er kisses on 'er ngulya. 'We not gonna let no old witch cook you up for dinner, Lil-Lil. No we won't.' I blow a raspberry on her djuda and she giggles.

Sarah come up then, tuggin' at my skirt, 'What old witch, sissy?' she ask ngulu-way.

'No witch,' Eva tell 'er, 'sissy just talkin' joobardi-way.' Eva frowns at me. 'You wanna be up all night with her crying 'cause she scared of old witch?' she growl me under her breath.

That night, with all our djuda mooga full with Mumma's stew, Ada help dig minya bit of dirt out to make nice comfy sand bed for us 'round the fire. She tired too, bin working doin' cleanin' all day. She throw blanketie over me and my sisters and sit down next to the fire. Lil-Lil in Ada's lap suckin' 'er mimmi, minya jinna stickin' out wigglin'. I want to lean over and pretend to bite them, they so cute, but Ada will growl me 'cause she tryin' to get baby to sleep, so I just stay there smilin' at my minya sister. All the grown-ups sittin' round the fire talkin' and laughin'. Uncle Murdi playin' 'is guitar and singin' old cowboy song, with 'is booba Yudu curled up next to 'im; Uncle Jerry and Uncle Wadu on other side with Papa rollin' buyu; Aunty Soossy and Aunty Ruthie sippin' tea outa big pannikins, and Aunty Nora got baby Jeremiah on 'er mimmi, layin' with the other kids, Polly, Sandy and Joshy. They only turned up late today, for more work tomorrow. Aunties Essie, Mim and Wendy back at the Mission but Molly 'ere, she playing with big long stick, pokin' the fire. She might goomboo 'er bed later. That's what Mumma says: 'Gidjida mooga that play with fire goomboo the bed.'

If walbiya mob here now, they wouldn't know what we yarnin' 'bout, cause we talkin' Kokatha lingo. When we by ourselves like this we Kokatha wongan anytime. If we on the Mission, walbiya mob growl us to stop talkin' in our lingo and make us talk English. Why they do that? They probably worried we talkin' 'bout them and don't nyindi what we wonganyi 'bout. So they say, 'Speak English' then they nyindi. But even if they nyindi Kokatha wonga, they wouldn't understand anyway, 'cause they different from us. It's like they gotta know everything and be boonri of everybody, all the time. I don't say nothin' to walbiya, 'cause if I do I get called 'cheeky little girl' and I get told off or flogged.

All the minya ones yawnin' and gettin' real tired now, startin' to go ungu. I close my guru mooga and layin' on the munda all warm next to Eva and Sarah, she got 'er arm over me, touchin' my face.

'What 'bout that bad ol' witch, sissy?' she whisper.

'Sissy look after you, don't be ngulu minya Sarah,' I tell her. 'Sissy chase witch 'way if she come 'ere. You safe now, go ungu, minya, sweet one.' I sing 'er minya lull-a-by. She close 'er guru mooga and go ungu.

Uncle Murdi's put 'is guitar 'way and there's only whispers and fire cracklin' now. I'm tired-way goin' ungu too, thinkin' what Eva said 'bout people bein' mudgie mudgie with someone else's mudgie, and fire and brimstone. Then I feel Ada quiet-way lay Lil-Lil next to me and tuck the blanketie under us. Lil-Lil feel soft and warm and I breathe 'er minya guling smell in my moolya but I still pretend I'm sleepin'. Then I hear car engine, and peek with one guru minya bit open. Ada walkin' outa the hut, and minya while after, car drivin' 'way. Where she goin'?

Later, I wake up when I hear car drivin' 'way again. It's real minyardu now and I can 'ear old rooster in the chook shed cock-a-doodle-doo-in'. Ada stokes up the coals, gets shovel and digs a hole next to me, then she shovels some coals into the hole and covers them up with munda. She go back to the fire and puts more wood on to keep it goin'. She lay down then in the soft warm sand and pick up Lil-Lil and put 'er on 'er mimmi and pull the blanketie over 'em. Lil-Lil snuggles into Ada's mimmi and Ada goes ungu. I snuggle into 'er too, she smell like gubby, ngug-gil and 'nother funny sweaty smell. Then I start thinkin', 'Who she bin with? Someone else's mudgie? Will she burn in hell with fire and brimstone like Pastor's talk 'bout the Ten Commandments and adultery?' No, the thought of Ada burnin' up with gugga uru all diggled, and smellin' like malu cooking on the campfire sound like lies to me. Ada a good weena, she try to look after us kids best she can. She growl us sometimes, but she always make sure we 'right and when she can't Mumma Jenna's there to look after us. No, Eva wrong, she don't know nothin'.

Next day, I tell 'er straight, 'You talkin' joobardi, Eva.'

She leanin' against the tin hut in the shade yarnin' with Polly and I can see 'er murra mooga goin' into fists. She's gettin' moogada with me. I cross my arms and squash my eyebrows together.

'Ada's not goin' to hell,' I tell her.

'I never said she was,' Eva yells back.

She moogada too now, she jump forward, and push me, and we into it then, pullin' 'air and screamin'. And my no-shame minya mouth swearin' loud-way, too. Can't stop once Eva get me moogada like that.

'You so stupid, Grace. Trying to get me in trouble again,' she yell. Then, she head for the moog tree near the farm'ouse. That's where we go when we moogada.

'God's not stupid,' I yell out after her.

She just throw 'er murra mooga up in the air and keep walkin'.

No. God's not stupid. He's smart. Mumma Jenna says he won't send us any troubles too big we can't put up with.

But sometimes, I think he sends us things that don't make sense, that we 'ave to find out for ourselves, like them Ten Commandments. God give us brains to figure them out, one by one, like riddles. I like riddles 'cause I'm good at workin' 'em out. Teacher give us riddles in class sometimes and I just deadly-way drill them other kids at school with the answer. Sometimes it takes long time, thinkin' 'bout it all the way 'round, but sooner or later, I always get 'em right.

I know where I fit in my family until I come to that place where my father should be. It's like one big riddle, mix my head up, and I can't work it out. Who's my mummatja? Sometimes, people ask me that, they say, 'Who's your father?'

I say, 'I don't know.'

'What, you illegitimate?' they say.

I don't know what that big word means, so I don't say nothin'.

'You must be bastard-kid then,' they say.

Then, I start kickin' and punchin' or swearin' at 'em, 'cause I don't like 'em callin' me that nasty word. I don't know what that means either, but I know it's not a nice word.

Who's who?

Who's my mumma? I used to ask myself that. I know that now. Ada's my mumma and I got lots of other mothers too – all Ada's sisters. Mumma Jenna's not really my mumma, she my granny. I nyindi that too, now. I got lotsa other grannies – grandmothers and grandfathers, too. Papa Neddy say that's Nyunga-way to 'ave big families, that's how we look after each other. He sit me on 'is lap and say, 'Girl, you a child of God and you got lotsa mothers and fathers that care for you. You don't need nothin' else but God's grace and you already got that too, with a name to prove it.'

'But Papa, who's my father?'

'Quiet now, Grace. Your father is the Lord God in Heaven.'

4

Secret-pretty-things

All the work finished on Williams' farm and the next
week we back in our minya cottage on the Mission. In the
mornin', us kids wake up and gotta get ready for school.
Ada usually feeds the minya ones, Sarah and Lil-Lil, while
Mumma and Molly get feed ready for Eva, me, Polly, Joshy,
Mona and all the other kids, if we got food. This week we
'ave 'cause all the grown-ups bin workin' on the farm.

'Get up, go wash your face and 'ave breakfast,' Ada tell
us.

We don't need to get dressed 'cause we already wearin'
clothes from yesterday. Us bigger girls get up one after
the other, rubbin' our guru mooga tired-way, go over to
the corner of the kitchen to the wash bowl with Velvet
soap on the side there, and we give our face a splash or
two. In the mornin' the water's always see-through but

by night-time it's a brown colour. Everyone use that same bowl to wash in, kids and grown-ups. We don't 'ave a flash bath tub like Superintendent and the other walbiya mob on the Mission.

Other than a tin one that the grown-ups use to clean the wadu mooga, we just got this one minya bowl and cloth and Velvet soap. Ada tell me 'bout the bath tubs she's seen cleanin' walbiya houses. Sometimes, I wonder what it'd be like to lie in a big bath of warm water with lotsa fancy smellin' soap and bubbles and stretch out. I s'pose I'd 'ave to be careful not to drown. Then, after we wash our face, we eat breakfast, if we got mai – piece of damper or Mumma's bread with drippin', or jam if we lucky. If we don't 'ave any mai we just go to school with our minya djudas growlin' hungry-way.

When it's time to go to school my sisters and brothers cut it out the door but I always stay behind. Sometimes, I sit on the bed in the kitchen where Molly squished my head that time when that ugly old Sister McFlarety come snoopin'.

Once all the kids gone, Mumma say, 'Come on, girl. Get to school too, now.'

'No. Not yet, Mumma,' I always say in my sweet voice. 'I just wanna listen to this song on the radio first.'

Papa's radio sittin' on the kitchen table there in front of me, with the music comin' out of its big material mouth. The buttons look like minya guru mooga lookin' back at me and even the top looks like an old-fashioned moona comin' down over its yuree. I love listenin' to the music hour, *Yours for the Askin'*, with that tjilbi with the flashy soundin' voice. I always laugh when I imagine 'is voice belongin' to Papa's radio. As if Papa's old radio would talk like that if it had a voice. It would most probably use Kokatha wonga, like us.

I love that radio program so much 'cause anyone can write a letter and request their favourite song like, 'Jimmy Crack Corn' and 'Danny Boy'. Lotsa deadly songs like that. I reckon even I could make a request if I had envelope and stamp. But where am I gonna get enough bunda to buy those wada mooga? Superintendent must 'ave them things 'cause he probably writes to welfare and tell them when to come and check on us. Us kids don't like Superintendent, we call 'im cheeky name, 'Tjidpa' behind 'is back. But he not gonna let me use 'is writin' things, 'specially if I'm meant to be at school.

Can you imagine it?

Knock. Knock.

Superintendent opens 'is office door, looks down at me, moves 'is guru wada on 'is moolya and 'is ngulya goes all wrinkly.

'Grace. What are you doing here? You should be at school.'

'Yes, Mr Tjidpa, I mean, Superintendent, Sir. But I wish to use your desk for a moment so I can write a letter, and ah . . . one-of-ya stamps too, if you please, Sir.'

'Is face'd go all red then, and he'd huff and puff like that big bad wolf in them stories at school. 'What?' he'd yell real confused-way. 'Get to school, now.'

'I'm talkin' 'bout *Yours for the Askin'*, Sir', and 'Jimmy Crack Corn'.'

Ha. Ha. Nahh. I'm only ngoonji bula. Tjidpa'd give me

a good floggin' and yank me to school by my yuree. But sometimes it's good fun thinkin' 'bout what I might say to 'im.

Sometimes, someone requests my favourite song, then I put my yuree to the radio and listen close-way with my guru mooga closed and sing along real loud. I learn them songs by heart and sing with Uncle Murdi when he play 'is guitar. Uncle Murdi reckons I can hold a tune. I s'pose that means how I can sing a song over and over, without stoppin', like I do on the way to school after I listen to *Yours for the Askin'*.

It's like that music carry me up, up and away into 'nother place. It feels so good that I don't wanna come back 'cause if I do I know I gotta go to school and face Teacher and Headmaster who will be real moogada with me for gettin' to school late. But sooner or later I know I gotta come back down again from that nice feelin'. So when the program finishes, I run off out the door. The other kids have left long time ago 'cause they don't wanna get the strap for being late.

Even though I try to sneak into class real quiet-way it never works. And sure enough, Teacher not too 'appy when I get to school late again.

'Grace Oldman,' she screeches. 'Come here *now*.' 'Er voice sounds like a garnga. 'Why are you late?'

I shrug my shoulders 'cause one of them Commandments say, 'Thou shalt not lie.' So if I don't say nothin' I'm not lying and I'm not breakin' God's rules. She point 'er finger to the other classroom and send me next door, where Headmaster teachin' the older kids.

Headmaster goes to 'is desk and take that dumb strap outa the drawer and walk back to me. Stupid boy called

'Arold sitting at the back of the class with a big smile on 'is ugly wah. If Headmaster's not lookin' I screw my face up at 'Arold when I turn 'round.

I hold out my murra. It's shakin' but not as much as Headmaster. I can tell he don't like givin' me the strap, I think it hurts 'im more than me. He always looks real sad when he see me, like 'is wrinkly face is sayin', 'Oh, no Grace, not again. This is going to be very painful, for me. You know that, don't you?'

Then I feel sorry for 'im, 'til he whack me.

It hurts like hell but it's worth it. I'd get the strap on my murra with all of Headmaster's strength any day if I can listen to *Yours for the Askin'*, if I can sing and go flyin' off to that special place. It's the deadliest thing ever 'cause I don't 'ave to worry about nothin' when I'm there.

When I meet Dee-Dee Doe in the playground at lunch time we go play on the swings.

'Hey, Dee-Dee Doe what ya doin?' I yell out to 'er when I see 'er.

'Talkin' to you, Gracie Oldman,' she say in her sweet minya djita voice and runnin' over to me. 'What ya know?'

'I know lots. What about you?'

'I know I know you.'

We both laugh.

'What don't you know, Dee-Dee Doe?' I jooju ingin as I swing.

'I don't know? How long's a piece of string?'

She laughs more and I laugh too but then I think 'bout what I don't know.

'Dee-Dee,' I say, slowing down my swing.

'What Grace?' she ask, slowin' down hers too, lookin' at me with 'er big brown eyes.

'Can you keep a secret?'

'Yeah, course I can. You know I can, Gracie, 'specially for you.' She put her jinna down on the munda and 'er swing twists 'round.

'Do you know who my dad is?'

'Your dad is Papa Neddy, your mum, Mumma Jenna, indie?'

'No, Dee-Dee, they our grannies. My mumma's Ada.'

'Oh, yeah, that's right.' Dee-Dee hits the front of 'er gugga with 'er murra. 'Aunty Ada your mumma.'

'So who's my mummatja, Dee-Dee, do you know?'

The swing stops now and Dee-Dee is leaning right over to me. 'No,' she says in a loud whisper. 'Tell me, Gracie. Tell me who.'

'Well, Dee-Dee Doe, to tell you the truth, I don't know either and that's the big secret that everyone's bin keepin' from me – and I wanna know.'

'Well, that's a pretty big secret,' says Dee-Dee with her murra on her chin like she thinkin' real hard 'bout it.

'Yeah, and I'm gonna work it out like Teacher's riddles.'

'Oh, Gracie, that's a deadly idea.' Dee-Dee jumps off the swing and starts dancin' round. Then she stops in front of me and takes in a big breath, claspin' her hands in front of her. 'I can keep a secret, can I 'elp you?'

'I don't know, I reckon I gotta look for clues at 'ome

mostly but maybe you can keep your guru mooga open for me too.'

'Oh, yes. Gracie, I will, I will. But if you find out first can you tell me?'

'Dee-Dee Doe, if I find out you'll be the first one to know.'

She hugs me then and we go off to play in the sandpit.

I know 'bout keepin' secrets 'cause I share them with some of my sisters and friends. It's our 'secret-pretty-things' that no-one knows 'bout, only us girls – me, Eva, Polly, Mona, Dee-Dee Doe, Dora Clare and sometimes other girls. Dora Clare's mumma's Hetty Clare. Dora's real nice when she plays with me even though 'er mumma curses our family all the time. We play nice-way at school together and even deadlier when we at 'ome out back or in the scrub near our cottage. We play other things together too, like makin' minya dollies with Mumma's wooden pegs. We paint sad or smiley face and bunch up old material from rags, tie them around their necks to make sweet minya bultha mooga for them. We make them look real pretty, them dollies.

'Look, she's nigardi.' Dee-Dee Doe giggles 'bout 'er peg dolly with dots for eyes, crooked smile and no clothes on.

We all laugh.

'Quick then, Dee-Dee,' I tell her, 'you better put bultha on 'er before Pastor see 'er nigardi and she get in trouble.'

We all giggle again at the thought of us goin' to church on Sunday with Dee-Dee's nigardi dolly and Pastor yellin' from up the front to the church, 'Peg Dolly, you sinner. Put clothes on now.'

Sometimes, we play House.

'I'm the mumma,' I say, 'and Dora, you the daughter.'

On some days we argue 'til we decide to take turns. Then we play Doctors and Nurses. We always 'ave good fun playin' together.

Sometimes, in the evenin', especially when the jindu duthbin, all the kids in our family go down to the tennis courts by the school and play brandy and 'Who's Afraid of Mr Wolf'? It's deadly fun on those nights 'cause everyone playin' together. No one sayin', 'You can't play with us, you whitefella kid.' That's 'cause we all family and we all look after each other. When kids be mean like that I just try to stick to my sisters and brothers and friends, people I feel safe with, so I don't get teased. My older sisters and brothers always tell me not to worry 'bout them idiots, 'cause they don't know any better.

My very special friends and sisters Eva, Polly, Dee-Dee, Dora, Ruby Downs, Janie Burns and sometimes others, we play together and share our secret-pretty-things. We don't share them with just anyone, only our very close friends that we trust. We make treasures together and bury them in secret places. They special. We dig a hole and put in pretty coloured paper, pieces of different coloured glass and maybe special rocks or leaves, things that mean something to us. Then, when we ready to go we cover the 'ole over again. We might put minya stone or branch on top so we know where it is. That's our special hidin' place that no-one else knows 'bout. When we ready to go we spit on our murra and shake, our spit oath that means we won't tell a soul 'bout our secret. When we come back later lookin' for our secret-pretty-things, we real careful-way sweep away the munda. Yeah, sure 'nough, our treasure will still be there. We feel real important when we see it's safe, 'cause no-one in the whole wide world knows 'bout our minya secret, only us. Not those nasty kids that call me names and make me feel wild, or sad or hateful. Not them adults that say mean things about our family. Not the Mission workers like Teacher, and especially not those walbiya mooga in town who pretend we're not there, or whisper 'bout us rude-way when we go past.

It's deadly to play with our secret-pretty-things 'cause they make me feel real good, strong inside myself, like I can put all the special things about me in that minya hole and in the munda and no-one can touch them. No-one can hurt me either 'cause only me and my sisters and friends know 'bout where that special place is and no-one gonna dig it up and make fun of it, or wreck it.

Today me and Dee-Dee Doe gonna bury our little special secret in the munda. We get some leaves, stones and a pretty dead butterfly, put them together and dig a hole in the sandpit and bury them. Then we spit oath to keep our secret to ourselves, and smile and nod 'cause when I work out who's my mummatja Dee-Dee Doe will be the first one to know.

5

Lookin' for answers

When you tryin' to work out a riddle that Teacher writes up on the blackboard, you gotta look at it all the way 'round and ask lotta questions 'til you get an answer that fits. Sometimes you get to a dead end. That means you can't go that way any more, and you gotta go back and look for 'nother way to go, 'nother question to ask or 'nother way of lookin' at it. Best place to start is right there, at the beginnin'. When I look back to the start, I see Ada.

So when I get 'ome from school one day I look for Ada, and see 'er out the back takin' the washin' off the line with Molly. I go up to 'er and ask 'er straight-out-way, 'Ada, who my mummatja?'

'Grace, don't be such a cheeky minya wunyi, talkin' to me like that.'

'I just wanna know who he is,' I yell.

She slap me then, and tell me to mind my own business. I run 'round the side of the 'ouse, 'cause I don't want Molly to see me cryin'.

'I know who your father is,' Molly says to me as she comes 'round the corner after me.

I turn 'way and sly-way wipe my tears.

'Your mummatja Mr Dempsey, that's why you had mimmi from 'is wife when you guling, and that's why he pay you to work with 'im pullin' up weeds.'

I look up, thinkin' 'bout what Molly's sayin'. Could it be true?

Molly wongan more. 'You really their daughter . . .'

I look at Molly. She sounds like she's tellin' the truth.

'. . . but they couldn't stand to live with you 'cause you such a nuisance, so they gave you 'way.'

My ngulya screws up then.

Molly smiles and bursts out laughin'. 'Nah, only tellin' lies.'

I'm gonna kick 'er real 'ard in the shins. But she puts her hand out and says, 'Nah, nah, only ngoonji bula. I'll tell you for real who your father is, listen now.'

I listen again. Molly could know 'cause she's older than us kids and she gets to hear a lot 'bout what the adults are doin'.

'Your father that walbiya from town there, who goes out to work on the farm.'

I'm tryin' to think which one, lotta men, walbiya and Nyunga go out there workin' at reapin' and shearin' time. I lift my gugga up, askin' 'er for more information.

'You know that real skinny one?'

I shake my head.

'...with the real ugly face. Can't you see the resemblance, Grace? Go look in the mirror.' She laughin' again.

This time I had it with Molly I run up and grab 'er arm and bite it hard as I can.

'Ah, you little cow.' She screamin' and start hittin' me on the head.

I make sure I make a big mark on her arm before I let go. That'll teach 'er, teasin' me and tellin' lies like that. Then I cut it 'round the front of the cottage to get away from 'er. As I walk 'long the path I see minya weeds startin' to grow out of the munda. I kick 'em as I go past. Then, I think 'bout everyone I asked and how no-one wanna tell me. Who can I ask next?

No good askin' Ada any more, she just growl me and give me floggin' for bein' cheeky. Molly's no 'elp, she just tells lies to laugh at me, she like makin' me moogada. Papa Neddy and Mumma Jenna probably know but they won't tell me. I could ask aunties or uncles, but they probably just do same as Mumma and Papa. Who else can I ask? I think 'bout all the places we go and people we see. Then it comes to me. The car came to our hut on the farm, last week, so it's probably one of them workers on the farm and Old Rod probably knows who was drivin' that car. When I see Old Rod next time, I'll ask 'im. He knows all 'is workers and he probably knows who's Ada's gu mudgie, too. Next time I see 'im I'm gonna ask, 'Old Rod, do you know who my father is?'

★

Few days later, Old Rod turn up in 'is car and toot the horn out the front of our minya cottage. He's walkin' towards the boot when I run out flat-out-way knockin' over Eva, Polly, Adrian and Sarah as I go. Dust flyin' up 'round me as I skid to a stop, grabbin' onto 'is jacket to stop me fallin' over as he opens the back of the car.

'Whoa! Slow down, girl,' he says in a happy voice.

I tiptoein', tryin' to see what he's bring for Papa and us. He got box of food by the looks, and pretty coloured ribbons in 'is pocket for us girls. I'll 'ave to find a fork later to comb the knots outa my 'air so I can tie them on.

He don't stay for long. After he talk with Papa 'bout more work comin' up on the farm, he start to walk back to 'is car. I know he's goin' but I feel too shame to ask 'im straight-out-way if he know who my father might be. He gets into 'is car then, and I get real moogada with myself for bein' scaredy-cat, so last-minute-way, I run up to 'is car.

A big wide smile go over 'is face and deep laugh come outa 'is mouth. Reminds me of lyin' in the sun, listenin' to the waves at Denial Bay, waves that swallow me up and spit me out, and I come up laughin'. Old Rod makes people feel like that.

'Why you be nice to us, bring us things?' I blurt out.

'Because you're a nice little girl, your Papa Neddy's a good man, and your family gives me a lot of help on my farm,' he say, messin' up my 'air makin' it more tangly.

Then he drives off.

That's not the answer I want. But then, joobardi-way I didn't ask the right question. Now what? I come to a dead end again. I go back into the kitchen to look for fork to comb out my knots but I can't find one, so I go to my secret hidin' place in the fireplace and put my ribbons there for later.

Some nights, mostly on weekends or 'olidays, Uncle Murdi play 'is guitar round the campfire outside of our cottage. Sometimes, when I'm sittin' next to 'im and my sisters and Ada, we all snuggle together. Ada stroking Lil-Lil's 'air and givin' 'er mimmi and we all singin' along to the music. But sometimes Uncle Murdi plays just for me to sing along. Other times I pick up 'is guitar and try to play it for myself so I can sing.

'Put that guitar down now, Grace. You'll break it,' Ada growls me.

'Leave the girl be,' Uncle Murdi tell her. 'She can carry a tune, maybe she play the guitar too, one day.'

I muck 'round with the strings, but my murra's too small to fit all the way 'round the end of the guitar.

It's deadly fun when more people from the Mission come and sit 'round the campfire like Uncle Deanie and Aunty Annie Campbell (they my godparents, and they live next door with Georgina and Desmond Clare), Uncle Wingard and Aunty Maria and Aunty Dotti (they our next-door neighbours on the other side). They come over and join us and we all sing 'round the campfire and the grown-ups yarnin' and tellin' funny stories from long time ago, all of us laughin'.

Behind our 'ouses, that neighbour livin' there's a mean old lady, Hetty Clare, Desmond's sister, Dora's mumma.

Even though they brother and sister they real different from each other. Hetty real mean, and Desmond real nice fella. Hetty never comes over, only to yell nasty things to us and cause fights when she goes too far. Mumma Jenna gets 'er crowbar out then and slams it into the munda. That means she's had enough of Hetty Clare's big mouth and she's gonna use it if that old woman don't shut up. Hetty Clare usually shut 'er big mouth then, turn around and go back inside 'er 'ouse. She do that 'cause Mumma's given 'er a floggin' lotsa times before, mostly when she talk real cheeky-way about Mumma's children, Ada and the others, sayin' words that us kids get a floggin' for if we said 'em. But when she see Mumma's crowbar then she shut up real quick-way.

Nyunga-way when weena mooga fight, sometimes they rip their clothes off. It don't happen that way at the Mission but when it does I get real scared and run away and hide somewhere safe 'cause I nyindi someone's gonna get hurt. After they finish fightin' it's all over, everythin' goes quiet till next time. Everyone gets on with their lives then. But sometimes people fight when they gubbydja. Papa says too much gubby is walbiya-way too, and it mixes everythin' up wrong-way, makes us lose our way.

Papa say we got Nyunga-way of doin' things, real strong way 'cause our Old People handed it down to us and it's more powerful than walbiya laws. When someone does somethin' wrong in walbiya law they get locked up in jail. It might be long time before they're let out and when they get out people might still be angry with each other. But Nyunga-way, if you do somethin' wrong you might get spear in your leg, you might get sick or you might even die, but it's over quick-way. After a fight, it's all sorted out, sometimes by gudji, 'cause they got their punishment.

But that old Hetty Clare just don't seem to learn. I reckon she must be jealous like what Ada say: 'Them mob just tease and be mean to you kids 'cause they jealous of how we get work and mai from the farm.'

Next to Hetty Clare's 'ouse lives Granny Laura Dean, she Papa Neddy's sister. She live behind our 'ouse, where the strong wind blows from. Papa's always tellin' us kids, 'You be nice to that old woman, now.' And he send us over 'er place with kuka and damper. Granny Laura's real nice to us kids too. Poor old lady havin' to live next door to mean old Hetty Clare. But Hetty Clare wouldn't wanna pick on Granny Laura 'cause she'd cop it from Papa.

I think Hetty Clare must like gettin' a floggin', the way she always carryin' on.

'You Oldmans think you so good,' she scream like an old witch at us one day. 'You all nothin' but . . .' (lotsa words I can't say – too rude). She screamin' at all of us.

Ohhh, she so gonna get 'nother floggin' from Granny Jenna. I'm wonderin' where to hide before Granny gets 'er crowbar out.

Kids at school can be mean like Hetty Clare too.

'You stinkin' white kid,' they yell at me. 'Smelly white-arse,' and other filthy names like that. Sometimes, they real mean to us kids that are a minya bit fairer.

'Can I play that game with you?' I ask some kids with a ball that they hittin' up against the school wall or playin' rounders.

'No, whitefella's kid.' They spit at me real mean-way. 'Why would we wanna play with you? Now, go 'way and let us be, you white arse'ole.'

Some days I fight them, other times I just put my gugga down and walk off and go an' play by myself on the jungle gym or find my sisters or brothers or friends that will play with me. When kids wongan to me like that, it makes me feel real shame and sad. What's wrong with me? Why they so mean like that and call me them names? I never be mean to them. But then I tell myself, no you don't wanna be like them arse'oles. They call me 'whitefella kid' cause I'm fairer than them. I hate the colour of my skin. I hate being different. Why aren't I like them?

But Old Rod's always tellin' me and my sisters we're different from them other kids on the Mission too. He squats down like the big old giant Papa talks about in our old Kokatha stories, grabs my arms with his frypan hands, looks me right in the guru and says, 'You different from them kids on the Mission. You remember that. You different from them.' His voice booming like big malu tail hittin' the munda, goin' full-pelt. Like he's tryin' to hammer it into me, or really wants me to understand what he's tellin' me. When he talks like that my djuda goes all squirmy like maggots in stinkin' burru and I feel funny-way, 'cause I know I'm not different from them other kids, not the way he thinks we are. My skin's only a minya bit fairer, that's all. That's when I start thinkin', he's different from us, Old Rod. That old man doesn't really understand our ways but he cares. He's always lookin' out for me and my sisters.

Why did God make me different from them other kids? If Old Rod sayin' I'm different he must know why. When I see 'im maybe I can ask 'im why he tells me I'm different from other Nyunga kids? But what if he growl me like Ada and Mumma?

Old Rod treat us Nyunga mooga real well, looks after us real good. He come to the Mission and give us food. Sometimes he takes me and my sisters in the bush with 'im and give us good feed of fruit until our minya djuda mooga full to burstin'.

'Eat,' he tell us. 'Eat as much as you can because I know you're going to 'ave to share this food with the rest of your family when you get home.'

Then he take us 'ome with the rest of the fruit. He brings lots of different things sometimes: vegies, eggs, rabbity, malu. Papa real pleased with 'im sharin' 'is food like that. That's real Nyunga-way. But sometimes he buy bultha for us to wear too. In summer time and in winter time, Ada goes into the shop in town and gets clothes for us kids. Old Rod tell 'er, 'Tell Mrs Tareen to put it on my account, no questions asked.'

One day when I was little, Ada picked out a pretty minya dress and matchin' shoes for me and Eva at Mona Tareen's Frock Salon. After, Old Rod picked us up near the beach where he always dropped us off just outa town; we always wait there for 'im to pick us up. This day, I jumped into 'is car and real proud-way showed 'im my dress.

'How come you buy dresses for us?' I asked real shy but

excited-way, smoothin' out the yellow flowery material, imaginin' I'm wearin' it there and then.

He threw 'is head back and laughed. 'I've just reaped one of the biggest crops in the district, so I think I can afford to buy you pretty girls something a little bit special.'

The way he wongan, it was like he could 'ave bought us a million dresses if he wanted to, but I was so 'appy just to 'ave that one. It was so pretty and I felt like the most special minya wunyi in the whole world.

Could Old Rod be my mummatja? No way. He's a tjilbi, he must be nearly Papa Neddy's age. Like he said before, he treats us nice-way 'cause he's real pleased that Papa Neddy and 'is kids 'elpin' him on 'is farm to reap lots of crops and that's why he's got soft spot for Ada and us kids too, 'cause we Papa Neddy's mob.

Looks like I've come to 'nother dead end. Tryin' to work out this riddle's sendin' me joobardi, goin' 'round and 'round in my gugga, 'til my djuda feels real funny-way.

So, I don't think about it for a while and just go on doin' what I always do: go to school with my sisters and brothers, fight the cheeky kids who be mean to me, play with my friends, and try to stay outa trouble with my 'cheeky minya mouth', as Ada and Molly call it. But Christmas is comin' up soon and that's a real deadly time on the Mission.

6

Ngoonji bula: God, Jesus and Father Christmas

The days seem to drag on like years while we waitin' for the last day of school to come. Dee-Dee and me countin' on our murra mooga, as the days go by.

'Nine days to go, Grace,' Dee-Dee say.

'Yeah,' I say, pointin' at her fingers, 'nine days to go.'

Then a few days later say, 'Seven days to go, Dee-Dee.'

We take in turns like that 'til it one more sleep. Then that next mornin' we wake up on the last day of school for the year.

'Yippee.' Me and Dee-Dee jumpin' on our old bed with our murra mooga closed like we gonna punch each other. 'No days to go. No days to go,' we laughin'.

All the kids jump on the bed to join in. Mumma and Ada growl us then, to stop breakin' the bed and get ready for school.

We all cleanin' up the school yesterday and this mornin' and then it's recess. When I look back, I can see I learnt lotta things at school this year – readin', writin' and mental maths but now I can put it all away and just play, play, play. I'm sittin' on one end of the seesaw and Dee-Dee Doe's on the other end. We the same size so the seesaw goes just right. Dee-Dee pushes me up into the air and I can see all the kids playin' 'appy-way in the playground. Them mean kids playin' with the ball against the wall. I stick my tongue out at them even though they can't see me. From way up here on the seesaw I can see others on the slippery dip, jungle gym and swings, playin' marbles, skippin'. There's Polly. She just come off the maypole and spinnin' round dizzy-way, then she falls over.

'Ha. Ha. Ha.' I move my lips in Polly's direction and Dee-Dee starts laughin', too.

Polly sees us, and she come over to pull us off the seesaw. But me and Dee-Dee go up and down when she comes for us, so we always up off the ground when she gets to us. Polly's runnin' 'round the seesaw tryin' to grab us. We all laughin'. We so 'appy 'cause it's the last day of school. Seesaw go down on my side and Polly cut it 'round and trick us. She grab me and drag me off and Dee-Dee goes BANG on the munda and hurts 'er jinjie. We all roll on the ground laughin'. No point fightin' even though Dee-Dee's jinjie's real sore, 'cause tomorrow's the 'olidays and I can sleep in and listen to *Yours for the Askin'*, all the way through without gettin' in trouble. But most of all 'olidays mean Christmas and campin' down the beach. Christmas Eve and Christmas Day's the best days in the whole year.

Even the kids from the Children's 'Ome get to go and stay with their family. Well most of 'em, anyway. Us kids lucky we get to stay 'ome all the time.

'Olidays are good fun, we play all day and come 'ome when jindu duthbin, and if we lucky Mumma got big feed waitin' for us. Sometimes, walbiya workers come to Mission to fix up buildings and some of them want us kids to sing for them. One day us gidjida mooga playin' over in the pepper tree near the Children's 'Ome and they call us over. We all go to the walbiya workers there and some of the kids sing their minya hearts out. But not me. I'm too shame even though I sing real deadly. Then they throw money at us. Some of the kids pick the money up and go to the shop and buy lollies. But not me. I don't want their bunda, even if I could buy sultana cake or lollies.

'Go on, take the money,' they tell me. 'You can have it if you want.'

But I stand there, shakin' my head. I don't want to take their bunda. I'm too imbarda.

Time's flyin' by real quick-way and we so excited 'cause soon it's the day before Christmas. After a big day of playin' we all clean and dressed up nice-way for church in the night. It's a special church tonight 'specially for us kids and all the grown-ups that're gonna be there too, and it'll be packed. There's a big Christmas tree in the church and one in the hall. 'Cause me and some other kids are readin' the Bible, we get to sit up the front on chairs. I feel real important sittin' up there and hope them cheeky kids are havin' a good look and see that I bin picked to read and not them. My murra mooga's shakin' and my jinna's swingin' under the chair 'cause I'm real nervous. It's a bit scary up there in front of everyone. I might forget my words then everyone's gonna laugh at me.

Pastor reads from the Bible, tells us about Mary and Joseph and that donkey who took them to Bethlehem where Jesus was born in a minya shed like Old Rod's cow shed, I reckon. I like that story 'cause Jesus gets presents from wise fellas who follow that star in the sky to find 'im. We got stars we follow too. Our stars are our Old People, our Seven Sisters and the big giant man that chases 'em. Papa Neddy, Mumma Jenna and Ada, and the aunties and uncles take the horse and cart outback and we clean our rockholes. They our Seven Sisters too. Our Old People are in the sky, in the waterholes and on the ground, they everywhere, just like God and Jesus. But Pastor tells us we only allowed to worship God and nobody else. But we know them Old People, they look after us and we look after them too. Us kids watch Papa Neddy and Mumma Jenna and the others pull out sticks and dead animals with big branches, 'til them rockholes are clean again. Just like Jesus died and washed us clean from our sins like Pastor talks 'bout in the Bible. How he wash 'em 'way, I don't know. Maybe he use soap and water and a big tub, like when Mumma Jenna, Ada and the Aunties wash all our clothes. Lookin' after our rockholes means we keep real healthy and strong, too. That's what the Old People teach Papa Neddy and our other Grannies and we watch 'em and learn too.

After church the kids get minya bags of lollies, ginger-bread biscuits and nuts. They real yummy and us kids all go joobardi. Everyone go over to the Children's 'Ome, then.

All the parents of the kids in the 'Ome get invited there, too. It's real good to see all the kids with their family, they real 'appy. All us kids jumpin' up and down real excited-way when we go inside 'cause we gonna get clothes from the big table and presents from under the tree.

Dee-Dee Doe look at me, 'er guru mooga wide open like they gonna pop outa her head.

'Ooh, Grace. Look. Father Christmas bin give us kids presents.'

I look over to the biggest mob of presents, all wrapped up. I'm smilin' now, and lookin' round the room, it's real bright and pretty with all the streamers and biggest mob of balloons hangin' from 'em.

All the kids goin', 'Ooh! Ahhh!'

I start runnin' real fast-way on the spot and Dee-Dee's got 'er murra mooga pushed together like she's gonna pray but 'er guru mooga still nearly poppin' out and she jumpin' up and down next to me.

'Mmm,' I say.

I stand still then and cross my murra mooga. I'm worried 'cause Father Christmas don't give nothin' to naughty kids. Mumma, Ada and Molly reckon I'm naughty sometimes, 'specially with my filthy minya mouth.

'Father Christmas's just a big idiot anyway,' I curse 'im under my breath then. 'He's probably not even left me nothin'.'

'Why you swearin' like that for? You get in trouble in a minute,' Dee-Dee tells me quiet-way.

'Nothin',' I tell 'er, shakin' my gugga. Anyways, if stupid Father Christmas not givin' me present, he's not givin' lotsa other cheeky kids nothin' either. Lotta kids cheekier than me and all of them real dumb, idiot kids, anyway.

Pastor ask us to pray then. Everythin' goes real quiet.

'Heavenly Father, we thank you for your provisions here this night, that we can come together in fellowship and praise of your name and give our thanks to you for sending us your only beloved Son, Jesus. And on this day we remember his birth and that he died to save us from our sins. In the name of the Father, Son and Holy Spirit. Amen.'

'Amen,' all us mob say together.

Then I jump in at the last minute in case their yuree still open and listenin' after Pastor finish talkin' to them. 'God and Jesus and Father Christmas, if you still listenin' can you please let me 'ave a nice present and I promise to be a real good girl and not swear for a long time.'

'Please be seated,' Pastor tell us.

So we all sit down on the munda and Teacher starts calling out the names. I'm watchin' them other kids go up and get their present and wonderin', what's goin' on here?

'Hey!' I say to Eva sittin' next to me. 'Real naughty kids gettin' presents, there.'

'So?' Eva say, jerkin' 'er gugga back, lookin' at me like I'm joobardi.

'Father Christmas only meant to bring presents to good kids, indie? But look there.' I stickin' my lips out, pointin' at them kids out the front. ''Arold's an arse'ole of a kid. And look at them others, they the rotten kids who call me filthy names all the time. Why Father Christmas givin' them presents?'

Eva laughs at me so I punch 'er in the arm.

She punches me back twice as 'ard in the leg and yell, 'Father Christmas's not real, stupid.'

'Shhhut uuup.' Polly pushes us in the back.

Teacher's lookin' at us, 'er guru mooga gone real small like she ready to growl us.

I scratch my gugga. I do that when I got gooloo, but this time it's cause I'm thinkin'.

'If Father Christmas is not real who buys the presents?' I whisper to Eva out the corner of my mouth 'cause I can see Teacher's still lookin'.

'Them walaba ladies from Adelaide who got plenty of bunda to send them over for us.' Eva cough out the answer behind 'er murra.

'How you know that?' I say through my teeth, so Teacher think I'm 'appy and smilin'.

'Pastor just said so. If you weren't so yuree bamba you would 'ave 'eard it, too.'

'That's true,' Polly say real quiet-way from close up next to me.

I turn 'round and Mona's there, with a sad look on 'er wah, noddin' too. I look for Dee-Dee but she's gone up the front.

Sometimes Eva's wrong, but Polly and Mona, they sayin' Father Christmas's not real too. Why don't they tell me before when we play with our secret-pretty-things? We don't keep nothin' secret from each other, 'specially important things like Father Christmas. My guru mooga go all watery and I feel empty inside. Why grown-ups tell us Father Christmas real when he's bloody well not?

'If you children be good maybe Father Christmas will

pay you a visit this year and bring you some presents,' Teacher say.

When I think about that, I get moogada then. They lie to us kids and God say in 'is Commandments, 'Thou shalt not lie'. They all full of goona.

'Grace,' Teacher calls out.

'What?' I yell out real moogada-way 'cause I'm still thinkin' 'bout 'er lyin' to us kids.

All the kids laugh at me, then. Shame job.

'Come up and get your present. Quickly, please.'

I jump up flat-out-way and fall into Dee-Dee comin' back from out the front with a big present in 'er arms. Stupid bloody kids still laughin' at me.

Teacher gives me a real minya present.

'Thank you, Miss Peabody,' I say. And as I walk back through the kids I say to myself quiet-way, 'Thank you God and Jesus. But Father Christmas, you can go and get stuffed.'

Before I sit down my present's already unwrapped and I'm real 'appy 'cause I got a pretty minya bracelet same colour as my secret-pretty-things. Only Eva, Polly, Dee-Dee, Sandy and Nora know what colours my secret-pretty-things are, except for God and Jesus. It makes me feel real special that God and Jesus give me a special present like that, that they know I'll like it. They see everything, they can even see inside our hearts and know what we thinkin'. They know all the secrets in the whole wide world. Everybody's secret. They must know the clues to workin' out Old Rod, and Mumma and Ada's secrets, too. Tonight, when I go to sleep, I'll pray to ask them to share their secrets.

Dee-Dee's tuggin' at me, again.

'What?' I say real loud-way.

Miss Peabody looks over at us with moogada look on 'er face again. 'If you children can't keep quiet you'll be sent home.'

We put our gugga down and whisper real quiet-way behind our murra mooga after that.

'Look, I got a real dolly,' Dee-Dee say.

She so excited she bouncin' on the spot. Dolly bouncin' too, 'er guru mooga's jumpin' openin' and shuttin' like she real excited as well.

'Deadly,' I say, lookin' and touchin' dolly's guru mooga, seein' how they work. 'But Dee-Dee,' I whisper, 'your peg dolly's gonna get real jealous now you got a real dolly.' Then, I smile at 'er silly-way.

'No,' she say, shakin' er gugga. 'Peg dolly's got Mumma dolly now to look after 'er. Make sure she put 'er bultha mooga on when we go to church so Pastor don't growl 'er for goin' nigardi.'

We close our guru mooga real tight and laugh loud-way on the inside, so Teacher can't hear us.

That night, I lyin' in bed and lookin' at my pretty bracelet. I move the shiny colour beads round on their string. It's real special, this bracelet. I feel all warm inside 'cause God and Jesus know me, they know 'bout my secret-pretty-things and they know everyone's secrets. I pray then.

'Dear Lord Jesus and God, it's me, Grace Dawn Oldman. Thank you for my bracelet, it's the most bestest present I ever had in my whole life but I don't need to tell youse that, do I? 'Cause youse already know that. Youse know everything. I nyindi that. I nyindi that youse know what's in my heart and Mumma's and Ada's and Old Rod's heart too. I'm just a minya wunyi and I don't know as much as youse do. Anyways, can you please give me things to work out that riddle, and please show me the secrets that Mumma and Ada hidin' from me. And one more thing please, can you make me not goomboo in the bed tonight. Amen.'

Next mornin' sun shinin' bright but I pissed the bed again. My sisters are moogada with me, as usual, and Ada yellin' for us to get outa bed so she can change the blanketie. Well stuff you, God and Jesus. If you not gonna 'elp me with my riddle and findin' out secrets, I'll 'ave to do it myself. Maybe youse just big lies like Father Christmas.

I stomp outa the room then, into the kitchen where Mumma already got 'er turkey and jookie jookie in our old oven. And Aunty Essie and Aunty Mim bringin' in the red and green jelly from off the top of the water tank at the side of the house. When it gets cold at night it sets the jelly and make it go hard. Those jellies look so yummy jigglin' on the table there in the kitchen now. I can't take my guru mooga off them while I walk past goin' outside to wash my face. I wanna stick my murra in there, to 'ave a taste, but Mumma's workin' there in the kitchen with my aunties and they'll see me and growl me. So I just take a big whiff of the deadly smells, my mouth waterin', my djuda grumblin' as I go outside to wash my wah. Mumma sure is a good cook.

Eva and Mona run past with all the minya kids runnin' behind them playin' chasie. Polly tryin' to catch 'em.

'You "It".' Polly slap me on the back.

'Ouch!' I yell out, cursin' her. Then I run quick-way after her. I'm gonna slap 'er real hard like she slapped me, so she'll be 'It' again. She trips and tumbles in front of me. I nearly got 'er now, I dive down and grab 'er. Next minute all the sky and the munda whirlin' 'round and I feel lotta pain in my jinna.

'Ahhhh.' I'm cryin' and grabbin' my jinna 'cause it hurts like hell.

I look down, my leg achin' and goin' red down there under my knee. I rub it real 'ard 'cause it's real sore like it's achin' from the inside. My guru mooga squeezed tight, tryin' to make it stop hurtin'. Maybe God and Jesus punishin' me for bein' cheeky to them.

'You 'right, Grace?' Polly's sayin' sittin', up rubbin' 'er arm.

'Yeah,' I tell 'er but I don't really feel 'right.

All the kids stop runnin' and come 'round me to see what's wrong.

'That's the same jinna you hit on that water pipe on the way 'ome from school the other week,' Polly say.

I nod at 'er with sorry look on my face. Then, I look 'round with big smile on my face, 'cause there are one, two, three, four, five, six, seven, eight kids, all in slappin' range for chasie and they don't even know it. So, sly-way I start to get to my jinna. All the kids lookin' at me real sorry-way and helpin' me get up.

Now, who do I want to be 'It'?

'Ahhh,' Polly scream out in the distance 'cause I'm already cut it 'round the side of the house, sore jinna and all.

'You're "It", Polly.' I'm laughin' so hard I nearly can't breathe.

'Hey, you kids, why you not ready for church yet?' Papa Neddy growls us.

He's standin' there with 'is stock whip in 'is murra. I keep runnin' straight through the door behind 'im. Stuff gettin' hit by that ugly big whip. He cracks it real loud. CRACK.

All the kids stop dead in their tracks then, and flat-out-way cut into our cottage to get ready.

'What? You want to keep the Good Lord waitin' on 'is birthday? After all he's done for you?'

Papa's real strict 'bout us goin' to church and bein' respect-ful to God and Jesus. He'd give me a good floggin' if he'd knew I bin cursin' 'em. But Papa Neddy can't look into my heart to see what's there, not like God and Jesus, if that's not a lie like the rest of them lies grown-ups bin tellin' me.

Us kids all lined up now ready in our Sunday best. I got a deadly minya dress on that Old Rod bought me but I can't find my boogardies so I go jinna nigardi like most the other kids.

When we get to the church, I'm real moogada that I gotta go and listen to Pastor and say prayers and thank you very much Lord Jesus for bein' born and dyin' on the cross to save us from our sins.

Instead I curse them under my breath. 'I'm not thankin' you, Heavenly Father, for bein' a pig-head and not 'elpin' me. You can go'n get stuffed. Amen.'

After church, our mob crammed into the kitchen, all hot and sweatin', my mouth waterin' lookin' at Christmas dinner on our kitchen table full with Mumma's fresh cooked bread, turkey, jookie jookie, roast vegetables, steam comin' up off 'em. And that jelly, that deadly jigglin' jelly with custard.

Papa gets ready to say grace. 'Let's thank the Lord now.'

We all put our gugga mooga down.

'Count one to ten, drop your dacks and pick them up again,' I whisper along with Papa's grace.

Sandy elbows me.

'Amen,' I say real loud-way with everyone else.

'You'll go to hell talkin' like that when Papa's prayin'.'

I shrug my shoulders. Hell might be a lie, too.

Wiggle welly, wiggle welly jelly in the plate. I like jelly, it's good for your belly. Wiggle welly, wiggle welly jelly in the plate.

Everything goes quiet then, 'cause everyone's hoein' into their tucker. Even Yudu's havin' a good feed 'cause I'm throwin' 'im bones under the table.

Before Christmas, Papa Neddy and Mumma Jenna bin ridin' in their jinka 'round the farms gettin' turkey and jookie jookie mooga to buy for Christmas Day. Papa got two boonie mooga, Jess and Bob. One pulls the jinka. They real big friendly horses that got feet like 'airy boogardies. Sometimes Papa lets us kids ride them but only slow-way 'cause he don't want us to get hurt.

My most favourite horse is Thundabolt. He's Granny Hector's horse. Granny Hector's Papa Neddy's brother. He's not called Thundabolt for nothin', he's a real wild boonie. Us kids're always fightin' over who's gonna take Thundabolt for a drink at the trough. One day, not long ago, when it came to my turn, I was gettin' on but 'cause he's real thirsty, he didn't give me a chance to get on properly. He just took off like a thundabolt, just like 'is name. Bloody mongrel. I was slidin' all over 'is back, hangin' on to 'is mane tryin' to stay on 'im.

'Ahh. Look out, Thundabolt,' I screamed. 'The berry bush.'

I could see them prickly berry bush mooga whizzin' past me, my jinna just missin' 'em. I tried to slow 'im down, pullin' real 'ard on 'is 'air, but Thundabolt kept gallopin' faster and faster. We was goin' so fast everythin' was real blurry. I could see the windmill and the underwater tank there at the bottom of the hill, and the big water trough at the end of the path. There was nowhere else to go. I thought, this is it, we gonna crash right through it and I'm gonna die. But right at the last minute that boonie Thundabolt slammed 'is brakes on. Them jinna mooga must 'ave skidded on the ground 'cause there was all this dust flyin' up in the air and next thing, I was flyin' like a minya djita – until SPLASH! I landed right in the middle of that stinkin' animal trough and there was Thundabolt havin' a real good drink next to me like nothin' happened. Granny Hector must've worked that boonie real 'ard that day, to make 'im that thirsty.

When I got outa the tank all drippin' wet the other kids were all laughin' their 'eads off. I was pretty moogada and wanted to fight them to start with but then I could see the funny side too, and later we all 'ad a laugh.

Papa Neddy and Granny Hector didn't think it was funny though. They growled me and I got in big trouble.

'What the hell did you think you were doin' girl?' they yelled, like I meant to do it or somethin'. That boonie got a brain in 'is 'ead. I never told 'im to do it.

When I got 'ome Mumma and Ada growled me too, but then they start laughin': 'You won't need a wash today, will you, Grace?'

Then, I sneak off to the bedroom, to get outa their way.

Molly sticks 'er big ugly moolya in then, and cheeky-way reckons, 'Why you wanna drink from the stinkin' trough with the animals for?' She smilin' at me with 'er gumberdy teeth. 'When we got fresh water tank out the back there?'

I chase 'er into the kitchen and I'm gonna kick 'er but my other aunties, Mim and Dorrie, grab me and tell me off, tell me to be good.

After dinner, Ada tells us girls to come to our bedroom, she got presents for us. We all real excited.

'Look what I found under the bed,' Ada says. 'Father Christmas must've left these for you kids.'

My guru mooga goes real small and I stick my nyimi out at her. 'Why you lie, Ada?' I yell at her, 'Father Christmas's not real.'

She grab me by the yuree and pull me outa the room.

'Why are you spoilin' this for your minya sisters?' 'er breath real hot in my yuree. 'You so bloody naughty, Grace,' she say to me.

My yuree's still hurtin' like hell so I'm hangin' on to it, now.

'You bloody liar, too,' I yell back. 'The Commandments say, "Thou shalt not lie", and you lie so you gonna end up in hell 'cause Father Christmas, he's not real.'

Ada slap me then, and I run outside cryin' and go an' sit near the laundry tub hidin' in behind the big drum. It smells like piss. Probably my piss from our blanketie. I get more moogada then and stomp me feet on the munda real hard-way. Why Ada tell lies to me all those years? Father Christmas didn't give us girls those presents. Ada got no bunda to buy us presents, where did she get 'em? Then, I remember Mumma sayin' Old Rod came over and dropped off some boxes of food for us for Christmas when I was playin' out in the scrub the other day. Old Rod again. He's the one who gave us 'em.

Ada comes out after to talk to me, sits down next to me to say sorry for hittin' me and tell me that, as usual, my cheeky minya mouth got me in trouble again.

'I know Old Rod bought them presents for us,' I tell her. 'And I know you keepin' secret from me and I'm gonna find out.'

'What ya talkin' 'bout?' Ada say, gettin' moogada again. 'You talkin' joobardi now, Grace.'

'No I'm not,' I tell 'er, shakin' my head. 'You the one lyin' and keepin' secret, that's why you growlin' me.'

Ada throw 'er murra mooga in the air then and say, 'I give up, I bloody give up with you. You cheeky filthy mouthed minya wunyi. If it wasn't for you kids I'd 'ave my freedom.'

Then she took off out the house. She always says that when she moogada with us kids, it's like we always to blame for her bein' stuck with us. When she say that I always think, 'Go on then, go. 'Ave your freedom. I don't care. Good riddens.' But I never say it out loud 'cause I'd get a floggin'.

I know now I can't get any clues from Ada, Father Christmas, God or Jesus, so now the only one to ask is Old Rod but this time I ask him the question right-way.

7

Goin' away

Next day, Ada just pretends nothin' happen. We all up early and gettin' ready to go to Denial Bay on the Mission truck for 'olidays. S'pose them walbiya mob on the Mission need a holiday too, to go see their family in the city or other places. I'm usually real 'appy to be goin' away from the Mission for 'olidays but I feel rotten right now. I keep thinkin', who else's tellin' lies. I'm even wonderin' if everythin' grown-ups say is lies. How do I know what they say is true or ngoonji?

I'm in our bedroom lookin' up in the fireplace for my minya stash of lollies that I saved from the Christmas party when I 'ear Aunty Rose's voice, she must be back from Mount Faith. Then, I 'ear Aunty Dorrie raisin' 'er voice. Dee-Dee Doe come runnin' in callin' me, real worried-way and I 'it my gugga on the fireplace tryin' to get out in a hurry.

'Gracie, my Mumma Rose's 'ere. She wants to take me with 'er long way away.' She hug me. 'I wanna stay 'ere with you and my mumma Dorrie.'

Dee-Dee's cryin' now. I'm cryin' too.

'We can run away into the scrub 'til she's gone,' I say.

'No, Grace. Papa Neddy say I gotta go 'cause Rose's my proper mumma.'

Dee-Dee Doe and me hug each other real tight. We can 'ear Aunty Dorrie cryin' in the next room; she's been like mumma to Dee-Dee since she was real minya wunyi.

'Please,' she's sayin'. And Papa he sayin' again, 'No, Dee-Dee's Rose's gu wunyi, she has to go with 'er mother and that's it.'

'Spit oath, Dee-Dee. Spit oath that we will never forget each other and we will always remember our secret-pretty-things and all the deadly things we shared together.'

We spit oath with our murra mooga then.

'Dee-Dee,' Papa callin' 'er.

'Grace, I really 'ope you find out who's your mummatja?'

'Dee-Dee, you meant to be the first one I tell when I find out. Now 'ow am I gonna tell you?'

'Catch a butterfly and whisper in its yuree, then let it go and it will fly to me and tell me.'

'Oh, Dee-Dee, you funny minya wunyi, and you my bestest friend. I'm gonna miss you.'

'Me too,' she say.

Then Dee-Dee Doe turns 'round and runs out the door. And she gone, just like that, and I feel like there's a big hole in my guddadu.

★

When the truck takes off from the Mission to Denial Bay, we're all on the back, clean and dressed real nice-way. What's the point? We always dusty and dirty by the time we get to the beach. But no one cares 'cause they free from the Mission, free to drink and lie without Pastor tellin' them off, and free to make more secrets to hide.

On the truck I'm real miserable. Dee-Dee's my bestest friend in the whole wide world, now she gone. I put my gugga under the blanketie and cry then.

When we get to Denial Bay, the truck dumps us at the old water tank stands. Everyone piles off the back. We're all excited 'cause we don't get off the Mission very much, don't need to, 'cause we got minya store there that sell lotta things, except for malu and wadu burru, men gotta go huntin' for them, and all the bush mai that Mumma, Ada and the aunties take us in the scrub for a good feed. But I reckon Superintendent and Pastor make us all stay on the Mission for long time to keep eye on us. Sometimes us Nyunga mob leave the Mission when the men do wheat lumpin' work on the big ships when they come to the Thevenard jetty. Sometimes, if Papa or my uncles go for work at the jetty, Mumma, Ada and some of the aunties go too and take some of us kids. We always camp near the Ceduna cemetery at night and go down near the Thevenard jetty where the big boats come in every day. It's deadly there 'cause we near the beach and go swimmin' and there's a shop that sells everythin', even bullseye lollies, they my favourite.

Sometimes, if I'm lucky, Ada or Mumma might give me bunda to buy lollies or ice-block over at the shop. I like that shop. It's got two big doors, one for sellin' hot feed for the workers, and another door for other things like lollies, ice-blocks and fruit. Sometimes Mumma goes there and buys bread and other tucker. I love takin' big deep breaths in that shop, lotsa different smells all mixed together, mostly nice. When I go through the door to get lollies there's a minya bell that rings to tell the lady I'm comin' into 'er shop.

It's like that minya bell say, 'Hello, Grace. Good to see you today. Come in.'

Then, this lady comes to the counter and smiles at me real nice-way. She don't talk much English, she got 'nother wonga like us Nyunga mooga. She's a walaba weena but she's different from them white mob in town who stare at us, or pretend we're not there. She's a real nice lady, smilin' at me all the time. Then we play this game, I tell 'er what I want and she gotta guess what I'm sayin'. It's always lollies but sometimes I like to get different ones. She go to this jar and smile, pointin' at the lollipops, I shake my 'ead. She go to the jar and point, smilin', and I shake my gugga. Then, she go to the bullseye jar and I nod. Then she gives me extra ones. She don't know much English but she good at knowin' what people sayin' usin' other parts of their body like us Nyunga mooga do. I like that lady, 'er smile say, 'You a special minya wunyi and I like you very much,' and it's the same feelin' like when Mumma and Mrs Dempsey give me a big hug. I always give smile back at 'er that say, 'I like you too, walaba lady, I like you a real lot.'

Denial Bay got shop too, but it's smaller and smells different from the shop near Thevenard jetty. The lady in Denial Bay store don't smile much. But she helped us once when we in trouble, when there's too much gubby 'round our camp, and a Nyunga man went joobardi, screamin' round the place, rippin' 'is clothes off, and runnin' 'round nigardi with a knife in 'is murra sayin' he was gonna kill everyone. Us kids were real ngulu, shakin' under the blanketie, all huddled' together there.

'Go away you stupid, ugly man,' I whisperin', one murra over my yuree and my guru mooga squeezed real tight, other murra hangin' onto Sarah who's screamin' in my other yuree. Then, he jumped right over us kids lyin' on the munda, wavin' 'is knife 'round. I'm thinkin' he'll stab us through the blanketie, directly. Ada gets real ngulu, then, too, so she grab us and run over to the place where that walaba shop lady lives.

'Tessie,' she calls out loud-way, bangin' on the door. 'Tessie.'

The door opens and that Tessie weena looks real moogada at Ada. She don't like us wakin' 'er in the middle of the night, most probably.

'Man goin' crazy over there with knife. Please, 'elp us.' Ada beggin' her. 'I'm real scared my girls gonna get 'urt.'

My minya baby sister, Lil-Lil's screamin' in Ada's arms there, and Ada nearly cryin', too, and Sarah sobbin' into Eva's shoulder while she nursin' 'er. Us girls all huddled into Ada.

Even though I'm sobbin' too 'cause I'm so ngulu, I feel shame. How come Ada knockin' on a walaba weena's door and not even callin' er by Miss or Mrs? Ada got no shame. Maybe she know her? Who is she? I don't know her.

First the walaba weena growl Ada but when she look at us kids, all scared and cold, she let us come inside, take us into 'er kitchen, gave us drink of cordial and biscuits. Us kids sittin' there real quiet-way then, and look 'round 'er kitchen, guru-manardu-way. Sure look flash, all sparklin' clean with shiny floor and flash stove and pots and things. Not like our kitchen. Ours got hard concrete floor but mostly dirt and one old burnt-out pot for stews. Walbiya mob sure live flash-way.

When the yellin' dies down, Ada says thank you to the nice weena and we go back to our camp near the beach. That was real good of that Miss Tessie weena to help us that night.

Some walbiya mooga all right to us but I don't trust them walbiya men that come late at night with their car lights turned off, sneakin' round like tjunu mooga in the grass. 'Cause that's when some of the weena mooga go off with 'em and come back later with gubby, and fightin' starts after that, after everyone's gubbydja. I reckon big secrets happenin' on those nights that no-one dare tell Superintendent or Pastor about when they get back to Mission. Sometimes our minya camp ends up with some gubby too.

When we jump off the truck at Denial Bay all the kids run for the beach and the grown-ups unpack and make camps and light fire. Then they make the sand soft with a stick and move the seaweed 'round to make nice soft bed for us to sleep on later. They put the blanketie down then, and it's real nice. I just walk off on my own down the beach and start kickin' the seaweed 'cause I still moogada with Ada and God and Jesus for lyin' and not helpin' me. And now Dee-Dee gone. 'Ow come they let that happen? I pick up minya stones, put all my moogada feelings in them and throw them real hard-way onto the wanna so they skip on the top, then disappear. That makes me feel better.

I look over to the shop and houses and wonder who's that nice walaba weena Miss Tessie, that helped us that night. Ada knew 'er, 'cause she called 'er by 'er name. Maybe she works for 'er cleanin' sometimes? But she should call 'er Miss or Mrs.

'Grace,' Eva yells from a big clump of seaweed down the beach. 'Biggest mob of wanna mai, nyumu mai 'ere. Come and 'elp me get them for feed.'

I start runnin' towards Eva, laughin'. The wind whooshin' in my mouth, carryin' my breath away. Even though we bin comin' 'ere ever since I bin minya wunyi, just like Ada and Mumma Jenna when they minya wunyi mooga, I never get tired of it. We can run and run without no fences stoppin' us, we free. That's cause our mob use to come here long time ago before walbiya mooga. We go here on holidays 'cause this our country and walbiya go back to their homes – just for a minya while anyway.

Eva's scoopin' 'em into 'er dress, it's real full. My mouth's waterin', my djuda growlin' too, cause I 'aven't 'ad anything to eat since this mornin', only minya bit of damper.

We both laughin' when we get back to camp with our dresses dripping wet and full of mussels. We've bin actin' silly-way, pretendin' we gubbydja staggerin' back to camp holdin' on to our dresses, heavy and full up with nyumu mai. Then, I trip over at the last minute and them mussels go flyin' all over the sand near the fire. Eva drop hers too and we rollin' on the ground laughin', 'er nyumu mai all over me and the munda too, and our dresses caked in sand mud.

'You two must be gubbydja carryin' on like that,' Ada say, shakin' 'er gugga at us.

Mumma smilin'. She 'appy 'er grannies are 'appy.

We pick up the shells and put them in the hot coals 'til they sizzle and open, then we 'ave good feed. Oh, they taste beautiful.

Minya while later, Eva gets tired of playin' with our minya sisters and brothers. We walk along the beach with our arms 'round each other and talk 'bout how deadly it is that we on 'olidays, at least we off the stupid Mission and can go swimmin' and collect our own tucker and run for ages along the beach with no-one tellin' us what to do.

'Hey, you stinkin' whitefella kids. Williams' pigs.' Two mean boys kickin' up sand in our faces as they run past. 'Why don't you go 'ave a wash in the wanna to get rid of your boongada.'

'Get lost,' I scream out after 'em. 'You the stinkin' ones and real ugly too.'

'I hate it when they call me names,' I tell Eva. 'Make me feel like piece of goona. Just 'cause our mob get work on the farm 'cause we good workers.'

'You not the only one who get called names,' Eva tell me. 'Them arse'oles pick on me too. Sometimes, I just wanna knock 'em in the gugga.'

'Yeah,' I say, 'me too.' I look over at my sister, we feel the same way. I spit in my murra then. 'Let's do special truce, cross our hearts and hope to die, that we stick up for each other 'gainst them rotten kids, no matter what.' I hold my drippin' murra out to her.

Eva's lookin' back at me now, big smile spreadin' over 'er face. She does a big spit in 'er murra too, and we shake on it, our spit all squishes together. That mean we'll keep our promise to each other, no matter what. Eva's got real pretty face with 'er blondie brown 'air fallin' over it. I never noticed 'er 'air was different from us other kids before.

'Where you get that blonde 'air from?' I ask 'er.

'From inside my 'ead. It grows out of it, stupid,' she tell me with one side of 'er face screwed up.

'Yeah, but who got 'air like that in our family?'

'Aunty Essie and some of 'er kids got white colour 'air.'

I nod, then. Some mob in our family real muroo but some of us got lighter colour skin too, not only me and Eva.

We go wanderin' off into the bushes then, to look for more mai. It's like that spit oath's stopped us from fightin', made us good friends. We talk 'bout lotta things, like how we feel different from other kids and left outa things a lot, and how sometimes we don't feel like we belong 'specially when them kids tease us. As we pick the berries off the bushes and eat 'em, we talk 'bout how we feel sad and moogada and sometimes not very nice inside, like somethin' missing. I never knew Eva feels just like me. Then I wonder if she knows 'bout Old Rod and Ada and Mumma's secrets. She might know who our mummatja is. No-one else wants to tell me, they just get moogada with me when I ask.

She squats down then, and pulls the top off a pig-face flower, and sticks the round juicy part in 'er mouth and squashes it. I sit down next to 'er on the munda and we both 'ave a good feed of the pig-face. It's real nice and juicy and tastes real good.

'Eva, who's our mummatja then?' I ask.

'We don't 'ave one,' she say. 'That's why we're bastard kids.'

'Don't call us that,' I growl 'er, pushin 'er back so she fall in the tjilga bush. 'I'm no bastard kid.'

'Ouch. Right, you little cow, that 'urt.'

Eva's ready to punch me, then she must've remembered our spit oath and stops to pull the tjilga off 'er bultha. I start pickin' at one of my scabs below my knee, they always clear up when we on 'olidays swimmin' in the wanna. Then tears start fallin' on my scab, makin' it all soft.

Eva just shakes 'er gugga at me, then puts 'er arm 'round me again.

'Why don't we 'ave a mummatja like other kids?' I ask her.

''Cause we can't, 'cause of God's Commandment.'

'Maybe Old Rod will know who our mummatja is,' I say.

'Don't even talk 'bout 'im,' she says.

She spit on the munda in front of us. I look at the spit curl up into a ball with dirt floatin' 'round it.

'But why's he so nice to us?' I ask, lookin' at an ant tryin' to climb on the spit ball. 'Give us things and that?'

'We better get back to camp. Ada and Mumma will be wonderin' where we are.'

She's tryin' to get out of answerin' the question, just like Ada and Mumma. She 'elps me up and steppin' over the spit ball, I ask 'er, 'Is he our mummatja?'

We walk along the track in the sand towards 'nother clump of bushes without sayin' nothin'.

'I already told you, Grace, we not allowed to 'ave a father, so he's not.' Eva stopped walkin' and turned to me. 'In other words, Grace, no.'

I start cryin' again then. Eva's my big sister and she knows lotta things. Sometimes she's wrong but I know this time she's tellin' me the truth. I know she won't lie to me after a spit oath.

Eva hugs me then. 'Look, my sissy. We don't need no stupid mummatja. We got Papa Neddy and lotsa uncles who're our fathers Nyunga-way, they look after us and I'll look after you, too.' She grabs me by the arms then, and looks me in the wah. 'I'll make sure nothin' happens to you and our minya sisters. And just look out if them kids call us any filthy names again. We'll give 'em a hidin'.'

'Yeah, I reckon,' I say, wipin' my murra under my nose and sniffin' the snot back up. 'We'll give it' to 'em.'

I do boxin' punches that I seen Papa do when he playin' 'round with my uncles. Eva pretends I hit 'er and falls back on the munda again but not in a tjilga bush though. Then she gets up again.

Laughs are comin' outa my mouth now, I'm feelin' better.

Then, Eva started laughin', too.

We both laughin' so 'ard we fall back over together, almost outa breath. We lay there quiet-way for a while. From the bushes we look out over the white sand beach and the dark blue wanna. No-one can see us there tucked behind the bushes on the warm munda, 'cept for the minya ant mooga, no-one can hurt us here, me and my big sister. I wanna stay here forever, I think, and sink into the warm sand.

'Jindu duthbin,' Eva whispers, moving 'er lips towards the sun goin' down over the saltbushes behind us. The waves almost drown out her voice. 'We better get back to camp.'

★

Next mornin' I wake up and I've pissed the bed but it don't even matter, the seaweed smells anyway, and no-one even notices. I do a big yawn and look 'round at my sisters on our seaweed mattress. They all look like minya djita mooga in a nest there. A big smile comes over my face. I see Eva smilin' back.

She throws 'er 'ead over towards the wanna, 'er tangled 'air blowin' in the wind.

Lookin' over I can see the tide way out. My mouth's waterin' and I run my tongue over my lips.

'Are you thinkin' the same as me?' Eva say.

We both jump up and run to get a stick from the bushes, then cut it flat-out-way down the beach. Sarah cryin' for us to wait for 'er.

'Come on, sissy,' I yell out, 'We gonna 'ave a good feed of gulda marra for breakfast.'

'Hooray.' Sarah claps her hands as she runs after us.

We don't need nets to catch crabs like them walbiya mob, when the tide's out like this we go out on the flats with a stick. When we see dark patches in the white sand we poke the stick in and tap the crabs' backs and straight 'way they stick up their nippers. Then we flat-out-way grab them by their claws and take them to camp and throw them on the coals to cook. Ada's always in a real good mood when we catch gulda marra 'cause she like havin' a good feed too. She pick out the meat to give to my younger sisters, for them to 'ave a feed too. Sometimes all of us go out together to get gulda marra so we get a big feed for everyone.

Later, all us kids go to our special spot by the old Denial Bay jetty, to get more numu mai. Then, with our toes in the sand, we feel 'round for cockles and get periwinkles off the rocks too. We put all of the wanna mai in a big pile on the beach, and when we finished we take them back to camp and cook them on the coals. We get salt water and boil the periwinkles in a billy can, and get a safety pin to pick out the meat. Some grown-ups and bigger kids go up the jetty to catch fish and if we lucky we get to 'ave a good feed of fish cooked in the coals. Mumma always cooks damper too.

I love 'olidays at Denial Bay so much, I never want 'em to end, I just want 'em to go on for ever and ever.

One night, snuggled up to Mumma 'round the campfire, I say, 'It's so deadly here. Was it like this when you were a minya wunyi?'

'Well, when I was minya wunyi like you, I lived on the Mission too, but we moved 'round a lot more.' Mumma Jenna stoked the coals with a stick. 'When we not on the Mission, in summer we come down to the beach and eat wanna mai and bush tucker like our Old People 'ave for long time. Then, when winter comes, we go back that way.' She points with 'er murra, back towards the Mission. 'And eat other mai. Mulu, wadu, rabbity, joongu joongu, things like that.' Then Mumma smile like she gone back to when she's a gidja, and the fire there make 'er look like she's shinin'. 'I used to play in the wanna here, just like you kids, now,' she tells me.

The fire crackled like it was agreein' with 'er.

'I reckon it's rotten how them Mission mob keep us cooped like jookie jookie layin' eggs,' I say to Mumma.

'You know,' Mumma say gentle-way, movin' 'er murra through my 'air, 'my Papa, your Granny Charlie Freedom, he was a strong man, he spoke up for us Nyunga mob when the Missionaries treat us bad-way. He even wrote letter to government boonri mooga in the big city askin' for them to take over 'cause the church mob not treatin' us right-way. Lotta people starvin' and gettin' sick, gidjida mooga too. Not enough work or rations. It was a real bad time for us mob.'

'What happen then?' I ask, amazed that my Papa Charlie and other Nyunga mooga would do that, stand up to wal-biya mob like that.

'Well, nothin' at first, but Papa Charlie rounded up the men with their picks and shovels and walked down the road on the Mission there, in front of the boonri's 'ouse, and demand that we be treated right-way.'

'Wow, that's deadly.' My guru mooga nearly poppin' outa my gugga.

'Hey, look out!' Eva laughed.

'Yeah, them Missionary mob got real ngulu after that, thought somethin' bad was gonna happen to 'em. They shit themselves.'

Us kids all look at each other and giggle.

'Some things changed but some things stayed the same.' Mumma looks into the fire. 'You can't change some things, girls, but you mustn't stop tryin' either. Us Nyunga mooga stuck together and some things changed for the better. You always remember that story now, and when you grow up, you will get more wisdom to know what you can change and what you can't. The Good Lord will give you that wisdom if you pray and ask 'im for it.'

I put my gugga down then and feel shame how I bin real cheeky to God and Jesus lately. But I only be cheeky 'cause they won't answer my prayers. I sit quiet-way after that and think 'bout all us Nyunga mooga comin' together on the Mission to help each other. I think about all the fightin', 'specially when they drunk and arguin' now, and I just can't see everyone doin' what Papa Charlie done long time ago.

Mumma put more wood on the fire, it crackles like biggy ngunchu burru in the oven.

'Mumma,' I ask her, 'why some of our own mob treat us real bad-way, call us nasty names?' I thinkin' 'bout them boys on the beach kickin' sand at me and Eva earlier. 'Why lotta people fight on the Mission an' 'urt each other?'

She makes one big sigh and crosses 'er murra mooga, like she's thinkin' 'bout what she's gonna say next. Then she open 'er mouth and 'er words come out real slow-way.

'Sometimes, when you pushed down too low and put down all the time, you start believin' you're low and dirty and scum of the earth. Then you look 'round at your own mob and you start thinkin' the same 'bout them too. So you start actin' that way towards yourself, with no respect, and towards your own mob, disrespectful-way. That's how it works, girl. But you clever minya wunyi mooga, indie?'

We make big nods with our gugga. I agree with Mumma. I'm smart minya wunyi.

'So you nyindi to be respectful and carry yourself with pride like your Papa Charlie and speak out when you need to. And like the Good Lord, treat all men as equals, and always stand up for what's right for Nyunga mooga.'

As I curl up next to Ada and my sisters that night, I feel real strong inside, like nothin' in the whole wide world's gonna hurt me. 'Sticks and stones can break my bones but names will never hurt me,' I whisper as I fall to sleep, thinkin' of Papa Charlie and all them brave Nyunga mooga. Makes me feel real strong and proud to be Nyunga, and now I nyindi why them kids treat us mean-way 'cause Mumma give the answer to work it out.

Us kids real sad when we see that stupid Mission truck burnin' down the dirt road comin' to round us up and take us back to the Mission, like sheep dog with nyarni mooga in a paddock. Take us back to that dirty, cramped minya cottage with the stinkin' mattress that smell of goomboo and those rotten bedbugs all skinny and hungry-way waitin' for us.

'I wanna stay here,' I yell at Ada.

Goin' back to the Mission reminds me of all the ngoonji promises and grown-up lies.

'Don't start, Grace,' Ada says with a look on 'er wah that says she will crack me if I muck 'round.

I swear under my breath, but Ada 'ears me. I've done it now.

'What did you say?' She's yellin, slappin' me 'round the yuree. 'Your filthy minya mouth gettin' you in trouble again, Grace, and we not even back at the Mission, yet.' She 'it me a couple more times. 'Keep it up and I'll really give you somethin' to whinge about.'

I run away from 'er and stand behind a jinditji, lookin' back at the houses near the jetty.

'Hurry up and get on the truck now,' Ada hisses through 'er teeth at me.

I frown at 'er and kick the leaves of the bush, then run past 'er quick-way before she can slap me again. Grown-ups 'elp me up on the truck and I go sit between Eva and Polly.

On the way back to the Mission I ask Eva, 'Who's that Tessie weena whose place we went to that night when that drunken Nyunga went joobardi with the knife?'

'She's Old Rod's sister,' Eva say, then turns away from me like she don't wanna talk no more.

Before the truck gets back to the Mission my leg start hurtin' real bad again but I'm sick of worryin' if God's punishin' me so I just think about all the fun we had at Denial Bay to try to forget about the pain.

When we get 'ome I'm lyin' on our bed cryin'. Ada thinks it's 'cause I got the goonas with 'er for slappin' me but my leg's hurtin' real bad.

Mumma comes in to see me. She sits down on the bed next to me and brushes my tangled 'air off my face.

'What's wrong, girl?'

Mumma's voice always feels like honey goin' down a sore throat, real soft and soothin'.

'It's my jinna, Mumma,' I tell 'er, movin' my murra down my leg to where it's achin'.

'It must be the pipe you bin tripped over on the way back from school the other week, that Polly tell me 'bout,' she say.

I nod my gugga.

Mumma put 'er murra under 'er armpits and wipe out the smell from there, then with 'er murra mooga rub my jinna where it's sore.

'Nguggil make your leg strong,' she say, rubbin' 'er murra hard round my jinna where it hurt.

'It's feelin' better now, Mumma,' I say, after she's bin rubbin' it for a while.

'See, that's Nyunga-way, the Old People teach us that.' She's smilin'. 'We got word that your Jumoo Rick Joanus comin' soon, he might 'ave a look when he comes.' 'Er face look real serious-way then. 'You might 'ave mumoo in there.'

My eyebrows go up on my ngulya.

'Nunkerie can see right inside your jinna and take that mumoo out if it in there.'

'No mumoo in my jinna, Mumma,' I tell 'er, sittin' up.

But I'm just sayin' that 'cause I don't want to believe it. Nothin' else but mumoo would make my jinna hurt like hell, like this.

'You just lie down there now and don't worry, Grace. Jumoo will know what to do. He'll be 'ere soon to 'elp.'

Mumma go out the room then and Ada come in.

'You right, my girl?' she ask in a nice voice.

'Jinna's real sore,' I tell 'er.

'Yeah, I nyindi.'

She sits down next to me. She looks at me sorry-way and brushes my fringe out of my eyes and tucks it behind my yuree.

'I'm sorry I growled you today, Grace.'

'That's 'right, Mumma Ada,' I say, 'I can be proper naughty minya wunyi sometimes.'

Ada nods and we both smile.

'You rest now,' she say quiet-way before she goes out the room.

I lie there scared-way, thinkin' 'bout mumoo runnin' round in my jinna, makin' it hurt real sore-way, makin' my jinna minga. I think about how mumoo can act funny-way sometimes, how they jump right into you if you run 'round the wrong places and step on one.

I try to think of somethin' else, somethin' nice and calm to stop thinkin' 'bout mumoo mooga. I close my guru mooga and I see Old Rod's face smilin' at me with a big box of fruit and I start stuffin' my face. Then, I see us drivin' into town with 'im in 'is car and we crossin' the railway line. I reckon there's a mumoo that lives on the railway line that likes to jump in and out of Old Rod when he drives past, when he takin' Ada and us girls into town. 'Cause he sure act different when he goes over that railway line. Oh no, I'm thinkin' 'bout mumoo again, it must've jumped from my jinna into my gugga.

I just want that mumoo to go 'way so I pray.

'Dear God and your Son Jesus. I know I bin real naughty minya wunyi lately, cursin' youse and all, but I promise if you make this mumoo go away, I'll be a good girl from now on and even if you can't I'm gonna try my best to be good minya wunyi from now on. Amen.'

8

Mumoo jumpin' 'round

As I'm lyin' in my bed waiting for Jumoo, I start to think about solvin' my riddle again and Old Rod's there in my gugga, or mumoo pretendin' to be 'im. I look at 'im this way, and then that way. Slow-way, I try to work 'im out. Sometimes he acts like walbiya and sometimes he acts like Nyunga. Sometimes, he mixes it up and acts both ways. It's real confusin'. To work a riddle out you gotta look for things that match that are the same, and look for things that match that are different.

Like when Papa and my uncles go out huntin' they look out 'cross the munda and they can see malu movin' long way 'way. Walbiya mooga can't see what they see, they can't see the malu like Nyunga mooga 'cause they used to lookin' at the munda 'nother way.

'Where? I can't see any kangaroos,' they say. 'You must be imagining things.'

But muggah, our men nyindi the malu's there, 'cause they look with their guru mooga different-way, they look all at once, for everything that's the same, and for anything that's different. And sure enough, when they get closer, there's the malu 'cause they seen it long way back and they nyindi the malu's there. They might look for other clues too: fresh goona on the munda. If it's dry, malu bin there long time ago, if it's soft, then malu nearby. 'Nother thing's smell. The men use their moolya to smell for malu goomboo and goona but the wind gotta be blowin' right-way 'cause them malu mooga can smell too, and if they smell Papa and my uncles, they jump away. Then we go hungry. That's 'ow I bin lookin' at Old Rod, same way as Papa and my uncles when they go huntin' for malu and the same way that eagle watches them rabbity mooga.

When I look close-way at Old Rod, I see some things the same, and I see some things different. I notice that Old Rod treats us nice-way on the farm and when he take us campin' outback to check 'is stock or fix fences, but when he takes us in town, that's different. He acts funny-way, like he don't know us.

Why's he do that?

When he acts different, it's always just after 'is old truck crosses the railway line headin' into town, over them railway tracks at the crossing, always then. It's like them railway lines're a big mark in the munda where things change. Not like them lines or tracks Papa Neddy and Mumma Jenna or the other grown-ups, draw in the munda with a stick or their murra to tell us stories 'bout our Old People or animal footprints. Not them tracks. More like them lines Eva draws when she gets moogada with me for annoyin' 'er. She stand in the hut on the farm and stretch out 'er arm with a big stick and draw a circle 'round in the dirt and says I'm not allowed to go over that line or she'll 'it me. And I just gotta put my jinna over that mark in the munda to see if she tellin' ngoonji. Then, when my big toe crosses over that line, that's it, everything changes, real quick-way. We fight and I go cryin' to Papa Neddy. Then Eva gets in trouble from Papa and she's even more moogada with me then and teases me, 'Ah, you Papa's minya pet.'

That railway line's like that. When Old Rod crosses it, everythin' changes, 'is eyebrow drop over 'is guru mooga and them wrinkles in 'is ngulya go all deep and squash together. That's when he reaches under 'is seat and grabs a bottle of gubby and drinks it down quick-way. Then he starts to growl Ada 'bout minya things. Things that don't even matter. Like the minya stain on Eva's dress or me jinna nigardi. Ada always puts 'er 'ead down then and don't say nothin'. Me and Eva do the same. But I still look up, sly-way, outa the corner of my guru, to watch 'im. Try to figure 'im out, that tjilbi. Try to work out why he acts different-way, after we cross that railway line.

When we get into town, he always drop us at the bushes, near the 'ospital, by the wanna, and we 'ave to walk into the main street from there like he don't want other walbiya mob to see us with 'im.

'I've got business to do,' he always tells Ada. 'You meet me back here with the girls, later on.'

And he has a big important voice when he say that, when he talks about 'is big business he's gotta do. Like, it's so important that the sun might not come up the next day, unless he do that business right away. He gives 'er bunda then and we always 'ave to meet 'im at the same place later.

If Ada sees 'im in town and asks 'im how long he's gonna be, he talks real quick-way to her, then flat-out-way leave us then, like he don't even know us. He act more like the other walbiya mob in town. They pretend we not even there, or just stare at us, whisper behind their murra, real funny-way. Makes us feel shame when they do that. I know Old Rod's different from them whitefellas but he acts like them when he's in town. It's like when he's 'round 'is own walbiya mob, he act like them and when he's 'round Nyunga mooga he act more like us. He look after us though, gives Ada bunda, buys us things, gives us food to eat, and gives us rides in 'is big truck and sometimes 'is moodigee.

On special days, not very often though, Old Rod drops us at Mona Tareen's Frock Salon and goes in and talks to the boonri weena.

'You buy a good dress for yourself, and clothes and shoes for the girls,' he tells Ada.

When me and Eva were real minya she bought minya moona mooga for us too. Every summer and winter we get new clothes and Ada has to look after them bultha and boogardi mooga, otherwise Old Rod gets real wild and tells 'er off.

When I was minya, three or four, I didn't see how Old Rod acted different-way to us when he's 'round walbiya mob, but as I get older I notice more. Since I've bin lookin' for clues I see more things now too.

★

It was good fun goin' with Old Rod into town and even deadlier if we went with 'im to the Ceduna Show. Ada would dress us up real flash-way in our clothes from Mona Tareen's and us kids'd look real deadly. Ada'd dress real nice-way, too. We'd be so excited, waitin' for Old Rod to pick us up at the Three Mile Gate, that it'd be real hard to keep clean. We'd be runnin' 'round Ada playin' catchy, slidin' 'round on the munda, fallin' down and actin' real silly-way. But Ada give us good growlin' to make us keep clean. We'd start jumpin' up and down when we see Old Rod comin' down the road in 'is flash green Holden or 'is big truck if he got pigs, sheep or bullocky to put in the show. He's always winnin' first prize with 'is animals. He pick us up, drive us to the show and give us bunda to go on the rides and play games. My favourite ride's the hurdy gurdy and I like puttin' the balls in them clown's mouth too. But I never win anythin', only jidla toy, 'cause they cheatin' mob, them fellas that work there at the show. We go flat-out-way 'til we got no more bunda. Then we look for Old Rod again. We go 'round the animal fences, through the legs of all them walbiya mooga, all them farmers there waitin' for the judgin' of their biggy ngunchu or sheep or bullocky, yarnin' with each other. They all look the same with their boogardi mooga, trousers, overcoats and their moona mooga on their heads. So we gotta scoot 'round lookin' up and tryin' to find Old Rod's wah. It's a long way up to find 'is wah when you real minya.

When we find 'im, I tug at 'is overcoat 'cause I don't know what to call 'im. Then he turns 'round and looks down at us. 'Is eyebrows close together and ngulya all wrinkled.

'What do you want?' he'd say real quick-way, like he's busy.

'Can we 'ave more money?' I'd say in my sweetest minya voice.

I tilt my gugga sideways and screw up my face, sort of like a smile. I feel shame askin' 'im but I gotta get more bunda to go on more rides and to play more games.

'I've already given you money,' he says.

Then, shakin' 'is gugga and smilin', he reaches into 'is pocket and pulls out a handful of coins, shillings and two-bob coins, if we lucky. Then he tells us not to come back again, and wait with Ada when we're ready to go 'ome.

Back then I never noticed how he acted different-way to us 'round walbiya mooga 'cause I was too young, too busy havin' fun. But since I bin lookin' all the way 'round at 'im, I see other things too, like how things are different when we with Old Rod, to when we doin' things with our Nyunga mob. With Old Rod 'round, us kids get growled to behave and we don't talk our language much. When we with our own mob us kids can play 'round and do more things and we talk anyway we want, Kokatha wonga too. But we never go hungry when we with that old man. When we on the Mission, it's different, sometimes our djuda mooga get real hungry from no food. That's why I hide my minya stash of food in the fireplace.

When us Nyunga mooga go into town together it's good fun, no one growls us 'bout what we wearin', no one's actin' like they don't know us or droppin' us off in the bushes by the wanna. Even though families fight sometimes, us Nyunga mob stick together when we leave the Mission, we 'ave to, to look after each other. That's what Papa says. He says it's not safe to go walkin' 'round on your own in town.

I think 'bout when us Nyunga mooga go into town together for work or on the ships or special times like the show or circus, we go on the back of the Mission truck. Wind blowin' our gugga uru all over the place. People smilin', jokin' and laughin'. Everyone 'appy 'cause we don't go to town much. We stuck on the Mission like nyarni mooga in the paddock. 'Baah. Baah.' So when we get to go out it's real good fun.

Like the time when I was really minya and the Mission truck was waitin' to take us somewhere special. Just before, Matron from the Children's 'Ome give us second-hand clothes. Mumma Jenna spread them out on the kitchen table there. All us mob start goin' through 'em then. Next minute, I see this deadly overcoat, checked one, with all green colours and black too. It's real flash, no buttons but it's got a belt that goes 'round the waist. I quick-way grab that overcoat and 'old it up to me.

'It's too big for you. That'll fit Eva,' Aunty Dorrie say, holdin' 'er murra out.

'No it don't. It fits me better,' I yell at her.

'Come on now, Grace. It's way too big for you,' Aunty Dorrie says, comin' over to grab it off me. I see from 'er face that she moogada with me, 'er one guru squish smaller than the other one and 'er lips point out and 'er voice is gettin' louder too.

'No. It's mine.' I run into the bedroom. 'I'll grow into it. Anyway, you just sayin' that 'cause you want it for yourself,' I yell out cheeky-way.

'Gorn, it too small for me. You just a selfish minya wunyi.'

I slam the bedroom door and take my clothes off. Then I put my arms through the sleeves and do the belt up really tight-way in a big knot. I know no-one can take it off me 'cause I'm nigardi underneath and they'll get in trouble from Papa and Mumma. I nyindi it's too big, that the hem's even touchin' the ground and when I put my arms out I can't see my murra mooga. But I don't care. I've seen it first, so it's my coat.

Even though it's hot I walk 'round in it all day. Mostly so no-one can steal it from me but also so they can see me wearin' it and get ngudgie for it, and want it for themself.

Later when Eva sees me she say, 'That's a nice coat. Where you get it from?'

I flick my 'air back snooty-way as I walk past her. 'It my overcoat and you not gettin' it.'

'You can 'ave your stupid coat,' she says. 'I don't want it but don't be so cheeky.' She goes to hit me but I cut it quick-way 'round the corner. No-one gonna get this coat off me, no-one. I'm a real stubborn minya wunyi. It might not fit me but no-one else's gonna 'ave it.

That same day, the circus comes to town, and last-minute-way Superintendent get the truck ready to take us kids there. 'Cause I playin' outside, I find out just when the truck's ready to go. My skinny minya jinna goin' flat-out-way inside.

'Too late now, girl. Truck goin' soon,' Mumma Jenna say. 'And you not even dressed. You just got that silly big coat on.'

'Nooo,' I scream and run into the bedroom.

I'm scratchin' 'round for somethin' clean to wear, but can't find nothin'. No clean clothes anywhere. Then, I start to cry 'cause I'm gonna miss the damn circus and I can't even find any clean duthu to wear under my coat. I still nigardi underneath.

Outside, the truck's startin' to go, leavin' me behind. No way I'm gonna miss out on the circus.

'I'm goin' anyway, Mumma,' I yell.

I run out the door after the truck. The dust flyin' up everywhere makin' it hard for me to see. Flat-out-way I'm runnin' after it through the dust, screamin' my head off with my overcoat flappin' in the wind, yellin' out for them to stop. Then they slow down to turn the corner and someone see me.

'Wait,' a voice yells out from the truck. 'Wait, one more little girl comin'.'

That big truck stop then, and they pull me up onto the back.

When we get there not everyone got bunda to pay to go in, so some of the grown-ups pull the tent up at the back and we crawl underneath. Then other Nyunga mooga pull us up from the seats and then all of us can see the circus. I pop up just behind a little walaba girl so I follow her, maybe there's a spare seat next to her. I can smell sawdust. Lookin' out to the middle of the circus ring I see all the pretty colours under the big bright lights, then when I look back that little girl in front of me has gone. She disappear into thin air. I look 'round. Then I hear a cry under the planks of wood and look down. She's there, on the munda. I can see 'er through the piece of wood I'm standin' on, one of our Nyunga mob helpin' 'er, pushin' 'er back up. I giggle and grab 'er hand and help 'er. She wipe 'er face on 'er pretty pink cardigan sleeve and smile at me.

'Lucky lion didn't get you,' I say, smilin' back.

Her guru mooga get real big and a weak minya scream come out 'er mouth then. She turn 'round and walk real careful-way after that.

Then I see our mob at the back and go sit with 'em.

Oh, that circus deadly fun. All them men and women swingin' from ropes and swings and doin' fancy things way up in the air; them joobardi clowns with red noses and boogardi way too big for them. They make us kids fall over laughin'. The animals doin' all them tricks. The pretty lady with all 'er sparkles ridin' on the big horse. But us kids crack up laughin' when that boonie do a big goona in the circus ring and that joobardi clown gotta get 'is shovel and scoop it up and 'nother joobardi clown squeezin' 'is big red moolya like it's the most boongada goona ever.

But my most favourite, that deadly minya Shetland Pony. That pony was so beautiful.

'I want one of those. They so cute,' I whisper quiet-way to myself.

So, I just can't believe it when at the end the man with the flash moona on 'is head call out for the kids to 'ave a ride on a pony. Real quick-way I run over to line up but them bigger kids beat me and I way back in the line.

'Hurry up, hurry up,' I'm mumblin' under my breath. 'They takin' for ages.'

I'm waitin', waitin', stompin' my jinna on the ground. Things always take long time when you minya.

'Come on,' I yell out to one of the kids. 'Don't be a hog of that pony. I want a ride too, you know. We goin' 'ome in a minute.'

'Oh, shut up, Grace,' yells 'Arold, one of the older cheeky boys, standin' behind me. 'Just 'cause you whitefella kid don't mean you special. You just goona oona. Wait your bloody turn like the rest of us.'

My lip stick out then and my eyebrow go over my guru mooga starin' at 'im. No-one can call me that name and get away with it. I swing my jinna long-way back, then swing it forward, kickin' 'im in the leg.

'Ouch!' 'Arold yells out.

He go to hit me then, but Molly who standin' behind 'im, grab 'is arm and pull it back real hard, nearly make 'im fall over.

'Why don't you pick on someone your own size,' she say, lookin' at 'im right in the face.

'Arold look like he in pain, but goojarb.

Molly let go then, and he fall forward, grabbin' 'is arm.

'Yeah. That'll teach you a lesson, pickin' on a minya wunyi like me,' I tell 'im, lookin' at 'im moogada-way, screwin' up my face and crossin' my arms.

'Arold squint 'is guru mooga at me like he gonna try and hit me again but I know he won't dare. Then I look at Molly and give 'er a big smile. Molly can be a real pain sometimes but this time she all right. That's 'cause our family look out for each other.

At last my turn. The man 'elp me up and I swing my jinna over the pony. I try to hold my overcoat when I get on but then that pony take off runnin' fast-way, and blow me down, if my overcoat didn't start flyin' up and down so everyone could see my goonanyigindi. I can't hang on to my coat or I'd fall off. All the kids are screamin' out and laughin' and pointin' at me, all them grown-ups too. At first I feel shame and curse 'em under my breath but after a while I don't care. I just throw my gugga in the air and ride that minya pony like it's mine.

When I get off the pony 'Arold say, 'Grace, you got no shame flashin' your jinjie for everyone to see.'

'I don't care,' I say to 'im. 'At least I'm not a scaredy-cat of girls, like you, big sook.' I poke my tongue at 'im then.

When I turn 'round, all the Mission mob are laughin' at me behind their murra mooga. I just straighten up my coat, flick my 'air over my shoulder and walk past them with my gugga held high. So what, I think, least I got a ride on my pony and I'm wearin' the deadliest overcoat on the Mission.

Even though kids tease me sometimes and the Mission mob laughin' at me that time we went to the circus, most times we go out we all get on all right. But it's a different story when we in town 'round walbiya mob, different story altogether. That get me thinkin' about Old Rod again. Them questions still swishin' round and round, in my gugga all the time. It's like Mumma on washin' day with 'er stick stirrin' and scrubbin' blanketie in them old concrete tubs at the side of the house. Blanketie usually need washin' cause I wet the bed again. I can't 'elp it, goomboo just comes out when I'm 'sleep.

'Grace, you goomboo minyi,' my sisters growl me in the mornin'.

Make me shame when they wongan like that. I know Ada real moogada too. She don't say nothin' though, she just real rough-way doin' things. She rip blanketie off the bed and throw it in the corner for washin'. Morning, the worst time in bed, all wet and cold with that stinkin' stale smell of goomboo in your moolya.

Night-time in bed better, before we go ungu. My most favourite place in the whole world's lyin' in Mumma Jenna's bed, snugglin' into 'er soft mimmi, like old Mrs Dempsey. My second favourite place in the whole wide world is our bed with Ada and my sisters, night-time when the bed all dry and warm. Blanketie pulled up over our heads on those minyardu nights in winter. Squished together like sardines, it feel all warm and safe. I like it that way, all close-way, just Ada and us girls. Nothin' can hurt us there in our bed. Not sticks or stones, or even names, 'cause that's our special place, all squished in together safe-way like that.

After my sisters stop whingein' and wrigglin' and settle down for the night, it gets real quiet. That's when I lie there and think 'bout things, everything that happened during the day. Sometimes I start thinkin' 'bout Old Rod again. At Denial Bay, Eva said he not our father, but lotta things don't make sense. Like why he 'elp us so much? And as far back as I can think in my gugga, he always bin there with us, not like Nyunga family, just always there in the background. I lie there quiet-way but it get real annoyin' swishin' round and round in my gugga like blanketie on washing day.

One night I decide I'm gonna ask Ada 'bout Old Rod when she fallin' 'sleep the next night. She bin real nice to me lately, with my jinna still sore, waitin' for Jumoo. I bin waitin' long time for 'im. He must have lotta people he visitin' to make 'em better. He like walbiya doctor, only he make people better Nyunga-way. My jinna still real sore but it feels bit better since Mumma Jenna rub nguggil on it all the time. Anyways I'm gonna try to get answers from Ada while she tired-way, 'cause usually she don't wanna talk 'bout Old Rod.

Next day, I try to put 'er in good mood.

'I'll change baby's nappy, Ada,' I tell 'er real sweet-way, and grab my baby sister out 'er arms.

'You right with your jinna, Grace. It's still sore, indie?'

'It feel minya bit better,' I tell 'er, takin' Lil-Lil from 'er.

'You be careful with them safety pins there, Grace,' Ada tell me.

'Yeah, I'm 'right.'

I real careful-way push them pointy wada mooga through the nappy there. Then I walk slow-way outside with the fire bucket to empty last night's ashes and fill it with hot coals from the fire in the backyard. Most of the time, grown-ups do this in case kids get burnt but I wanna help Ada so she gives me answers later. We always do the fire bucket this way when it's cold at night. It keeps us real warm like them flash radiators walbiya mooga use.

That fire at the side of the house work real hard day time and sometimes at night-time too, if we got plenty of wood to keep it goin'. We use it to heat up billy tea, damper, gulda, malu and sometimes even wadu.

Later, that fire will be heatin' up water buckets for Mumma, Ada and the aunties to do the washing. Them tubs the best place for hide-and-seek with blanketie pulled over you. But look out if Mumma or the other mothers find you there, you get big hidin'. Like that time the other week when I throw blanketie back and jump outa the tub.

'Ahh!' Mumma Jenna scream, jumpin' back and grabbin' 'er guddadu. 'You nearly give me 'eart attack.'

'It's just me, Mumma. I'm playin',' I tell her.

Mumma grab the big stick to hit me but I too quick. I cut it flat-out-way to find 'nother hidin' spot.

'Don't come back, you little rat. I could've poured boilin' water over you,' she screamed, real panic-way.

When they wash nappies, blanketie and our bultha, they put the hot water in them tubs with Rinso or Velvet soap all grated up. Then they get a big stick and stir it 'round and 'round, then flat-out-way scrub with washboard 'til everything real clean to hang on the clothes line that Papa put up at the back with two big sticks and fork stick to lift it off the ground. That's outa bounds too, that clothes line. Mud pies and clean nappies don't mix. You try that one, and you get good beltin' with that big washin' stick. I know that from first hand. It hurt like hell.

The fire buckets keep us warm at night, like Mumma's damper in the ashes, all warm so butter would melt on us. Then we nice and warm 'til mornin' even though old Jack Frost is out there. In the mornin' we warm, unless goomboo in the bed, then we all wet and cold. But we can get up and warm ourselves by the stove in the kitchen, 'cause Mumma Jenna always lights it up, first thing in the mornin'. When it's cold, sometimes Uncle Murdi will let Yudu sleep on 'is bed to help keep 'em warm. But we don't 'ave a booba, we just got each other.

Later that night, when we all cosy cuddlin' up in bed under the blanketie, and my sisters 'ave stopped wrigglin' 'round and started to go to sleep, I turn quiet-way to Ada. I know I can't ask 'er straight-out-way 'bout Old Rod or she'll growl me to go to sleep. So I ask 'er round-about-way question.

'Ada,' I whisper, and wait for 'er reply.

'Mmm.' She nearly 'sleep.

'You know that place we use to camp, at back of that old Catholic church in town?'

She say nothin'. Maybe she's sleepin'.

I think back to when I'm a minya wunyi and Ada and us kids in town camping on that munda behind that church on the edge of town. Sometimes our family camped there. It was a safe place to go in the 'olidays where no Mission walbiya mooga bothered us. We stayed in a wuthoo we made out of some iron and any tin we could find and branches and leaves from the trees, real cosy inside. Even if it's windy outside we warm inside. It's our special place. I feel real proud 'cause Old Rod came 'round and say, 'This is for you, Ada, this land is yours and the girls'. I bought it from the Council so you've got somewhere safe to live in town. No-one can kick you off this place.'

'Why Old Rod say that place ours?' I askin' 'er, a minya bit louder this time.

''Cause he bought it for us, that's why.'

'Why'd he do that?'

''Cause he wants somewhere for us to stay, to get us off the Mission.'

'Why aren't we stayin' there now?'

''Cause when Council found out he bought it for Nyunga mooga they gave 'im back 'is bunda. Said no blacks 'lowed to own land or live on land bought for 'em, they 'ave ta live on the Nyunga Missions and Reserves.'

I lie there quiet-way then, and think about that. That's not nice for Council to do that. Just 'cause we're Nyunga. Then I think 'bout how walbiya mooga treat us in town. They must think we like biggy ngunchu in a pigsty that we can't 'ave the same flash things as them, that we can't live in town like them with flashy wada mooga hangin' in their windows. Why they like that for? Whitefellas got funny ways sometimes. Old Rod, he good fella, though. He bought us a place to stay. Why he different from them other fellas?

I think again 'bout that special block of land that Old Rod bought us. When we minya, Eva and me use to go down to the church tank and get water in our billy can for Ada to make cuppa tea and for washin' and cookin'. Lotsa Nyunga mooga would come to our camp and sit 'round the campfire at night. We'd make our campfire real big and while we sittin' 'round gubarlie mooga were tellin' us minya ones 'bout our Seven Sisters, our weena mooga Ancestors and the big giant man, our wadi Ancestor, sparklin' up there in the sky. Sometimes there'd be a corroboree 'round the campfire. When the men doin' their corroboree us weena mooga and kids 'ave to cover ourselves under the blanketie. That's men's business, we not allowed to see what they doin'. Under the blanketie, I smell campfire and dust, and hear the men singin', and clappin' their boomerangs and jibin, together. It was real excitin' and minya bit scary too, for a minya wunyi like me. The sound and feel of the Nyunga mooga gu jinna, thumping on the munda real close-way, make me ngulu but I wanna see what's happenin' so I find a minya hole in the blanketie and peek through and start singin' make-up words to join in. '*Yudi, yumba, yarni. Yudi, yumba, yarni.*'

I remember Ada slap me then and pull the blanketie up so I can't see no more.

'You naughty minya wunyi. Don't be so cheeky,' she growl me quiet-way. 'That men's jooju ingin. You wanna get in trouble?' she tellin' me wild-way. 'That's imin. You wanna get sick, girl?'

'Nooo. I don't wanna get sick, Ada,' I whisper grabbin' my jinna.

I was only minya wunyi. I didn't understand them sorta things back then.

Anyway, it's real warm in our bedroom 'cause the fire bucket's still glowin' bright.

'Ada, why Old Rod buy us that block to live on?' I got to work this old man out so my gugga can rest when I go ungu later. 'He just 'nother walbiya, indie?'

Ada start kickin' me with 'er jinna.

'Don't be so cheeky, Grace. He does a lot for you. He feed you and clothe you.'

I pull my jinna 'way so she won't kick me and pull the blanketie over my gugga. Two of my minya sisters, Lil-Lil and Sarah start to cry. I musta woke them up when I moved my jinna.

'He's not just 'nother walbiya,' Ada yells. 'He's a bloody decent man to us.' She stopped kickin' me then. 'If it wasn't for 'im we'd be starvin', Grace. You remember that before you open that big cheeky mouth of yours.'

I lie there sobbin' but my minya sisters' cryin' drowns me out.

'Now, look what you've done. You woke up your sisters,' Ada says nasty-way.

Squeezin' my guru mooga tight I try to disappear into the dark. I push the back of my murra into my teeth and bite as hard as I can 'til I taste blood in my mouth. Then I let go and float up into the sky. I don't care if mumoo get me. I don't care if I never come back again. I fall into deep sleep. Then, out of the dark I see Old Rod's face glowin' like our fire bucket, all warm.

'Who are you old man?' I ask 'im.

He don't say nothin'. He just holds 'is murra moogas out to me.

'Why no one want to tell me 'bout you?' I ask again. 'It's like you one big secret.'

He open 'is mouth to talk.

'Grace, you bloody goomboo minyi.'

Why he callin' me goomboo minyi?

And I wake up then, wet, cold and miserable, and not one more clue for the riddle, only Eva screamin' at me.

'Eva,' I yell back, 'you just woke me up from a real important dream.'

That's when I thought of it again. Why don't I ask Old Rod the questions?

9

Walbiya gu minga: white man's sickness

On Sundays everyone on the Mission go to church and listen to Pastor talk from the Bible. That church bin there long time, it's older than me. Mumma Jenna say, her father, Granny Jimmy bin show the Pastor the right place to put the Mission long, long time ago and that's where we live now.

This Sunday, Pastor preaches to us 'bout how the devil can sneak up on you through gubby, gamblin' and what he says is bein' 'immoral'. I don't know what that flash word means, s'pose it means bein' a sinner.

That bloody devil must be everywhere then. He must be like a minya mumoo, sneakin' 'round, jumpin' in through people's windows and runnin' amuck on the Mission and nothin' Pastor can do 'bout it, 'cause all them adults just tell lies to 'im when he asks. Maybe the devil makin' 'em do it, whisperin' in their yuree. Anyways, I reckon them Ten Commandments just one big joke. Nyunga mooga must think they're to be broken.

I think 'bout how Old Rod and Ada give us girls gubby to drink to 'elp us go ungu some nights. And I wonder if the devil makin' them do that too, and are we sinners for drinkin' the gubby, even if the grown-ups give it to us? I don't even like the taste anyways, it burns when it goes down my throat and into my djuda. They bin doin' that since me and Eva minya girls, three or four years old. Sometimes when we park the moodigee at night and Old Rod and Ada sneak off together, it's real scary. Everythin' is quiet and black outside. I'm shakin' in my skin, so scared mumoo or jinardoo's gonna get me. You can 'ear the minya djita mooga when they get woken up by somethin' walkin' past their nests, they scared too. But then the gubby starts to make me real tired and I nod off to sleep. I don't like it when I wake up though, 'cause I need drink of water and my yudda feels like it's got cotton wool in it and my gugga hurt real bad. Why grown-ups wanna drink when they feel like that next day?

Just the other day, some uncles snuck into the Mission six bottles of wine in hollowed-out loaves of bread from town. And a weena brought new pack of cards in baby's nappy, had to wash them though, 'cause baby done a goona before they got 'ome. And other weena mooga met with some walbiya farmers, bullocky mooga, out past the back paddock so they can get more gubby for cards night comin' up soon. And poor old Pastor don't even know nothin' 'bout any of it, 'cause when he ask, everyone real polite-way tell 'im lies, straight to 'is face. Make me feel sorry for 'im. He think he's doin' a good job for God and Jesus, but nothin'.

Only trouble is, gubby means big fights and I hate it when people start fightin'. I get so scared but there's nowhere to hide where I feel safe. My minya sisters get real scared too. It's like all the old arguments the grown-ups had with each other, that are gone, come up again, oozin' up like a big red boil ready to pop. And look out when it does, 'cause it's real rotten. There's screamin', big punch-ups and sometimes people bleedin' and gotta go to 'ospital. It's real scary. When you minya wunyi you feel like you can't do nothin'. It's like the devil bin send this big fight and Jesus and God not there to protect us. When you look and see someone gonna get hit in the gugga with big bunda you want to tell 'em to stop. But you can't go there to tell 'em 'cause you too frighten, screamin' your head off and with your murra mooga over your yuree hopin' to make it go away.

Sometimes, Ada run away with us, take us to Old Rod's farm, where it's safe.

Sometimes Pastor and Superintendent come and try and break up the fightin' and call the wultja mooga. If the wultja mooga don't come straight 'way, they come next day to look for them fellas who bin fightin' to take 'em to jail but our mob real cunnin' 'cause they tell 'em wrong way to go to look for someone when we all know they bin went the other way. Then wultja mooga give up and no-one gets put in jail.

★

When I see the grown-ups playin' cards, I decide to use old pack of Mumma's cards that I pinch when she not lookin'. Then I set up card game with the kids. Whoever's got minya bit of bunda can play, we only play a penny a go. Most of the kids're real stupid though, so I win lotta money, enough for a good feed of lollies, anyway. If Papa catch us he'd give us good beltin' for gamblin' but he don't growl the grown-ups. 'Im, the Uncles and other men on the Mission, got a special spot in the bush, out the back of our oval where they play two-up. I hide in the bushes and watch 'em sometimes. They get real excited over two minya pennies bein' thrown up in the air. I don't know why they get so excited for.

Doesn't matter who wins, no matter what sorta gamblin', cause the money always get shared back 'round anyway. That's how things work on the Mission with Nyunga mooga. If someone's starvin' and 'nother person's got enough food to go 'round, they share. 'Cept for me. When I win my bunda, I sneak off to the shop and buy lollies and hide them in my secret hidin' place so I don't ever 'ave to go hungry. Only sometimes my stash runs out, 'specially if I get in real generous mood and decide to share it with my sisters and brothers, Nyunga-way, but that's hardly ever.

'Where you get these lollies from?' Eva ask me.

I tell 'er I found 'em. I just don't tell 'er where I found 'em, in the fireplace in my secret hidin' spot, otherwise she raid them next time and I won't 'ave any for myself.

Mumma tells me that sometimes when Superintendent catches Nyunga mooga gamblin' he call the wultja mooga, 'specially if they bin given warnin's before. Then, they gotta go to court and get big fine and if they don't pay, they go to jail. Stuff that. So when I play with the other kids we do it real sly-way and get one of the minya ones to look out for us. If anyone's comin' they whistle and we quick-way put the cards away and hide our bunda.

Card night the worst night, old Hetty Clare come over to play but she bin gubbyngarl all afternoon, so she already mouthy when she gets here. She lose all 'er money and Ada cleanin' up with royal flush. Hetty real bad sport and start cursin' Ada. Us kids walkin' round the house, and playin' chasie out the back in the dark but when we hear Hetty start screamin' we cut it inside and hide under the bed 'cause we know trouble comin'. I can see 'er through the bedroom door.

'You think you so good, Ada Oldman, don't you? You just walbiya gu burru. That's all you are.' She stand up then and sway on 'er jinna. 'You just a big bloody shame job, that's all you are. Your own father so shame of you he flog you while you joonie thuda with that first bastard kid of yours.'

Ada hang 'er 'ead shame-way. Then Hetty jump forward and grab Ada's 'air, yankin' real hard-way with one murra and hittin' 'er in the face with the other. Ada screamin' an' thrownin' punches at 'er to let go.

I'm so scared hidin' under the bed there, with my sisters and brothers, I curl up into a minya ball and start punchin' my yuree to try to make the screamin' stop. My minya sisters screamin' too, clingin' to me when they hear Ada bein' hurt, cryin' out in pain. I just wanna run out there and make it all stop, but I'm so scared, I can't move except for the shakin'. I can 'ear things bein' thrown in the kitchen, sound like Mumma's big pot, then glass smash. I hate it here on the Mission, I just wanna run a million miles away and take my minya sisters away too, so we safe.

Mumma Jenna jump up then and grab Hetty by scruff of 'er neck and throw 'er towards the door.

'And us decent Nyunga mooga didn't want you 'ere either,' screams Hetty. 'That's why we threw bunda mooga at you when you came back with your bastard kid,' she yell out over 'er shoulder.

As Mumma boot 'er out the door, Hetty take a swipe at Mumma but Mumma grab Hetty's murra and send 'er flyin' through the door instead.

'Go 'ome or I'll get the crowbar onto you Hetty,' Mumma tell 'er. 'You can't come 'ere carrying on at my family like that.'

'Ahh,' Hetty Clare scream, stumblin' out the backyard. 'You all just a bloody mob of bastards, especially your arse'ole kids.'

Ada run off to our room cryin' then. I'm so glad she all right. She start grabbin' our clothes and blanketie and shovin' them into a sugar bag.

'Come on, you kids', she yell at us hidin' under the bed. 'Get outa there, we goin' to Old Rod's place.'

We walk for long time in the dark. Me and Eva helpin' Ada, carryin' our minya sisters. They whingein', complainin', they tired and hungry.

'We'll be right once we get to Old Rod's,' I tell 'em. 'He'll give us good feed.'

In the darkness ahead I can 'ear Ada sobbin'. I feel real sorry for 'er. Hetty can be real nasty weena, 'specially when she's drunk. Was it true what she said 'bout Papa beltin' Ada when she got joonie thuda for Eva, 'cause he's shame of her? And surely, Mission mob wouldn't be so mean as to throw bunda at 'er and minya guling. I wanna ask Ada if that's true but I know better. She might give me a floggin'.

As we walkin' along in the blackness, I look for our Seven Sisters in the sky, and think about everythin' that people 'ave bin wonganyi lately. If it's true what Hetty sayin', where was our father when this was happenin'? I think again, about when Eva say we don't 'ave one, 'cause he's not allowed to be our father. What's that mean? He should be 'ere to look after Ada, 'elp 'er look after us kids, to stick up for 'er. I get real angry thinkin' 'bout that and decide I'm gonna be more 'elpful to Ada from now on and not so cheeky. And just wait if I ever find out who our father is, I'm gonna give 'im a mouthful.

As we walkin' along I think about the time that some of us girls were minya. Me, Eva, Janie Burns, Raylene and some others left the Mission and cut it to Uncle Jerry and Aunty Dianna's place at Loffenhauser's farm. It was a real long way past the Mission on the way to Koonibba siding, where some Nyunga men worked on the railway line. When we got there they gave us cuppa tea and some bread but when we got 'ome me and Eva got a beltin' from Ada and all the adults were yellin' at us and tellin' us off about how dangerous it is for minya wunyi mooga to go wanderin' off like that without a grown-up. But I reckon walkin' behind Ada now with all the minya ones is far more dangerous. What if wild dogs get us? Ada must be real upset to do this, put us in danger like this.

When we get there, Old Rod's a real arse'ole to Ada. 'Why have you come here this hour of the night?' he yells at her.

Can't he see Ada's upset and got marks on 'er face from that ugly old battle-axe, Hetty Clare? Poor Ada got 'er gugga down like she always do when he growl 'er.

'Where am I going to put you and the girls tonight?' he yells. 'You need to give me warning, Ada, so I can arrange things.'

'I'm sick of all the fightin',' Ada say. 'Sick of livin' on the Mission, Rod. I wanna move off there.' She sobbin' then. She look so sad, like 'er 'eart breakin' in two.

Stuff tryin' to find out clues 'bout why Old Rod's different from other walbiya mooga and why he treat us nice-way, I think, lookin' at 'im walkin' up and down real moogada-way. He's just like them other walbiya mooga, mean, nasty old arse'ole.

After a while, he calms down and finds a place in the old caravan in the big shed for us to stay and then he brings us some bread and burru for a feed.

I never seen that side of Old Rod, he acted real mean. But at least he let us stay and we had a good sleep.

Next day, when Old Rod drops us back off at the Mission, my leg start achin' again. I'm thinkin' it's because of the big walk over to Old Rod's farm last night. Not long after, I'm curled up on our bed in pain again. Uncle Murdi come in and play 'is guitar to me, but it's still really sore. Mumma come in and shakes 'er gugga. Ada looks worried.

Mission Nursin' Sister come to see my leg when she find out. She move 'er murra over my jinna different-way to Mumma. 'Er hands are cold and stiff and she poke at my jinna like it's a piece of burru that she's tryin' to work out if it's fresh enough to eat. She sniff and fold 'er arms.

'It's not broken but I think it's best to get Doctor to have a look at it.'

Mumma and Ada both noddin'.

'You need to feed her more, Ada, she's far too skinny.'

I turn my gugga and look down at the munda, movin' my mouth from one side to the other. I hate it when walbiya mooga come into our cottage. They always so rude and bossy over us.

Ada and Mumma nod again. They don't tell Sister 'bout Jumoo, the nunkerie comin' to look at my leg, 'cause she won't understand, she don't nyindi Nyunga ways. She might even growl them for not puttin' their faith in the Good Lord and the walbiya doctor. But Mumma doesn't trust walbiya nurses and doctors ever since one of 'er grannies come 'ome with maggots in 'er ears, cause Sister didn't wash 'em properly. Mumma's a good midwife, she's delivered hundreds of babies, and she nyindi when a baby's not bein' looked after properly when they born.

They got funny ways them walbiya mooga sometimes, they treat us like booba mooga. Once when I was real minya, 'bout four, Ada sent me to get nyarni burru that the Nyunga butchers were cuttin' up over at the shed. She gave me bunda and said, 'Go get kuka for us and ask for nice pieces, you know, like chops. In this part,' she pointin' to 'er jinna.

At first, I didn't want to go 'cause it was real early in the mornin' and there was ice on the grass and I was only a minya wunyi and I knew my toes and murra mooga were gonna be freezin' but I knew we could be eatin' a nice stew or soup for tea. So off I went.

When I got there I was real shy and waited until they asked me what I wanted.

'I want some burru,' I say to the Nyunga workers.

If it was whitefellas cuttin' up the meat I'd be usin' manners. 'Can I 'ave some meat, please,' I'd say. Like I bin taught to do 'round walbiya mooga and to wongan to them proper-way in English, 'cause sometimes Mission mob growl us if they 'ear us talkin' Nyunga wonga. But 'cause it's our own mob I can talk how I wanna.

They try to give me horrible pieces from inside the nyarni but rememberin' what Ada told me, and worried she growl me, I shake my gugga and point to the leg part like she showed me.

'I want that meat there,' I say quiet-way with my guru mooga lookin' at the munda.

They laugh at me then, like I'm an idiot and I just wanna run all the way 'ome and hide under our bed, for shame.

'I'm sure you'd like that piece, but you can't 'ave it. That's for the Superintendent and 'is family,' they say, still laughin'.

Then they take the money Ada give me and hand me the fatty ribs.

Ada real moogada when I come 'ome with the 'shit burru', but I tell 'er what happen and she just shake 'er 'ead. Whether at me or them Nyunga mooga butchers, or the walbiya mooga, I don't know. But it wasn't my fault.

They really think they high almighty, walbiya mob. Like they own us or somethin'. Our Old People would 'ave somethin' to say to them, 'specially Granny Charlie.

'Nah. Don't worry we already got someone comin' to see my leg,' I call out to Sister as she walkin' outa our bedroom with Mumma and Ada.

Ada turn and give me moogada look that say, 'Grace, shut up, and don't be so cheeky.'

Mumma frown at me and lead Sister into the kitchen talkin' 'bout appointment with Doctor and things like that so Sister don't take notice of what I just said.

When Jumoo come to see me I'm real pleased 'cause I bin in bed for long time not even able to walk to go to the goomboo-wally unless Ada or Mumma 'elp me. My jinna in pain all the time now and I'm sure there's a mumoo in there and I want 'im to take it out straight 'way. The sooner it's out the better, 'cause all the grown-ups bin growlin' me.

'See, you wanna run 'round where you shouldn't be, 'round dangerous places, 'round campfires, course you gonna tread on mumoo,' they tell me. 'Goojarb, you got nobody to blame but yourself, Grace.'

I feel real shame and real guilty. Must be my fault I got mumoo in my leg for not listenin' to the grown-ups and runnin' round everywhere. I must be real naughty girl that's brought lotta shame on myself and my family. After a while I don't fight the pain, I just let it take over me. Maybe I deserve it, I tell myself.

When Jumoo come, he standin' there in the doorway lookin' round our bedroom. I wonder what he lookin' at. Nunkerie can see lotta things we can't, he can see inside someone, just like God and Jesus. He can see the sickness inside and with 'is murra he can take that sickness outa a person's body. He's a real special man. When he come over to the bed I can see Jumoo got a beautiful glow 'round 'im. 'Is guru mooga shine like the reflection on the water at night and like the stars in the sky. He put 'is murra on my head and feel my ngulya. Then he move 'is murra up and down my leg to feel for mumoo. 'Is guru mooga go real close together like he tryin' to see inside my jinna. Can he see a mumoo? Is it the same one that jumps into Old Rod's car when we cross over the railway line? Maybe this time that mumoo jumped into me.

'No. No mumoo 'ere,' he say as if he 'eard the question I was just askin' in my gugga. 'I can't fix this. This not Nyunga gu minga, this walbiya gu minga. You got to go to walbiya doctor to fix this one,' he tell us.

I'm real pleased I 'aven't got mumoo inside but worried at the same time. Walbiya gu minga must be real bad if Jumoo can't fix it. And how come I got it anyway if it belong to walbiya? Maybe Old Rod gave it to me? Or one of the walbiya Mission mob. Superintendent, most probably, he look like he would carry walbiya gu minga inside 'im the way he go round frownin' all the time. He can 'ave it back, I don't want it. How doctor gonna fix me? I start to worry then. Mumma and Ada look real worried too, 'specially later when Doctor tell 'em I gotta go on plane to Adelaide and it's so far away it's gonna take over one whole hour. Papa Neddy's not very 'appy that I 'ave to go away but he reckon I'm gonna be fine 'cause I got the Good Lord lookin' out for me. I better stop bein' so cheeky and start prayin' again, I s'pose.

10

Healin' jinna minga

Before I go to Adelaide, Sister check my 'air for gooloo in the Mission 'ospital, Superintendent standin' next to 'er. Sister pushes my gugga sideways real rough-way and start scratchin' round the back of my gugga uru. After a while she look up at Superintendent, 'er mouth open like she seen guldi or somethin'.

'This child has no head lice,' she tells 'im.

Superintendent's guru mooga open up wide-way, like he can't believe what she just said.

I shrug my shoulders and think, your gugga would 'ave no gooloo too, if Ada tipped stinkin' kerosene over it every time she seen you scratchin'. It stings like bloody hell too. Sometimes I'm sure them gooloo all long-dead and I'm only scratchin' cause that stinkin' stuff make my gugga itchy but she tip it on anyway, just in case. And when she's not doin' that she's holdin' us down, pullin' out the dead gooloo, slappin' us if we move. Sometimes the aunties do it too.

Lookin' round the old Mission 'ospital ward I shiver, lotta bad memories here when I was minya wunyi gettin' sick with high temperature, fever and everythin', all the time. Lyin' on the bed there by the window's the worst place of all, 'cause I nyindi the minya room where they put the dead people is just outside the window. I awake at night in the 'ospital bed, guru mooga wide open in the dark, sure I hear guldi breathin' real heavy-way in the empty bed next to me. Then I squeeze my guru mooga shut tight-way, frightened I might see somethin'. I hate this 'ospital so much, and I hate bein' sick.

Like that time I was 'ome with a fever. Ada goes out and see if she can find me somethin' to eat 'cause we got no mai at 'ome. Minya while later she come back with piece of bread and I cheeky-way throw it on the munda 'cause I'm too sick to eat and she tryin' to force me. Then Molly come in the room, goona stirrin'. I'm so moogada with 'er 'cause I just wanna be left alone but she keep goin' on and on. That's when I grab a penny near the bed and throw it real 'ard at 'er. It hit 'er right on the lip and bounce off, then she start squealin' like a minya biggy ngunchu and even though I feel as sick as a booba, I 'ave a chuckle behind my murra at her. I got big smile on my face, and I feel better then, 'cause I got 'er a good one, and I know she'll leave me 'lone to 'ave some rest now.

That Mission 'ospital's not so bad when Dr Dewer's there though. She's real nice doctor who take my appendix out one time and treat me real special-way. Sister bin put that stinkin' thing on my mulya and asked if I could count to ten. I thought she's stupid, course I can count to ten. But when I wake up I think I didn't count to ten, now she'll think I'm a baby and can't count. Then I feel the pain and forget about Sister. 'Nother pain this time, not like the djuda minga I had before, this one's different. I felt my djuda and there's a big sticky plaster on it and that's where the pain was coming from. Anyone who came to see me wanted to have a look at my djuda. Must've bin the most popular djuda in the whole world. Even after the plaster came off, everyone wanted to see my scar. I'm still real pleased to show it off when anyone asks 'bout it. I hope the doctors in Adelaide are nice like Dr Dewer.

I never bin on plane before so I'm real ngulu when Superintendent take me to the airport. When Papa see the big planes in the sky, he shake 'is gugga and say if we were meant to fly the Good Lord would've given us wings like wultja mooga. That's the eagle hawks that fly 'round our rockholes, lookin' out for 'em. I'm thinkin' what if the plane crashes to the munda or into the wanna and I die. But once I'm on the plane and the nice plane ladies there lookin' after me, I feel all right, 'cause they talkin' real nice to me and spoilin' me with pencils and colourin' book, givin' me drink and mai, makin' me feel real special.

When I get to the Children's 'ospital in Adelaide, though, I don't like it. Everythin' smells funny-way, and everyone's wah looks real serious and they talk like the walbiya mooga on the Mission boonri boonri-way and sometimes real rude, not like Mumma's nice voice. My bed's real hard with cold, scratchy white sheets, no hidin' if I goomboo. I wonder if nurses will growl me when I wet the bed and make more work for 'em. All these years I've bin hidin' from welfare, sly-way trickin' that fat old cow Sister McFlarety and now 'ospital mob got me, takin' me long-way 'way from my family. I'm wonderin' if they ever let me go 'ome.

Lyin' down on the bed, I put my face into my pillow and start cryin', quiet-way. I miss snugglin' up to Eva and my minya sisters in our big old bed on the Mission, our warm bodies squashed up close. I even miss their smell, I never knew they smelt so good, 'til now. When I'm with them there in our bed, I feel so safe. But everythin' 'ere's different. I feel scared and I don't feel safe either.

They bring me nice mai but at first I don't wanna eat 'cause I can't stop thinkin' of 'ome. But then a nice doctor come in and tell me I 'ave to eat to get better, and the sooner I get better the sooner I can go 'ome. So I eat like real djudayulbi after that, like a minya biggy ngunchu. Dr Taylor's my doctor's name and I'm real 'appy he's a sweet old tjilbi, real nice like Dr Dewer. He tells me my leg's minga with ost-eo-mye-lit-is, that's a big word that means infection in the bone. When I 'ear that name I know Jumoo was right, that I got walbiya gu minga, 'cause we got no word for sickness like that in our language. They put plaster under half my leg and wrap bandage 'round it so I can't walk on it, I just lie or sit there in bed all the time. The minga in my leg moves up and down, I can feel it from the pain. Pain's there all the time. They give me lotta medicine they call penicillin to try to help fix it but it'll take long time to get better, Dr Taylor says.

Even though I'm real bored all the time, after a while I get used to the 'ospital. I work out which nurses the nice ones and which ones are grumpy. The nice ones smile when I goomboo in bed and wash me and put clean bultha on me and change my sheets. The grumpy ones just act real grumpy. I'm in Suzanne Ward, the red pyjamas ward, there's lotsa nice kids in 'ere but there's this one ugly, cheeky boy same age as me, seven, and I don't like 'im at all.

'How many sisters and brothers you got?' bully boy asks me one day.

I start countin' on my fingers, Uncle Murdi's kids, Uncle Jerry's, Aunty Essie's . . .

'Twenty-somethin',' I say 'cause I'm sure I might've missed out a few.

'You are such a big fat liar,' he yells real loud-way at me.

'No I'm not. True God, that's 'ow many I got.'

'You can't 'ave that many sisters and brothers. I never heard such a big lie in my whole life,' he growls me.

I feel real shame 'im yellin' out loud-way that I'm a liar like that. I do 'ave that many sisters and brothers. How would he know anyway? Joobardi city kid. I want to jump outa bed and flog 'im but my leg's in plaster so instead I just put my 'ead into my pillow and don't talk to 'im for long time.

One day, I get real excited when I find out I 'ave minya relation stayin' in Duncan Ward next door, with the same jinna minga as me. 'Er name's Terry and she's the sweetest minya wunyi with curly hair that bounces when she shuffles along. But sometimes she real nuisance and the nurses growl 'er and tell 'er to go back to 'er ward. She has plaster all the way up 'er leg with a minya 'ole cut in it for a sore on 'er leg to get better. Nurses always growlin' 'er to stop pickin' at it but she just can't stop 'erself.

'You shouldn't pick it, Terry,' I tell 'er like I would my own minya sister. 'It gotta get better. If you pick, it won't get better, you know.'

She always smile at me and laugh. When she come to visit, she like fresh air blowin' over me from the wanna, reminds me of 'ome. Sometimes we talk 'bout how much we miss our family and all the deadly things we remember back 'ome. Other than Mumma and Ada, the one I miss most is Uncle Murdi with 'is guitar and our singin'. I lie there thinkin' of 'im sittin' on 'is bed next to Lil-Lil, Eva, Sarah, Polly and Joshy, strummin' 'is guitar and 'im and me singin' together, 'im with 'is deep munyadi and me with high minya munyadi we singin' the old country and western songs. That's when I go off to that special place that make me feel so good. I really miss that most of all.

On special days, when the sun's shinin' real bright, Nurse Traeger take me outside in a wheel chair. If I'm real lucky she take me down the Torrens River that looks so pretty with all the colours, all the brightest greens. I never seen colour like that before in trees and plants, so different from 'ome where the paddocks out the back of the Mission look like tjilbi with gugga bunda, the bald head of an old man, and the colours of the mallee trees and saltbush, dusty green, grey and light brown.

Sometimes, I get a visit from an old walbiya man who works in the 'ospital doin' odd jobs. He collects all 'is pennies and brings them to me in a minya bag. He doesn't say much, but he's real nice to me. And the Salvation Army ladies in their uniforms come 'round and give me col- ourin' books and pencils and even comics, magazines and story books sometimes. And teachers come and visit me in 'ospital too. They give me lessons, English, Spelling and Arithmetic and leave me lotsa 'omework. I finish every- thing real quick-way 'cause I got nothin' else to do but sit in my 'ospital bed. I learn to read real deadly-way with Noddy books. He a funny little man whose gugga nods all the time and 'is best friend Big Ears. He called Big Ears 'cause he got yuree manardu. After I get tired of the Noddy books, I start to read other book by Enid Blyton and books without pictures that are more grown-up than Noddy. I can read and write real well now. Teacher Pea- body's going to get a big surprise when I go 'ome.

Time's going by real fast, lots and lots of months go by, and I feel like I've been in the Children's 'Ospital forever. Not many people come to visit me, though, and I don't even think of my family much any more. I've even stopped worryin' about when my leg will get better so I can go 'ome. People who were strangers, like the old handy man and Teacher and the Salvation Army ladies are the ones I now look forward to visiting me, and Terry too of course, who I see at different times, but sometimes with big gaps in between.

One day my bed is moved inside the big ward and I'm put in a special room. Everybody has to put on these white face masks, gowns and gloves. I haven't had any visitors for a long time. No Salvation Army lady or Teacher, nobody, only nurses with wada mooga on their wah and white gloves on their murra mooga. I feelin' sick, hot and my eyes hurt when the big lights on in that minya room. When I notice red rashy things on my body I asked one of the nice nurses, 'Why am I in this little room all by myself and what's these minya spots on me?'

'You have measles,' the nice nurse said, smilin' at me sorry-way, 'and you're locked away for a little while so the other kids won't catch it from you. That's why we are wearing these.' She holds 'er murra mooga up to me then.

I lie back in bed quiet-way and wait for the itchy red rashes to go away. Then after a while I get wheeled back into my room again. I'm even happy to see that bully boy again. My bed's outside on the balcony. It has sides on it like a cot but the nurses can pull them up and down when they want to.

Sometimes my jinna hurts and when they bring nice mai, I can't eat it because I feel too sick but them nurse mooga sit there and make me eat. They tell me I'm too skinny and gotta put on more weight and nice food will 'elp my jinna get better. My best mai's in the mornin' before dinner time when they give me nice drink with green leaf in it and apple and cheese. I really like that.

Walbiya visitors come into the ward not long after I come out of that minya room. I'm thinkin' 'what big sooks', what they cryin' for. Then when they go 'way, I see a minya stretcher being carried out by fellas who work there and it's got a sheet coverin' it. What're they carryin'? I wonder.

Not long after, I get a visit from my Burns Aunties, Vera, Bertha and Janet. They all live on the Mission but go away sometimes to work. When I see them walk through the door I'm so 'appy, it's like bein' back 'ome again. I feel really good inside knowing that they came all the way from 'ome to see me. They look real pretty too, like the movie stars I've been lookin' at in the magazines, with their lipstick and deadly clothes and high-heel shoes and the nicest 'ats on their 'eads.

'Oh, you weena mooga look real yudoo. Real pretty bultha too?' I say, touchin' the soft material on Aunty Vera's dress.

They laugh and give me hugs and kisses and tell me all 'bout what's happenin' at 'ome. They make me feel real proud that I've got such pretty, flash aunties who care about me.

Then one day, Old Rod comes to visit me too and even though he brings the biggest bananas I've ever seen in my life, and even though I'm real pleased to see 'im, I don't feel so comfortable with 'im, not like I do with my aunties. And I've still got that memory in my head of when I saw 'im last, growlin' Ada when she was real upset when we walked all the way to the farm in the dark. It sticks in my head like a prickle.

It's like he's really nervous, 'is hands're all fidgety when he's tellin' me, 'Your mother can't come to visit you because it's too far away for her to travel and she has your little sisters to look after.'

I nod my head. 'I know,' I tell 'im.

Sittin' in the chair next to me, holdin' his hat in his lap, he runs his murra through his grey hair, and leans forward, lookin' nervous.

'Are they looking after you well in here?' he asks, lookin' at me concerned.

I nod and give 'im a minya bit of a smile 'cause he looks real worried. He smiles back, but it's kind of crooked, like he's in pain. Lookin' at 'im sittin' next to my bed, he doesn't seem as much of a mystery to me any more. Enid Blyton's clues are more interestin' to me now. I wonder why he puzzled me so much before. He's just an old farmer who 'elps our family out because we 'elp 'im on 'is farm.

He looks down at the plaster on my leg, frowns and takes a deep breath.

'Does your leg still hurt?' he asks.

I shy-way nod.

His eyes go all shiny and he pats my hand. 'The doctor will make it better soon.'

A minya smile comes across my face. Old Rod's always got that way of making me feel safe, just like Mumma.

'I can't stay long,' he says, lookin' down at the floor and turning his hat in his hands. 'It's a long drive home and I've got sheep on the back of the truck, prize ones for breeding.'

I nod again.

'I got lots more bananas for your sisters too. I'll tell them I've seen you,' he says as he stands up.

A minya lump come up in my throat and I want to say 'thank you' to him, just like Mumma and Papa taught us kids to show manners around walbiya mooga, but nothing comes out of my mouth. So instead I just give a minya wave.

Then he's gone. I look down at the shiny floor and feel a minya ache in my chest.

Old Rod was right. Not long after he visited me, and after nearly a year of being in hospital, Doctor decides to operate on my leg. Afterwards the pain's even worse than before and I cry all the time for it to go away. But the nice nurses come and sit with me and hold my murra, and talk nice-way to me. Even though a long time has passed from when I left home, it's these times I miss Mumma, Ada and my sisters most.

When the pain starts to go away I 'ave to learn to walk again after not usin' my leg for so long. The nurses take me to another part of the hospital where they make me walk on a movin' machine. Real slow first, then later a bit faster. They make me walk up and down the stairs and that was hard and really hurt my jinna mooga too. But when I start to walk all the pain comes back again.

One day I 'ear the doctor say to one of the nurses, 'I think she's almost ready to go to Escort House.'

I start thinkin' they claimed me now and they gonna send me away, I'll never see Uncle Murdi, Mumma, Ada, Eva and my minya sisters again. It's like welfare, they got me now, so I'm finished.

Not long after that a big black car come to pick me up. The nurses pack my suitcase and a box with all my minya toys in it. I give them big hugs, 'cause they've been like my mummas at the 'ospital. Two men take me out to the black car and tell me we're goin' to a place in Sussex Street. What's that mean? Will there be Nyunga kids there that 'ave been stolen from their familes too, I wonder. Who are these people? I real frightened then. But when we get there a nice lady come and get me from the car and speak real nice-way to me and tell me I'm safe. She says I'm gonna go on the aeroplane tomorrow. They sendin' me 'ome. I'm goin' 'ome at last. 'Ome. I can't believe it.

After eleven months in 'ospital, I'm goin' back 'ome. I think about how much I've grown and wonder if they'll remember me. My birthday's close to Jesus' birthday and I left after Christmas last year, so that means I'm nearly eight now. I always forget my birthday 'cause it gets lost in all the things that happen 'round Christmas time.

When the aeroplane lands in Ceduna, Mr Dryner, a welfare worker, picks me up from the airport to take me 'ome. He takes my suitcase and box and puts them in the back of the car. Then he opens the door for me to get into the front seat. When he shuts 'is door he says, 'Well, show me where they did the operation.'

He's lookin' down at my legs. I feel shame, the scar's under my skirt and I don't want to show 'im.

'Well, come on then, lift up your dress,' he tells me. 'I want to see.'

I lift it just far enough for 'im to see.

'Lift it higher,' he says.

I clench my fists, I don't want to lift my dress any higher, he can see good enough from there.

'Lift it higher,' he says again, but this time in a firm voice.

I feel scared and angry, I wanna punch 'im, but I don't 'cause I don't feel safe with 'im. I lift my skirt a minya bit further just above the scar and no more. I feel really shame. It's a long and nervous drive back to the Mission and I'm so relieved when he drops me off out the front of our minya cottage.

Even though I'm 'appy and excited to be 'ome, I feel real shy, even a bit scared, 'cause I've been away for so long and everything's been so different being 'round white people all the time, except for little Terry. And now being back with my Nyunga family, it's almost like I've forgotten how to be the me that left a long time ago because the me now is a different girl.

'Grace's 'ome,' I hear Mumma's voice.

Uncle Murdi comes outa the house and picks up my suitcase and box. He gives me a big smile that say, 'Hello there, Grace. It's real deadly to see you again, girl.' That makes me feel all warm inside but I feel shame too so I put my gugga down.

Eva, Polly and Sandy come runnin' round the corner and stop. They starin' at me, smilin', but they can see I'm real shame.

Feelin' my eyes wellin' up with tears I turn away and pretend to straighten my dress. It feels real strange seein' them again too, and the longer I stand there the harder it is to move.

Then Aunty Wendy walks outa the front door wavin' 'er murra, wantin' me to come inside.

Still I don't move.

'Come and meet your new baby sister,' Aunty Wendy says, movin' towards me. 'Her name's Jane, like Tarzan and Jane, Queen of the Jungle.'

She's gently pushin' me into our minya cottage, and I limp into the bedroom. Eva, Polly and Sandy run past Aunty Wendy and gently tug at my dress. I've forgotten what our bedroom looks like, the old cupboard with the broken door in the corner and the big double bed covered with the same old stained blanketie. It smells quite bad in the room, I screw up my wah. Everything looks real drab and dirty. Near the bed's my suitcase and box that Uncle Murdi's brought in. I straighten my dress and carefully climb on the bed and look at my new little sister. She's such a pretty baby. I put my finger in the palm of 'er chubby, little 'and and she squeezes it real tight. I smile at 'er, then look up at Ada.

Ada's smilin' too. 'It's good to see you again, Grace,' she says. Then she asks to see my leg.

Just as I'm liftin' my skirt up again, the biggest mob of my sisters and brothers come runnin' into the room and start openin' my suitcase and box. My bultha go in all directions and they're grabbin' my brush and comb, books and toys. I can see dolly's head go flyin' and hear pages being ripped.

'No,' I scream, springin' off the bed. 'Don't take those things, they're mine.' I'm crying and trying to get my books and toys off 'em but I can't stop 'em.

''Ow come you talkin' like a real walaba?' Eva asks me, 'er 'ands on 'er 'ips.

What? I stand there with my mouth open. What's she talkin' about? I don't sound like a walaba, do I?

'They my things and you kids got no right stealin' 'em,' I say. I can feel my anger wellin' up inside.

'Hey,' Molly yell out to me, walkin' into the cramped room. 'You got real fat.'

'And you just the same, Molly, still real ugly,' I answer 'er back cheeky-way, my shyness giving way to anger as I tug-of-war Joshy with my book.

After I manage to grab back most of my things and push them under the bed, I look up and there standin' in the doorway is Mumma. I nearly cry when I see 'er. She's just as I remember. I stand up and she walks towards me with 'er arms wide open and warm.

Mumma gives me big hug like she did when I was a minya wunyi. 'Hello, my girl. It's so good that you back with us again.'

She squeezin' me tight and jigglin' me 'round. I squeeze 'er back.

That night, Mumma makes us a nice big feed and we light the fire outside. There's lots of laughin' and singin' to Uncle Murdi's guitar. All the kids runnin' 'round the backyard, but not me, my leg's still gettin' better and I'm so tired from the plane trip.

I'm 'ome at last but I'm not sure if I want to be.

When I go to bed I can't sleep, the old goomboo smell's still there and the blanketie's rough and scratchy on my skin. I'm used to them clean white sheets at the 'ospital. And what's that bitin' me? Probably them bedbugs and fleas. They never stop me from sleepin' before but now I can't sleep for the itchin'.

In the mornin' I think, 'Oh, no. My goomboo minyi ways are back again.'

In the 'ospital from 'alfway through stayin' there I hardly

ever wet my bed, and now on my first night back, it's wet. Damn. No one growls me though, they must be pleased I'm 'ome.

As soon as I get back from the 'ospital, Mumma Jenna decides she's gonna get me to eat as much bush tucker as she can to help my leg heal.

'Make your jinna strong again, girl,' she'd say, giving me Nyunga mai to eat all the time when we out back in the scrub.

Mumma Jenna teaches us kids a lot about how to survive in the bush, what mallee roots will give us water, how to look for the joongu joongu and what food to collect in the different seasons. Spring's the best time for plenty of mai like boorar. We eat the thin layer of skin on the outside and sometimes we crack open the hard seed and eat the nut on the inside. Some of us kids even use the boorar seed for marbles too. Mumma shows us how to look for special bark of the mallee tree to peel back from the trunk to find honey sap. We lick the sap and it tastes delicious. Honeysuckle bushes are one of my favourites, we pull the little flower off the stem and suck the honey from inside. I always think of the minya bees suckin' the sweetness out to make the honey for the bee-hive. Us kids really like womoo too, it's small fluffy white bits that are sweet to eat and real easy to find on one side of the mallee leaves.

Then, there's the ngoonyin bush with see-through berries. They real sweet too, and they're tiny, only the size of a match head. Another favourite is walga, the bush tomato that grows between spring and summer. In the winter time there's the big mushrooms that grow under trees where the bark falls on the munda. They're not like the other mush-rooms you pick in the paddock, they're real tough ones, and have a strong smell and taste, a minya bit like wood or bark. If we found a big mob of them, we might light a fire and cook them to eat right there. They're so yummy.

Mumma takes us kids out all the time and we have a good feed so even if we got no mai at home, our djuda mooga always full when Mumma takes us out, most of the time anyway.

When it comes to kuka, Mumma always takes us to dig for rabbity mooga too. The first thing is to check if their goona and tracks are fresh. Then we walk along and cave in all the minya gudle mooga, so they can't get away. Mumma's got a long stick that she breaks off the mallee bush and sticks it in the main hole to see which way it goes. Then she takes 'er crowbar and digs along the hole. We can tell when the rabbity mooga are gettin' closer 'cause when she pokes 'er stick in and pulls it out and their fur's on the end of it, she knows they not far. Then she reaches down in the hole and grab the rabbity and stretch it from its neck to its legs real quick-way. When you hear the neck snap you know the rabbity's dead. On a good day, she might get as many as six out of one hole. At the right time of the year they're real fat and juicy too. After she catches 'em, she guts and skins 'em, then pushes a jibin through their skin to thread up the hole in the guts. When she gets 'ome she singes off the hair then puts the rabbity in the oven, same as malu tail and gulda. If we real hungry we light the fire straight 'way, heat up the munda underneath and make a ground oven by diggin' a hole in the shape of the rabbity mooga. Then we cook up enough to 'ave a feed, then take the rest back for the others.

When the men go out they hunt malu all year round, gibara and gibara eggs, but wadu only sometimes. When they come home from huntin', we all 'ave a good feed. Walbiya Mission mob don't mind us goin' out bush for food 'cause there's never enough mai to go 'round for everyone an' the bush tucker gives Nyunga mooga a good feed.

My leg keeps healin' and gets stronger all the time from me havin' good feeds of Nyunga mai. Mumma keeps rubbin' her nguggil into my leg too, to make it strong. That walbiya gu minga's pretty much gone now.

11

Some things stay the same, some things change

When I go back to school, just as I thought, Teacher's surprised how far I've come with my reading, writing and arithmetic. This year, I come top of the Mission school with my marks 'cause of all the schoolin' I've had at the 'ospital and as usual the teasin' kids are still cheeky. But it's real frustratin' sometimes, because Teacher won't let me play any sport or move 'round too much in case my leg gets sick again. She treats me like someone who can't walk but after being in the 'ospital bed for so long I just want to be like the other kids again. I think of how us kids use to run flat-out and throw ourselves at the bottlebrush trees to see how far they can fling us back. These big strong bushes can chuck us way up in the air and we lucky if we land on our jinna again. I wanna do that, I wanna run with my sisters and brothers. Instead I just skip along behind 'em.

My life on the Mission seems different now. It's like I've grown up five years in the one year with what I've learnt and what I know about life outside the Mission. It's like I'm this minya fish in a fishbowl that's jumped into the wanna, swam around for a bit, then jumped back into the fishbowl again. I'm startin' to feel safe, and all right again at 'ome just where I want to be. Or is it?

Improving at school work means more teasin' from the nasty kids, more 'whitefella kid' taunts. Even more kids get jealous now that I sit back and read a big thick book while they struggle with their times tables and ABCs.

When the teasin' gets too much I just get a book from the classroom or the school library and sit down somewhere quiet and read. Being stuck in a hospital bed for so long with nothin' to do, I started to make friends with books. Like when I sing with Uncle Murdi or along with *Yours for the Askin'*, I go to another place, another world away from all the hurt. Books take me to a peaceful place. The more I read the more I understand about the world and people outside of the Mission. But there are still some big gaps I want filled. One thing the teasin' does is make me want to find out who my father is again and with all my reading of Enid Blyton, I feel I'm more prepared than ever. My fair skin must have come from somewhere, I reckon.

Then a little walaba girl about my age comes to the Mission with her family. Her name's Gerta and she sits near me in class. She thinks I'm a walaba girl like her 'cause of my fair skin and she's nice to me. Every time there's a test for spelling, arithmetic, or speed and accuracy we try to outdo each other. Sometimes I beat her and sometimes she beats me. It makes me want to do better and for a while I forget about the teasin' and put all my thoughts into my school work. I think Nyunga mooga can be just as clever as walaba mooga and try to prove it every day.

One day somethin' happens that makes the teasin' worse, makes me real scared, and changes lotta things on the Mission. A truck pulls up with strange Nyunga mooga. They real wild-lookin' mob with dust all over 'em like they been travellin' long time out bush. Some of 'em 'ave red bands on their gugga like jinardoo and that frightens me. After Superintendent pulls up in the truck, he jumps out, gets people off the back real quick-way and starts buzzin' 'round like blowfly organisin' things, orderin' people 'round, bein' real boonri boonri. He wanna be careful one of the old fellas don't put mumoo in him, if he get too cheeky with 'em. He's tellin' some of our Nyunga workers to get wood for fire and sheets of iron to make shelters for these people. Then he jumps in the truck again and takes off to get another load of people.

This goes on for long time 'til we got the biggest mob of strange Nyunga mooga on the Mission. They look real confused and worried, talkin' their language flat-out-way. Some of the minya gidjida mooga are clingin' to their mummas and cryin' and I feel sorry for 'em 'cause they look real sad. Maybe they 'omesick like I was when I first went to 'ospital in Adelaide. Where's their 'ome, I wonder. Then, all the kids get taken to the Children's 'Ome for a wash and for clothes, 'cause they all nigardi.

Kids in our family lucky we don't get put in the 'Ome. Papa and the uncles work on Old Rod's and other farms, shearin' and reapin' season and fencin' other times to get food for us. Mumma, Ada and the aunties work too. Papa real strict with us kids to make sure we behave. He would fight them Mission mob if they tried to take us 'way. He would say, 'My family good Christian people, hard workers. We keep our children fed and clothed. We the best ones to look after our kids.' I don't know why them other kids get put in the 'Ome, maybe Mission mob think they not good enough Christians, or not gettin' enough food, or not wearin' clean enough clothes? Who knows what them walbiya mob think, I can't work 'em out.

Lotta us Mission mob come outa our houses and talk quiet-way to each other. There's lotta whisperin', shufflin' of feet and askin' questions. 'Who that mob?', 'Why they bringin' 'em here?' It's real strange to see our grown-ups lookin' all worried and nervous, makes me think of all them scary stories I hear about tribal mob. Even though some things are the same, they different from us Mission mob. They look different, more wild, they only talk their language, and they do things like the real Old People. They must know lotta things like the Old People too, like Nyunga magic. Pastor talks about them old tribal ways like they hand in hand with the devil. And thinkin' about that makes 'em more scary. I'm too ngulu to go near 'em, lot of us on the Mission are too ngulu to go near 'em, even some of the Camp mob that stay just on the edge of the Mission in wuthoo mooga and tin sheds. Sometimes Pastor goes out and gives them devotion and reads his Bible.

Camp mob are same as us Mission mob but different too, it's like they wanna stay by 'emselves with nobody to bother 'em. Welfare still goes snoopin' 'round Camp mob and takes their kids just the same. Some Camp mob stay because their kids are in the 'Ome and they wanna be near 'em. But them tribal mob that Superintendent bring 'ere, they're real different from the Camp mob too, they can get their mai from the bush like the Old People. So why they here? What country they from?

'Look out,' Molly whisper in my yuree as I peekin' out the window at tribal mob walkin' past. 'You better not leave any gugga uru in your deadly new 'airbrush or old Nyunga might sing you for 'is wife.'

I punch 'er in the arm and tell 'er to stop lying. But we always careful not to leave our hair lyin' round, 'cause we know that if Nyunga get hold of it and use magic, he can make us want to be with 'im even if we think he's real ugly. That's how strong Nyunga magic is. So, when Molly say that to me, I ngulu-way go inside and get all my hair outa my brush and chuck it in the fire 'til it shrivels up and disappears. No old Nyunga gonna sing me for 'is wife.

Soon after, I find out that some of them tribal mob are related to us on Papa Neddy's side, they Kokatha mob, and sometimes they come and sit 'round the fire with 'im talkin' in language. Then I ask Papa Neddy why tribal mob have been brought to the Mission. He says the government mob dropped big bomb on their country and Superintendent drove out to pick 'em up before they all jinga. I reckon that government mob's real bloody idiots. Why they wanna go do a stupid thing like that?

After that, I make good friends with one minya tribal girl called Ooji. She lives in the Children's 'Ome with all the other kids Superintendent brought to the Mission. I feel real sorry for 'em locked up there away from their parents, 'specially one day when Superintendent takes away all their grown-up family somewhere and I hear some grown-ups talkin' about Tallawan and Ooldea. That horrible day for Ooji and them other kids in the 'Ome. They all go joobardi, screamin' and cryin' for their family leavin' on the truck. I would too if my family bein' taken away. Mission mob doin' to these grown-ups what welfare mob did to some kids, stealin' 'em away. The poor kids locked up in the 'Ome at night might never see their family again.

'Why Superintendent takin' 'em away?' I ask Ooji.

She just shake her gugga, cryin'.

I put my arm 'round her then. 'You'll be right, Ooji. I look out for you,' I tell 'er.

But I know nothin' I say is gonna make her feel better. How could it?

Later, I ask Mumma why they do that to Ooji and her family. Mumma put her 'ead down sorry-way. 'Walbiya got funny ways, Grace, real funny ways. Ooji just lucky she gotta friend like you.'

Ooji's a good friend to me too but some of them tribal kids treat me real mean. They make my life hell more than ever before with their teasin' 'cause now them as well as the others make it double the teasin'. The new kids swear at me in their Pitjantjatjara wonga, using really filthy names and sometimes I feel real miserable, 'cause there's nowhere to hide or get away from 'em. It makes me feel further away from everyone and confused inside. Sometimes it hurts so much I feel real numb and empty. Sometimes Ooji growls 'em in their wonga but they don't listen.

After a while I get real sick of the teasin' so when I hear 'em sniggerin' at me, I look over the top of my book and throw my cheeky look at them with my guru mooga, then they get real wild. Sometimes they stick their finger up at me and in a high voice say, 'Boi, walaba goona muroo.' That means, you think you're just it don't you, but you're just a white woman with a black arse.

'You just smart 'cause you got stinkin' whitefella kid blood in you,' is the new sayin'.

'What? You don't think Nyunga mooga are smart or what? You think stupid?' I ask 'em, rememberin' what Mumma Jenna told me when we were campin' at Denial Bay. 'Don't go puttin' yourself down like that.'

One boy, Tjoobin, he's the worst, teasin' me all the time. One day at school when Headmaster asks me to hold the door open for everyone to go inside, I real proud-way reach for the door but Tjoobin pushes past me and yanks the door open 'imself, nearly knockin' me over. I'm so moogada with 'im, I push 'im back. He hits me and I start punchin' into 'im. We're havin' a big fight right there in front of all the kids and Headmaster but I'm so moogada I don't even care and I give him a good floggin'. Headmaster's yellin' at us to stop and runs over and pulls us apart.

When we goin' into the classroom, Ooji grabs my murra and squeezes it. 'Bulya,' she whispers and flashes a smilin' look at me.

I know that means 'good' in her language. I know she's glad I stuck up for myself.

Tjoobin doesn't bother me much after that.

12
Riddle solved

One evening, out of the blue, not long after my fifth minya sister Maddy is born, Old Rod turns up at the Mission in his FJ Holden to pick up Eva and me to take us to the farm. Mumma invites him inside. He wants to look at my jinna and see how it's goin'. He squats down and runs 'is fingers soft-way along the pink scar from when the doctor scraped out the walbiya gu minga from inside my bone and even though I don't limp any more, he asks if it still hurts.

I shake my head. I feel safe with Old Rod lookin' at my leg like that, not like that welfare man who came to pick me up from the airport. I don't think he was interested if my leg was hurtin' or not. Old Rod can be a bit grumpy at times but I reckon he cares about us and does a lot of things to help us too.

He goes into our room with Ada, then closes the door and us kids aren't allowed to go in there. I don't know what they're talkin' 'bout, it must be a secret. We just sit outside waitin', then after a while he comes out, and tells Eva and me to get some clothes and come out to the car.

Mumma waves to us from the front of our cottage as Old Rod opens the car door so we can jump in the front. Eva and me are real excited that he's takin' just us two, Ada isn't even comin'. We feel real special. Old Rod jumps in the car then too, starts it up, switches on the headlights, 'cause the sun's just gone down, and we take off out of the Mission. It feels so good.

When we pull out onto the main road, Old Rod's talkin' about it bein' a bumper year for his crops 'cause of a special wheat some government mob are gettin' 'im to try out and it's growin' much faster than the other one he uses. He says he likes tryin' out new things to make the crops give 'im more grain, make the pigs fatter, and the sheep and cattle get more meat on them, and that he's even brought bigger animals from Adelaide to mix with his animals, to do that. That's probably why he's won all those prizes at the show.

Lookin' at 'im talkin' away there, he looks real sure of 'imself. Like he's an important man, the way he moves 'is strong murra mooga in the air when he's talkin', then puts them back on the steering wheel and sits there real tall and proud-way. And he seems to know a lotta people too, not jus' 'round where we live but in the city. He's always travellin' over there to do 'is business. And a lotta people seem to know him as well.

Once I saw him and Mrs Williams at a dance with all these people in the Charra Hall. I was standin' outside with Aunty Mim and Aunty Dorrie. Mrs Williams was real pretty and from her smile I knew she was a kind lady. Nyunga mooga can tell straight 'way, things like that 'bout a person. She was wearin' a nice flowery dress with lace on the collar. Her light colour 'air was tied up in a bun at the back of 'er gugga. Under the light, she looked like she was shinin'. Old Rod was playin' his button accordion and she was on the piano. They looked real happy, dressed real flash-way up there, playin' their music together while everyone danced. It was deadly music too.

Aunty Mim, who's now mudgie mudgie with Old Rod's son, Dave, told me that she heard that Old Rod argued with the big boonri mooga in Adelaide to get the telephone here. Just imagine that, the government draggin' them wires and poles all that way, just 'cause Old Rod told 'em we needed it. And another thing Aunty Mim told me was that Old Rod's the big boss when fire breaks out anywhere 'round the place. He gets all the farmers together and they put the fires out. He must be a pretty big important, clever man. So why does he want to hang 'round Nyunga mooga like us? I still can't make 'im out. I use to look at 'im as a riddle but he's not like the mysteries in the books I read. In them all the clues lead to the answer, sooner or later the loose ends are tied together, then the mystery's solved. But in my head Old Rod's still just one big knotted mess. Nice one, though.

It's real dark outside while we're cruisin' down the road in Old Rod's car headin' towards the farm, engine hummin', headlights shinin' bright so we can see long way ahead. It's real nice and relaxin' sittin' between Eva and Old Rod.

But all of a sudden, there's a loud crunchin' sound like metal scrapin', and next minute there's a screech of brakes and his car's swervin' off to the side of the road. Old Rod's strong hands are tryin' to grab at the steering wheel but it's spinnin' outa control, he's pushin' back against the seat with his jinna flat on the brakes but the car's still slidin'. Eva and me are flyin' towards the dashboard, but we put our hands out just in time to stop us hittin' the windscreen.

The car comes to a joltin' stop right in front of the biggest stump I've ever seen.

'You girls all right?' I hear a voice yellin'.

Dust is everywhere.

'Are you girls all right? Eva? Grace?'

I blink a couple of times. Everything's dark, but I know the voice is comin' from Old Rod, it just doesn't sound like 'im, it sounds real scared. I'm real scared too. I can feel my heart goin' real fast. Then I hear the door open and Old Rod mutterin' and scroungin' underneath the seat for his torch. Next minute, there's bright light shinin' in my eyes and the same question bein' asked.

'Are you girls all right?'

Eva squints in the bright light, rubs 'er eyes and tells 'im, 'Ahh. Yeah, I'm 'right.'

'I'm right, too,' I say after Eva, shufflin' my jinna and wrigglin' my fingers to check that everything's still there 'cause I feel like I'm somewhere else.

'What happened?' Eva sounds groggy.

'I just lost control of the car, couldn't steer it. Something's broken. Might be the steering rod.' Old Rod jumps outa the car then, opens our door and reaches his big murra mooga for us. 'You sure you not hurt?' he keeps askin' while he helps us outa the car.

He makes us stand there while he checks that we're all in one piece. 'Thank God you're all right.'

He's shakin' and all jittery. I've never seen him like this but then again, I'm feelin' a little bit strange too, like everything's catchin' up with itself after slowin' right down.

'We're all right,' Eva says, lookin' a bit annoyed. 'Just a minya knock on the gugga, that's all.'

Normally Old Rod tells us to talk English when we talk Kokatha lingo but tonight he doesn't seem to care.

Old Rod feels Eva's head and lets out a big shaky noise from his mouth. He must believe us then 'cause he stops askin' us the same question over and over and walks to the front of the car.

Eva and me just stand there shakin,' huddlin' together. It's freezin' outside.

I can see his face in the shadow of the torch that he's flashin' from the front of 'is car to the big stump and back again. He looks like he's just seen the scariest guldi ever. He puts 'is murra over 'is mouth and makes a sound like a dog when it's hurt real bad.

I feel like askin' him, 'Are you all right?' But Eva might thump me if she hears that question one more time.

Old Rod comes back then to where Eva and me are standin'. He grabs both of us, puttin' his big murra mooga on our 'eads and pulls us into 'im. I think I can hear him sobbin' but I'm not sure, then I 'ear 'im blow 'is nose in 'is 'ankie.

As we stand there, huddled together in the freezin' cold, a minya light starts glowin' over the horizon.

'Someone's comin',' Old Rod yells, switchin' on his torch and walkin' into the middle of the road, ready to wave them down.

Soon an old ute comes puttin' to a stop. Old Rod seems to know the driver.

A walbiya tjilbi gets out and goes to the front of Old Rod's motor car. He puts his hands on his hips, shakes his head and gives a low whistle.

'You damn lucky you stopped where you did, Rod, or you'd be dead now.'

Old Rod nods his head slow-way, agreein'.

We all get in the man's car then and he turns the ute 'round and drives us back to Old Rod's place.

Me and Eva think Old Rod's gonna put us in the shed or the caravan where we usually stay but this time he goes to the front of 'is house and opens the door. Me an' Eva stand still. He tells us to go inside.

Eva and me look at each other. All those years we've been visitin' the farm and we always wondered what was behind that door and behind them flashy lace curtains and now we're gonna find out.

'It's all right, you can go inside,' Old Rod says when we just stand there, not movin'.

Eva walks in first, real careful-way, slow steps as if she's steppin' over a grave. I follow, with my murra on her back. That spooky witch gubarlie, Old Rod's mumma with the minya glasses sittin' on 'er nose might be in there waitin' for us. We look 'round. It's real nice and clean inside with flash table and chairs in the middle of the room, a bed up against the window, a piano in the corner opposite the bed, and a big bookshelf with lotsa different lookin' books. My eyes nearly pop outa my head to see so many deadly books. This must be where Old Rod gets the ones he gives to us kids sometimes, all them books about mermaids and things under the sea, and the fairy stories. When I was a really minya wunyi I used to like the ones with all the pictures but the other kids would rip them up. Soon enough they always ruin everything that Old Rod gives us.

Old Rod moves us towards the fireplace and tells us to sit down and warm ourselves. Then he stokes the coals and puts a few more stumps of wood on top. The fire starts to smoke and crackle before minya flames jump out from the sides of the stump lightin' up the wood. Then he makes us a cup of chicory each and cooks some toast over the fire with a fork. I look at the fork and wonder if my hair's messy, so I pat it down with my hands then.

Even though we're both still scared from the accident, Eva and I smile at Old Rod and say thank you to him, quiet-way, like we've been taught to use our manners around walbiya mooga.

Mrs Williams comes out of a room off the side and sees us and Old Rod then steps back in again and closes the door. Old Rod follows 'er into the room and leaves the door a minya bit open so I can see 'im sittin' down on the end of the bed. He leans down and puts his elbows on his knees and cradles his head in his hands.

I take a sip of chicory and look up on the fire mantelpiece, then 'round at the cabinet on the other wall. They're covered in Old Rod's trophies and ribbons. I'm real surprised. I know he's won at the show every year but not this many, there's the biggest mob there.

Eva is warmin' her murra mooga by the fire that's really startin' to take off now.

There's quiet talkin' comin' from the room where Old Rod and his wife are. Maybe she's moogada that he brought us into the house. Why did he anyway? We usually just stay in the shed, next to the pigsty out back, light a fire in the middle, put blanketie on the ground and sleep in the dirt if all us mob are over, or maybe the caravan if it's just Ada and us girls. Maybe he's still all shook up from the accident. I still feel a bit jittery. Maybe if I listen close-way, I can hear what Old Rod and Mrs Williams are sayin', I think.

'We came that close to dying tonight, Betty.' Old Rod's voice is shakin' again.

I look at Eva, she's listenin' too.

'I could've lost my two daughters.'

I nearly drop my cup of chicory, a minya bit splashes on the floor. Did I hear right? Moppin' the spill up with my dress so Old Rod won't notice, I look at Eva, turn up my murra and shrug my shoulders to ask, 'Is that true what we just heard or what?'

Noddin' with a sad look on 'er face, she says, 'Yes, but we're not meant to know.'

'Why didn't you tell me?' I hiss real quiet-way in case Old Rod hears.

I put my cup down and lean back then, lookin' at the ceiling, starin' for a long time, not really believin' what I just heard. Old Rod's too old to be our father. All the grown-ups in our family must know if it's true. So why do they wanna keep a secret like that from us kids all these years?

Then suddenly everything starts to make sense in a strange blurry kind of way. What I just heard gives me all the clues to work out the riddle and show me the secret Ada and Mumma'd been hidin'. My guru mooga dart from one side of the ceiling to the other as thoughts tumble 'round in my head.

Ada and Mumma knew all along that Old Rod was our father. Every time I asked, 'Who's my father?' or 'Why my skin fairer than the other kids'?' they just growled me, so they don't 'ave to tell me. All the times them nasty kids yell at me, 'You bastard whitefella kid ... you Williams' pigs.' I always thought they were being real mean to me for nothin', just 'cause they jealous. But now I know they were callin' me those names because I did 'ave a walbiya father. And Old Rod's always sayin' to us, 'You're different from those other kids on the Mission. Don't forget that now.'

My guru mooga stop at a cobweb floatin' in the corner.

Old Rod musta been tellin' us that because he was our father. That's why he always had us stayin' over in the 'olidays and why he took Ada and us kids out in his back paddocks campin' and we'd go with 'im to drive the sheep along the road and go fencin' out the back with him. That's why he brought us food and clothes and presents all the time. That's why he took us into town and gave us money at the show every year. And it wasn't a mumoo at all that jumped into him when he crossed over the railway line, he was just nervous about what walbiya mob were gonna say when they seen him, big important whitefella in town with his black mudgie and his black gidjida mooga, that's why he always drop us off at the bushes by the wanna.

Sobbin' is comin' from the room, now. It sounds like Old Rod cryin'. I see Old Rod's head movin' up and down in his hands. I feel scared, I've never seen Old Rod like this before. Are we in trouble? What's happenin'? Is he all right? Are we gonna be all right? I look at Eva. Her eyebrows are real high in 'er ngulya and 'er guru mooga dart from me to the piano and back again as if she's tryin' to read Old Rod's thoughts or work out what's gonna happen next.

I look 'round the room with all its deadly furniture. It makes sense now why Old Rod bought that land for us at the back of the Catholic church and why the walbiya Council mob gave 'im 'is money back. They reckon black-fellas not allowed to own land even though it all belonged to us Kokatha before the whitefellas came. Maybe that's a law or rules walbiya mob made, that's different from Nyunga ways, like Papa told me about.

And Old Rod is always goin' on about not sittin' on the dirty toilets on the Mission and keepin' clean and takin' care of ourselves. But how can we with one minya bowl for all of us to wash ourselves in? The water's always real muddy. Not like the flash bath they probably have here somewhere in this house.

I remember once way back, when I was hidin' under the bed in the kitchen playin' hide-and-seek, I heard Mumma talkin' to the other weena mooga.

'Old Rod went to jail after Eva was born and that finished 'im then 'cause he wanted to be a big boonri in Parliament's House,' she said. 'And it just might've been, if he hadn't had his way with Ada and 'er havin' Eva. "Consortin'"', walbiya mob call it.' Mumma gave a laugh like she thought it was stupid.

I didn't know who Parliament was, and why Old Rod wanted to go to his house, or what Ada and Eva had to do with stoppin' 'im. It just didn't make sense.

So later, I asked Papa Neddy. I wouldn't dare ask Mumma, she'd only growl me for bein' nosey minya wunyi. 'Who's Parliament, Papa? An' where he live?'

Papa laughed. 'Where you been gettin' big words like that from, girl? That teacher's been learnin' you lotta things at school, indie?' He rubbed the scratchy gunja on his chin, like he was tryin' to remember the answer. 'It's a place where walbiya mob make laws that tell us what we can do and can't do.'

'Oh, so Parliament's not a person,' I said to Papa.

He smiled and nodded then, and a funny minya chuckle came outa his mouth.

Maybe, Old Rod wanted to make some laws to help Nyunga mooga like us be allowed to own land walbiya way, I thought. But I still didn't know what Ada and Eva had to do with Old Rod goin' to jail. Unless it was 'cause he already had a wife, Mrs Williams.

And what about what Hetty Clare said? Papa gave Ada a floggin' when she still had Eva growin' in 'er djuda 'cause he was shame of her. Maybe that was against the law too, and that's why Mission mob threw stones at 'er and baby Eva. Or maybe Mumma and Hetty just got their stories wrong. After all, Ada's still Old Rod's mudgie and five of us girls've been born since Eva. So, why isn't he in jail now?

I look back towards the bedroom door.

'Well, you do what you need to, Rod,' Mrs Williams say.

And if Old Rod's already married with a wife, how come him and Ada still together mudgie-way? It doesn't make sense. But now it makes sense why they kept this secret from us kids. Pastor would 'ave somethin' to say about it. He'd say the devil's well and truly got Ada and Old Rod tricked and they goin' to hell with fire and brimstone. But I know deep inside Old Rod's good, and Ada can be grumpy but she's good mumma the way she does 'er best to keep us clean and fed, and gooloo out of our 'air, so I know there's no way Old Rod and Ada gonna go to hell.

After a while, Old Rod lifts up his head, pulls a hankie out 'is pocket and blows 'is nose. He stands up then, and begins to walk towards us.

I can feel a warm glowin' inside me like the fireplace that's now so hot my face is burnin'. My excitement starts to grow, sittin' in this lovely room, sippin' a warm cuppa in this once mysterious old house. I just know things are about to change for the better for me, Eva and my minya sisters because now I know this man is our father.

'Dee-Dee Doe,' I whisper under my breath, imagining I'm whisperin' to a butterfly. 'I know who my mummatja is – you'll never guess who. It's Old Rod.'

And that butterfly in my mind fly off.

13

Lookin' through new guru mooga

'You can both sleep in here tonight,' Old Rod says in a warm, gentle voice. His guru mooga and face all red as he walks into the lounge room.

Eva and me both nod and smile at each other. We both thinkin' the same thing, we don't 'ave to sleep on the dirt floor in the shed or that damp old smelly caravan. We are sleepin' in this deadly house, a walbiya house.

But best of all that walbiya is our father. He is the other part of what I've been lookin' for all these years. That's why I've never felt like I fitted in anywhere, not with the other Nyunga mooga on the Mission, except my family and friends, and not with walbiya mooga. But somehow right in this strange moment sittin' on the floor in Old Rod's house in front of the fire, I feel like I belong. It's like all the emptiness inside me has just disappeared, like the fire that warms us now, it's just burnt it all up.

Old Rod pulls back the covers on the bed near the window. There's a big fluffy pillow, nice white sheets and clean blankets, just like in hospital. Eva and me both jump onto the bed and snuggle between the nice-smellin' sheets, then Old Rod pulls the covers over us and tucks us in.

'I'll play you some songs before you go to sleep,' he says, walking back towards his bedroom.

When he comes back his hands are graspin' a piano accordion. He plays a few notes that don't quite sound right before he starts to play wonderful music from this box that he seems to squeeze the air out of and tickle at the same time. Some of the songs I know the tunes from him singin' them to us before and some I don't know. He tells us some of them are old Irish songs that his mother taught him when he was a little boy. When he sings his voice sounds real nice, just like the voices on the radio. And even though I'm not singin' along like I do with Uncle Murdi, it still takes me to that real nice place where I go when I sing and it feels real relaxin' and nice. Before I know it I'm floatin' off to sleep.

Next mornin' I wake up with light on my face and feel around the sheets. I can't believe it. For the first time in ages I didn't goomboo the bed that night.

'Well, what do you know?' Eva says in a flat voice when she notices the same thing.

I smile real proud-way. 'Maybe we should stay over here more often,' I say. Lookin' around the room, it seems strange, like I'm still dreamin'.

'I would've been living 'ere if it wasn't for you,' Eva says with a moogada look on 'er face.

'What are you talkin' about?' I ask, sittin' up.

'I overheard Mumma talkin' once,' she says. "Bout when I was born.' Eva stops and points 'er lips towards the bedroom. 'They were gonna adopt me, bring me up as their own, but then you came along.'

'What are you talkin' about?' I say again.

I don't doubt what she's sayin' 'bout Mumma is true. I always find out stuff I shouldn't from listenin' in on Mumma's yarns but I was a real sweet minya wunyi. Even Eva's always sayin' that I'm Papa Neddy and Uncle Murdi's favourite, so why would they want to leave me out?

'Why wouldn't they want to take me as their own too?' I cross my arms, feelin' real put out.

'Well, it's simple. They must've thought Ada wasn't gonna 'ave any more kids with Old Rod so they could pretend I was theirs and no-one'd know. But after you was born, they must've thought, we can't keep goin' on adoptin' more bastard kids, so they didn't worry about it.' Eva kicks the blankets off rough-way. 'Anyways, some of us like you and me are real fair and could pass for walbiya but some of us are more muroo.'

'I wouldn't wanna pass for a walbiya anyway,' I snap back.

'Even if it meant livin' like this every day?' Eva asks.

I think about that for a while. 'I'd live like this and stay Nyunga,' I say.

Eva shakes 'er head and laughs at me. 'I don't think you'd have a choice, Grace. Old Rod would tell you what to do and you'd have to listen to 'im.'

I nod, thinkin' how sometimes he bosses Ada 'round and that time Ada took us kids and ran away to Penong with a Nyunga man who lived there, tryin' to get away from Old Rod. But Old Rod just drove up to Penong and made Ada get in the car and drove her and us kids back to the Mission. Ada was so sick of the Mission she would've done anything to get off it, but Old Rod wouldn't let 'er live on the farm, probably 'cause he still had 'is wife. He only lets us stay when it suits 'im.

'Even if I wasn't born,' I tell Eva, 'Ada and Mumma wouldn't let them take you away anyway. They'd fight for you to stay with 'em, no matter what. And if Papa put his foot down and said "no", that'd be it, 'cause he's the big boonri of all of us.'

'Old Rod's our father, isn't he? And he's walbiya. They wouldn't 'ave any say.'

I think about what Eva's saying. She's right. Walbiya mooga have lotta say over lotta things, even us Nyunga mooga. Old Rod could probably do whatever he wants as long as it isn't against the laws that they make in that Parliament House place. But just imagine sleepin' in a nice, soft, clean bed like this one without anythin' suckin' blood from you all night, always havin' plenty of food to eat and a father who's got plenty of money to buy you things like books and clothes? That'd be so deadly to live like that.

'Good morning, my girls.' Old Rod's words are like a song as he comes through the back door. 'Your breakfast is on the table and when you've finished we're going to go for a drive in my new truck to check the animals and the water troughs.'

There's the biggest plates of food waitin' on the table, bacon, eggs and toast and orange juice. Me and Eva smile real wide, this is the flashest breakfast ever. When we finish Eva and me go outside and play while we wait for Old Rod. Everywhere we go looks different. We play where we've always played but this time I see it new-way, like it's more real than before, like it's got different meaning now because Old Rod's our father. I feel like Sleepin' Beauty who just woke out of 'er sleep, tryin' to remember back, to make sense of what's happenin'. I jump and skip and laugh and sing. Eva looks a bit annoyed, but I don't care, I feel so deadly to be alive.

Soon, Old Rod is yellin' for us to hurry up so we can get goin', then he helps us up into 'is truck.

'Do you like it?' he asks, real proud-way. 'I brought it from Adelaide last week. It can fit five people across.' He slaps the seat next to 'im. His hand makes a loud sound on the new leather. 'Only one in the district,' he beams.

Bouncin' along the dirt track, Old Rod whistles away as Eva and I look out the window. We pass a paddock that I remember visitin' when we were younger. Eva and me were real minya wunyi mooga back then, in the front of Old Rod's old truck. Big bales of hay were piled on the back of 'is truck for the cattle feed. As we bumped over the paddock, Old Rod told us he was goin' to feed the cattle, and to do that he would slow the truck right down, jump on the back and throw off the feed, but we had to promise 'im that we wouldn't get outa the truck and we mustn't touch anything, no levers or buttons or pedals, nothing. He told Eva to 'just do the steerin'.

'Especially not this one,' he said, tapping 'is foot on a pedal. 'All right? Do you understand?'

Guru mooga wide open and makin' big nods with our heads, Eva and me let Old Rod know we understood.

Old Rod moved the gear stick so the truck crawled along at a walking pace. He reminded us once again we were not to touch anything. Then he jumped out of the slow-moving truck, shut the door and jumped onto the back to start throwing off the hay feed.

Me and Eva sat there real patient-way for a while, thinkin' about what Old Rod had told us but because we were so little we started to get bored and fidgety.

'Push that there.' I pointed to the pedal on the floor that Old Rod had sternly warned us against pushing. 'Push that one there.'

'Old Rod said we not 'lowed to touch anythin',' Eva growled me.

'Are you scaredy cat? Eva is a scaredy cat, Eva is a scaredy cat,' I teased.

'Am not.'

'Am too.'

'Am not.'

'Show me then,' I said, puttin' my hand on my hips and makin' a face at 'er.

Eva stuck 'er tongue out at me. 'All right, then.'

She slipped down the seat, stretched 'er foot over the pedal and gently pushed down.

Nothin' happened. So she began pumpin' her foot up and down real hard-way. The truck was jerkin' along then.

We looked out the back window and saw Old Rod stumblin' all over the place and nearly fallin' off the truck. We both started to kill ourselves laughin'. He looked like he was doin' a silly dance.

'Hey, hey.' He yellin' real loud. 'What are you little rascals doin' in there? I told you not to touch anything. Hey.'

We turned back round and giggled some more as Eva kept pushin' the pedal up and down.

Old Rod still bouncin' around on the back of the truck. He grasped for balance on the side railings cursin' us and the whole time we were nearly fallin' off the seat laughin' in the front of the truck.

But boy, did we get a big growlin' once Old Rod finally got back into the cabin.

'Grace told me to do it,' Eva cried.

But Old Rod growled both of us anyway.

Rememberin' back to that time makes me giggle again.

'What's so funny?' Old Rod has a big smile on 'is face.

'Just rememberin' a time we came out 'ere with you,' I say, shy-way.

'Yeah.' Old Rod pulls up at the next water trough and smiles. 'We've had plenty of good times together out here on the farm, haven't we?'

Eva and me nod.

After checkin' the water trough and makin' sure no sheep have been killed by dingos, Old Rod drives down to the next gate, opens it and drives through slow-way.

'Baaah. Baaah,' comes a sound from the back of the truck.

Old Rod looks over towards the corner of the paddock and sees a single lamb walkin' along by itself. It's lost its mumma. Me and Eva see it too, so we jump out of the truck and run over to play with it. Its wool is all wavy and soft as we run our fingers over its fluffy coat. But the poor little thing is real weak. 'Oh, it's so nice. Can we keep it? Can we? Can we?' we both beg Old Rod.

'Well, it looks like it's lost its mother, so it won't last too long out here by itself.' He looks around the paddock. 'Okay, you can keep it,' Old Rod finally agrees. 'But you'll have to feed it and look after it properly. You promise?'

'Yes. Yes. Yes,' we scream together, jumpin' up and down on the spot.

Old Rod picks up the lamb and puts it on the back of the truck.

'What will you call it?' he asks.

'Dolly,' I said, thinkin' of Dee-Dee's nigardi peg dolly's mumma dolly she got for a Christmas present.

'Okay, Dolly it is,' Old Rod says as he puts the truck into gear and takes off to the next trough.

When we reach the end paddock, Old Rod stops the truck and shares a bottle of water and some sandwiches with us. 'You know,' he says, turning to us, 'I first came here to the west coast when I was about four years old. That's when my mother and father decided they would move us here. First we stayed at Athena, then we moved here to Charra once my father and elder brothers had made the farm livable. I even went to school in the old Charra woolshed over that way.' He sweeps his hand towards

Penong way. 'Us kids getting a good education was really important to my parents. It's important to me too. So I want you girls to study hard at school to do the best you can. I'll get you off the Mission and make sure you're well looked after and go to a good school.'

'I come top in school last year,' I say proud-way.

Eva rolls her eyes.

'Yes, I heard,' Old Rod says. 'Good work, keep it up.' Then he looks over at Eva. 'And you too, Eva, you do the best you can, too.'

Eva nods, and kicks my jinna.

'Another thing that was important to my parents was workin' hard on the farm to build it up.'

We nod again. We know that, from how Old Rod talks about makin' 'is farm bigger and better all the time.

'Because of their hard work,' he continues, 'and the hard work we do now on the farm, we're one of the biggest land holders in this area.'

He's talkin' like what he's sayin' is really important, but I can't understand why he's tellin' us all this stuff. It's like he's braggin'. I yawn. I'm startin' to get bored. I turn to Eva. One side of her mouth goes up, makin' her cheek look puffy. I can see she's feelin' the same way.

'And when I die . . .' Old Rod pauses for a long time.

Eva and me both look up at him. Is he planning to die soon? He can't do that. I've only just worked him out, I've only just found out he's my father.

'I want Ada and you girls to 'ave some of this land too, the land out the back of the Mission. That will be especially for Ada and you girls.'

Wow, imagine that, I think. Our own place away from all them rotten, teasin' kids, away from all the drinkin' and fightin' on the Mission. A place of our very own.

Munchin' on our sandwiches that Old Rod's given us from the brown paper bag, Eva leans down and scratches 'er ankle, while I nod to myself. He's a real caring man, Old Rod. He gives us Dolly and now he wants to give us some of his farm when he dies.

'But I hope he doesn't die,' I quiet-way whisper under my breath as we head back to the Mission in Old Rod's new truck. 'I still got to get to know him as my father first.'

If he died would he go to hell with fire and brimstone? I hope not 'cause deep down inside he's a good man who really cares.

'Don't die just yet, Old Rod.'

14
The sins of the father

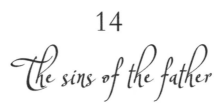

When Old Rod drops us off on the Mission with Dolly, a bottle and some powdered milk to feed her, all our minya sisters and brothers just go joobardi. Before we can tie her up, about ten kids start chasin' her 'round the house.

'Hey, you kids, leave 'er alone,' Eva yells at them. 'She's only a minya baby.'

But no-one's listenin'. They just keep chasin' her screamin', 'Come here, minya nyarni.'

Poor Dolly is boltin' in all directions tryin' to get away from them.

'You bloody idiots,' I yell. 'You're scarin' 'er. Now stop it.'

They all want to pat 'er, or feed 'er and some of the boys even want to see if they can ride 'er, even though she's real tiny.

Eva and me growl them again. Dolly is our special pet that Old Rod's given us, and he made us promise we would look after 'er real good and there's no way we gonna let anyone hurt 'er.

'Right, that's it,' I scream, frustrated that they won't stop. 'Next one not to listen is gonna cop it.'

I put my fists up.

Thump. Adrian is the first one to go down as he runs past. Then Joshy. I only manage to slap a couple of the girls on the arms because they see the boys on the ground and swerve around me.

'Hey, stop it.' Polly grabs 'er arm that's goin' real red from the slap.

'Let's get 'er.' Joshy waves his arms in my direction.

Then suddenly all the kids stop chasin' Dolly and head straight for me.

'Noooo,' I yell as a mountain of kids comes tumblin' in on me. Elbows, knees, fists hittin' me from all directions.

I'm swearin' with swear words that I'd never put together in one sentence before.

'Hey, who's the filthy mouthed little girl, swearin' like that?' Mumma comes out the back door, picks up a stick and starts wavin' it in the air. 'You kids stop fightin' now.' Her voice booms over the squeals and groans comin' from me and the pile of kids on top of me.

One by one, the kids peel back to reveal me at the bottom, still swearin' my minya mouth off. Mumma gives me a sharp hit on the jinjie with the stick and tells me to get inside. Ada is there waitin' at the back door and she give me a clip on the ear as I walk past.

'When you gonna learn, Grace? You just wait 'til I see Papa Neddy, I'm gonna tell him about your filthy minya mouth. Now get inside.'

Molly stands in the kitchen with a big grin on 'er face, sharpenin' the knife on a sharpenin' stone. 'So Grace, what? We havin' roast lamb for tea tonight? That's real nice of you and Eva to share like that.'

I turn 'round, ready to run at 'er and give 'er a big kick on the shins. Then I see Ada glarin' at me from the back door.

'You better leave Dolly alone, Molly, or you'll be the one bloody-well fryin',' I hiss at 'er between my teeth.

'Get into the bedroom now,' Ada yells. 'And don't come out 'til I tell you to.'

Moogada-way I turn 'round and kick the cupboard instead of Molly, stomp to the bedroom and slam the door as hard as I can behind me. It shakes on its hinges as I throw myself on the bed.

Ada is in the bedroom in a flash, givin' me a good hidin' until I start to cry.

'I hate you,' I scream.

'I hate you too, Grace, when you carry on like such a rotten kid.'

'Anyway, you a damn liar,' I spit back at her through my tears. 'I know your big secret you been hidin' from me. I know Old Rod's our father.' I punch at the bed. 'I might have a swearin' mouth but you're nothin' but a liar, Ada.'

Ada backs out of the room then and slams the door behind 'er.

I lie on the bed, sobbin' and thinkin' how much I hate Ada when she hits me like that. I hate my life on the

Mission. I hate havin' to share everything with the other kids who don't respect nothin', not even the special things Old Rod gives us. But most of all I hate this stinkin' bed that I goomboo in nearly every night and the bloody bedbugs that'll be havin' a good feed on me and Eva and my minya sisters again tonight. I wish I was back at the farm with Old Rod, my father, livin' in his farm'ouse, with him.

Next minute the door opens and I hear a little clip, clop on the floor. I lift my head and smile.

Eva has brought Dolly into the room. She is safe. The poor minya thing's still shakin' from those stupid kids scarin' 'er, but when Eva lifts 'er up and puts 'er on the bed next to me, she nuzzles 'er nose in under my arm.

'She knows what's good for her, what'll make her strong, nguggil,' I say.

'Yeah.'

Eva smiles and pats her, then asks me to look after her while she makes up some powdered milk. Not long after, Eva returns and hands me the warm bottle. Dolly greedily tugs at the teat, suckin' it, spillin' minya drops out the side of her mouth, her little tail goin' a million miles an hour.

Eva and me both laugh. It feels so good to look after a helpless minya lamb like Dolly, to feed her and protect her. I feel like her mumma. Holdin' Dolly close to me, I tell her how beautiful she is and that I will never let anyone hurt her, no matter what. And most importantly of all, I will never belt her or tell her lies or keep secrets from her, nor will I growl her if she goomboo the bed.

★

As the weeks go by, Dolly grows bigger and stronger and her wool grows thicker. Eva and me play with Dolly for hours, take her for walks and tie material around her neck and ribbons in the wool 'round her yuree. Even though Old Rod give us those ribbons for our hair we're sure he wouldn't mind us sharing them. After all, he did say to look after her real good and now she looks so pretty. We tell her how sweet she looks too, right up close to her yuree, in our nice, soft voices and she bleats back at us, like she's thankin' us for sayin' nice things about her.

Not only will we have to keep an eye on Dolly around Molly, who is always sharpenin' that damn knife, teasin' us, we have to keep an eye on the dogs too. They try to round her up and sometimes even bite her on the legs or the neck. When the dogs snarl at her, she comes runnin' to me or Eva to protect her. But after a while, the dogs get used to her and leave her alone and she gets used to them, too. When they come at her barkin' she nudges them to push them away. We're real proud of how Dolly's growin' up into a lovely young lady sheep. Old Rod will be proud.

One day, Old Rod comes to the Mission in his car. It's the same one that we had the accident in, Old Rod got it fixed. Makes me a bit nervous lookin' at it, even though it's workin' all right now. I still think about what happened that night, how we could've died. Ada was real worried when we got back from the farm after the accident but was pleased that Old Rod wanted to look after us girls more, too. After gettin' in trouble for swearin' I've been thinkin' a lot 'bout Old Rod, Ada and us kids. Even though I've been angry with her for lyin' I reckon it must be hard for Ada sometimes.

Again Old Rod goes into our bedroom to see Ada while us kids wait outside. When he comes out, he asks Eva and me to go for a drive with him. Old Rod's face looks real stern and even though I feel safe with him, I worry what Ada's told him 'bout my swearin' and if I'm gonna get a growlin'.

Eva must be thinkin' the same thing, she's got a big frown on her ngulya.

After Eva and me climb into the front seat, Old Rod closes the door behind us, walks around the back and gets into the driver's side. Then he starts up the engine and takes off slowly down the road. We don't get very far when he takes a big, deep breath, pulls up in front of a building and switches off the engine.

Raisin' our eyebrows, Eva and me look at each other, then back to Old Rod. Why's he stoppin'? We aren't even out of the Mission yet.

Old Rod clears his throat.

Closin' my eyes and holdin' my breath, I start countin', wonderin' how long it will be before his big, boomin' voice gonna start growlin' me.

But instead, a soft, caring voice comes out his mouth. 'There's something I want to talk to you girls about.'

I open my eyes and stare at him. He takes off his hat and is movin' the rim 'round in his hand like he's lookin' for somethin' on it, a loose thread maybe.

There's a long silence.

It makes me feel real nervous. Old Rod is never lost for words, he talks real deadly-way and always knows what to say. Why's he havin' trouble now? Maybe he's really angry with us?

'Ada tells me there's a certain little girl who's always using really bad language, who swears all the time.' His voice is flat and firm.

I put my head down, real shame-way. I can feel heat risin' up in my face until my ears burn. Tiltin' my head sideways, I look at Eva. She's sittin' there real proud-way, guru mooga as round as Tom Bowler marbles and a stupid big smile on her face that seems to be singin', 'I-know-who-it-is-and-it's-not-me.'

I want to punch her right now. Stupid bloody Eva with that smart look on 'er face, stupid damn Ada for dobbin' on me. And stuff Old Rod for tellin' me off and makin' me feel so shame. I swear some more at both of them in my head.

Then I stop 'cause Old Rod is startin' to choke up. He puts his murra mooga over his face and starts rubbin' his eyes with his pointin' finger and his thumb.

What's wrong? Did my swearin' really upset him that much?

'Your mother and I ...We ...' He starts to choke up again.

I feel real scared now. It looks like Old Rod's cryin'. I've never seen 'im like this 'cept the night of the car accident. Has something else really bad happened?

He starts again. 'Your mother and I, we have broken God's fourth Commandment. Do you know what that Commandment is?' He's lookin' at us with red, watery eyes.

We both nod, of course we know what the fourth Commandment is, Pastor drills the Commandments into us all the time at church, and then there's Teacher breathin' down our necks about it all the time: Thou shalt not commit adultery.

'That means you can't be with another woman if you already have a wife.'

Old Rod's words can hardly be heard through the tears that are now streamin' down his face. He fumbles at his jacket pocket and pulls out a hankie. Then he wipes his eyes and blows his nose for what seems like a really long time.

Now I know the full reason why Ada bein' Old Rod's mudgie had to be kept a secret. Now I know why Papa Neddy flogged Ada when she still had Eva growin' in her djuda, and why Hetty Clare said what she did, that night she fought with Ada. Papa was so shame of Ada, shame of what her and Old Rod did knowin' what Pastor and all the Christian walbiya mooga on the Mission and Nyunga mooga would be sayin' about him, his daughter, Ada, and our family. But worst of all, Papa who's a strong believer in God and his Commandments would have felt so shame in front of God, probably like he'd let God down for bringin' his daughter up not to take notice of his Commandments.

Hetty was right. Ada did bring big shame on our family havin' us kids. But she wasn't the only one to blame. Old Rod here too, he's the other one. He should've had more sense, he much older than Ada, closer to Papa's age, and a big Christian man, too. He was even once an Elder in his own church, he told me and Eva one time. He should know better than to commit adultery with Ada who looks like she's the same age as his and Mrs Williams' daughter.

Poor Mrs Williams, imagine how she must feel. Then, I wonder if his son, and his daughter, who lives in Adelaide with her aunty, know.

I suddenly feel shame and angry with Ada, and Old Rod, too. How could they do this to us kids? Bring us into the world like this, out of their act of sin, so everyone points at us and calls us 'bastard kids' and 'illegitimate'. I've heard those taunts as far back as I can remember, even before I knew what they meant. That's why we've been teased all these years by them nasty kids.

'I'm so sorry,' Old Rod sobs. 'I know life hasn't been easy for you girls and your mother and for that I'm so very sorry.'

Eva is lookin' straight ahead, out the window with a blank look on her face, her hands curled in her lap. She could be thinkin' anything.

'I'm going to make it up to you girls. I promise. Soon, I'm going to Adelaide to see my lawyer and I'm going to change my will to include your mother and you girls in it, to make sure that no matter what happens, you'll be well looked after and have a decent chance at life, to get you off this cursed Mission.' He wrings his hankie. 'I promise you that.'

When he drops us off out the front of our minya cottage again, I feel like I've been through the wash tub and hung out on the line, except I feel real dirty, like I have a million stinkin' smelly stains on me. No wonder God never answers my prayers. Look where I come from, the sins of my mother and father. I was born from breakin' God's fourth Commandment. God probably doesn't even see me as his own. Never in my life have I felt so dirty and filthy, as I do now that Old Rod's told me about his sins. It just kind of clings to me like a bad smell and now no matter what I do it'll always be there.

15

Dolly gets a haircut

I talk to Dolly 'bout everythin' and it makes me feel better. We sit out the back together, or go for a walk into the scrub and I tell her everything. She seems to understand when she looks at me with 'er big watery eyes and goes, 'Baah, baah.' It's like she's answerin' me, 'It will be aaaaall right, Graaaace.' I give 'er a big hug then and it makes me feel like everythin' will be all right.

When it's time for Dolly to have her first shearin', Eva and me are real worried. 'Who's shearin' her?' we ask Old Rod in a quiet, real concerned-way. We don't want just anyone cuttin' her wool. What if they're too rough on 'er? Or they slip and cut 'er throat instead or somethin' like that?

'I've got some of the best shearers in the district working for me,' Old Rod says, crossing his arms and standing up straight. 'You should know that, your uncles are some of them.'

Eva and me still aren't convinced, we've heard the uncles talk about roast lamb when they look at Dolly. I draw a line in the dirt with my big toe, and Eva puts her hands on her hips. They probably want to eat Dolly too, just like Molly.

'I tell you what,' Old Rod says, tiltin' his head slightly. 'I'll make sure Dolly gets well looked after by putting your Uncle Ted in charge of her, okay?'

Eva and me both nod, satisfied. Uncle Ted is real good with animals and we know Dolly will be in very good hands.

Uncle Ted is Old Rod's brother. We love him 'cause he's not like other grown-ups, he's more like us kids in some ways. Aunty Mim says that's because he had an accident when he was younger and God gave him a different way of seein' things. That suits us just fine. Eva, me, Sarah and Lil-Lil, we follow Uncle Ted 'round the farm when he feeds the animals and does his chores. Jane and Maddy stay with Ada, 'cause they're still minya. Uncle Ted never gets tired of us or growls us like the other grown-ups, or if he does 'cause sometimes us kids get up to a lotta mischief, he does it in a nice way. He doesn't talk much but he's always happy to listen to us. It isn't like I could have a big yarn with him or anythin', that just wasn't like Uncle Ted. When I was younger though, I would yarn away to him about my peg dolly and he'd listen real close-way, noddin' his head like he thought it was very interestin', but he didn't say anythin'. Most of the time we spend with Uncle Ted is real quiet. There's just this nice, warm feelin' that's always around us.

But Old Rod is the opposite to Uncle Ted, 'cause when Old Rod speaks it's in a sure-of-himself way, like his voice comes from deep inside him, where there's a lotta power that shines out in his eyes, and seeps outa him. He's like a big tractor and Uncle Ted's a pushbike. When Old Rod stands up and walks and moves, it even seems to flow through his arms and legs and when I was real minya I found this frightenin'. I couldn't take my eyes off him but at the same time I felt scared of him, and was drawn to him at the same time. I didn't know he was my father back then, course. If I did, would it have made a difference? I don't know. He was just this big man who was always talkin' about buildin' more things, makin' things work better, makin' his animals bigger and stronger. But a lota the time we shared together was in silence, too. Like it was enough just to be together so we didn't need words.

It's same-way with Uncle Ted, but he and Old Rod are like night-time and day-time. Uncle Ted plods around the farm lookin' after the animals and doesn't talk of big, highfalutin' things. In fact, he doesn't talk much at all and when he does, us kids often know what he's gonna say long before he's finish sayin' it, 'cause it comes outa his mouth real slow and careful-way, like he has to form the words in his mouth before his voice pushes the words out in first gear. In the quiet spaces between his words he's in neutral, tryin' to find first gear again, and sometimes he accidentally hits reverse and has to start again, it's kind of like that with Uncle Ted.

Even though Eva doesn't like it, I love the way Uncle Ted says her name, in a real slow and drawn-out-way:

'Eeeeeevieeeee. Come on, Eeeeeevieeeee,' he says. Sometimes, Eva gets real moogada and it makes me kill myself laughin'. If I can't hide my laughin' from her, Eva gets even more moogada then, and sometimes we end up havin' a big fight, all because of Uncle Ted's 'Eeeeeevieeeee'.

It's strange that we've always called him Uncle Ted, even when we didn't know Old Rod was our father. And we still don't call Old Rod 'Papa' or 'Father', even though we know who he is now. We don't really call him anything to his face, he's still Ada's mudgie when we're around Nyunga mooga, and Old Rod when us girls talk among ourselves. But we don't call him by any name when we're with him. To get his attention we say 'Hey' or ''Scuse me' or we just start talkin' to him or pull at his clothes to get his attention.

'Okay, it's time to get this sheep on the truck and back to the farm to be shorn.' Old Rod rubs his hands together as if they're cold.

Eva and me know Uncle Ted will be gentle with Dolly so we're happy for Old Rod to take her.

'Be careful now,' we beg him. 'She's our baby.'

Old Rod laughs as he ties Dolly's feet together with a rope.

'Do you 'ave to do that?' I ask, seein' the fear in Dolly's eyes as she bleats for Old Rod to let her go.

'Well, it's either this and she gets back to the farm safely, or no ropes and she ends up being knocked around in the back and maybe hurt.'

I nod and pat Dolly, reassurin' her everythin' will be okay and how much better she'll feel after a haircut, 'specially with the hot weather comin'.

174

Then Eva whispers somethin' into Dolly's yuree, strokin' her neck before Old Rod slams the back of the truck shut and drives off down the road.

Eva and me wave until the truck is out of sight then we put our arms 'round each other's shoulders and walk back to the cottage. We aren't good friends very much, we always fight, but we're both a bit worried about Dolly and it seems to bring us closer together, both carin' about Dolly the way we do.

'You reckon she'll be all right?' I ask Eva, a minya bit of doubt naggin' at me.

'Yeah, Uncle Ted'll be extra careful when he knows it's our Dolly.'

I smile, knowin' what Eva said is right. Uncle Ted wouldn't hurt a fly. He'll be givin' Dolly the royal treatment, lotsa water and good feed, he'll probably even be talkin' to her and givin' her messages to pass on to us when she gets back.

Dolly's away for a long time because after the shearin' comes the reapin' and everyone's flat-out on the farm workin' but still Eva and me don't worry 'cause we know she'll be fine. Papa and the uncles have gone to help with the work but Ada and Mumma have stayed to look after the minya babies.

After they finish reapin' the harvest, Dave, Old Rod's son, and Aunty Mim announce that they plan to get married. I'm surprised and excited at the same time. I never thought she'd get married because Old Rod and Ada never did and they'd been mudgie mudgie with each other for years. But then Dave didn't have a wife, did he? So in the end it made sense.

Aunty Mim looks beautiful in her white wedding dress as she walks into the Mission Church, Papa proud-way with her arm in his and Dave looks pretty handsome too, handsome like Old Rod, but in a different, younger-lookin' way.

Before the wedding, Molly's dead serious when she tells Eva and me that Old Rod's been keepin' Dolly on the farm 'specially for the weddin' dinner. She says that Old Rod has told her that he thinks now is a good time to eat Dolly because she's big and fat enough to feed a lot of people but he's asked Molly not to tell us because he knows we wouldn't be happy about his decision.

'But I just couldn't not tell you,' Molly says, lookin' real concerned-way, 'because I know Dolly is like your baby.'

For a minute, I think Molly is tellin' the truth. Tears start wellin' up, I gonna start cryin'. How can Old Rod do such a horrible thing to Dolly? How can he do such a horrible thing to us?

Then Molly starts snortin'. 'You should see the look on your face, Grace.' She blurts out words between explosions of laughter.

I run for her then and start punchin' into her.

Eva joins me, until Aunty Wendy and Aunty Dorrie come runnin' from one of the bedrooms yellin', 'Hey, come on now, you girls. You gonna really hurt Molly in a minute.'

'Ouch,' Molly screams as Eva and me both hit her on the same arm at once.

The aunties try to pull us off. Tryin' to break free of Aunty Dorrie's grasp under her arms, Eva yells, 'Goojarb, Molly.'

'You bloody little shits,' Molly curses as she nurses her bruised arm.

'That'll teach you. You big fat liar,' I say, straightenin' up my dress that has somehow twisted up 'round my skinny little body in the scuffle.

Eva and me sigh with relief when Old Rod brings Dolly back to the Mission. It makes me want to punch Molly in the arm real hard again, for bein' so mean and trickin' us like that.

When Old Rod lifts Dolly off the back of the truck she looks like a new sheep, all slim and white, now that her dirty old coat's been shorn off. And it looks like Uncle Ted did a good job of lookin' after her too, she looks real healthy with nice clear eyes. Dolly is so happy to see us she bleats out a minya song.

'So what did Uncle Ted have to say?' I whisper into Dolly's yuree.

She bleats sheep talk into my yuree.

'True?' I say, noddin' my head with my eyebrows raised. 'Well, next time you see Uncle Ted, you tell him I said the same back to him.' I laugh then, and give Dolly a big hug 'cause I missed 'er so much.

After Old Rod closes up the back of the truck, he goes inside and drops off a box of food to Mumma who's in the kitchen cookin' up a big stew. Then, as usual, he goes in to see Ada in our room. Later, when he comes out, he talks with us girls, about stayin' over again in a minya while, after he finishes some big jobs on the farm and has more time to spend with us.

Eva and me nod and smile. Even though it was pretty scary havin' that big accident in Old Rod's car, we really like stayin' on the farm with just him and us 'cause we get spoilt with hot chicory, toast, big feeds and Old Rod singin' to us while we snugglin' in between clean sheets and warm blanketie. Mrs Williams gets a bit grumpy sometimes, slammin' doors and bangin' dishes 'round, but she leaves us alone with Old Rod, and me and Eva always offer to help her with things. I think she's startin' to warm to us.

I feel so happy that we goin' to the farm again that after Old Rod leaves I jump in the air for joy. Eva just smiles and walks off to check on Dolly who's gone out the back to eat the grass that's grown while she's been away.

Dolly's back but Aunty Mim's gone, she moved off the Mission and went to live on the farm after the wedding. Her and Dave are now staying in the caravan in the big shed where Ada and us girls stay sometimes but their caravan is big and new. It was real sad to see 'er leave 'ome 'cause it feels like a part of me left with her, like it always does when family move out. It happens all the time, 'cause the weekly Mission rations are never enough to keep us from goin' hungry. Sometimes the uncles leave to do shearin', wheat lumpin', fencin' and things like that, and the aunties mostly leave to do cleanin' and washin' in walbiya houses, and milkin' cows and the like.

I remember when I was real minya goin' with Granny Laura, Papa Neddy's sister, to a Greek lady's house in Thevenard not far from the shops. Granny would work real hard scrubbin' her clothes in a big open shed with tubs like the ones at the side of our cottage. Granny would take me with her with the promise of a good feed, so as I watched her scrubbin' away, my djuda would be rumblin' and my mouth waterin' waitin' for the nice food. Then she'd hang out the clothes on the line and I'd know she was nearly finished. I was too minya to help her so I'd just stand there and watch, hopin' she'd be finished soon. When it was time for a break, the Greek lady would bring us the nicest food I ever tasted. Granny and me would sit down on the wood pile near the shed in the corner of the yard and 'ave a big feed.

Family come and go, and when they go they always send back money so everyone at home can eat, and there is always enough to go 'round.

But when Dee-Dee Doe left our cottage, it was different. I lay on our bed and cried for days, I felt so empty, and deep down inside I just knew I'd never see her again 'cause she was goin' somewhere that was a long way away with her mumma, Aunty Rose. It's a bit the same now with Aunty Mim because I know she won't be comin' back, but it's different too 'cause I'll see her every time we go stay on the farm and soon the farm will feel even more like home with her there.

So when Old Rod picks up Eva and me to take us to the farm like he promises, I'm lookin' forward to seein' Aunty Mim again. And we are pretty sure that we'll be stayin' inside the farmhouse, again. 'Cause we figured out that we won't be sleepin' next to the pigsty if there aren't any grown-ups with us, and now Aunty Mim and Dave are stayin' in their caravan in the big shed. 'Sides, I don't know what they did with the old caravan.

For the first time I think of Dave as our big brother, 'cause now I know we 'ave the same dad. Dave has been in the background, lived in the farmhouse with Old Rod and Mrs Williams, but I'd never really taken much notice of him 'til him and Aunty Mim started bein' mudgie mooga. And it seems strange that my aunty is now married to him. I think about that for a while. Ada is always beggin' Old Rod to get 'er and us kids off the Mission, but he wouldn't let her live on the farm all the time. Why not, I don't know, but that's what he always told her. And now Aunty Mim moves onto the farm to live for good. It doesn't seem fair for Ada. Me and Eva are goin' to the farm more often without her and the little ones. I feel sorry for her, but there is no way I'm gonna miss a chance to get off this stinkin' Mission with these rotten, nasty kids who still callin' me names all the time. And it's like those kids' taunts stingin' me all the more now because I know what they're sayin', and in some ways they're right. If I can get away from them and the teasin' remindin' me of Ada and Old Rod's shameful sins, I will, whether Ada's with us or not.

Now that I know everything, I don't want to know, but it seems like there's no gettin' away from it. The kids on the Mission remindin' us every day of our lives, the Pastor preachin' about adultery at church and when we go into town, with not only Old Rod but Dave and Aunty Mim now, the whisperin', turnin'-their-noses-up walbiya mooga seem to be even worse. Sometimes, I just feel like crawlin' into a hole and hidin' for the shame. Shame follows me everywhere, 'specially now that I'm startin' to get older and growin'. I'm no longer a gidja and nearly a teenager. I feel real imbarda and awkward, 'specially with my skinny minya legs that just keep growin' and don't seem to fit the rest of me.

Eva and me sleep at the farmhouse for two deadly nights on the weekend. Other than Mrs Williams still bein' a bit grumpy with us sometimes and slammin' her bedroom door behind her every now and then and stayin' in there for ages, it feels real good to be there.

In the mornin' we catch up with Aunty Mim. She is so happy to see us that we yarn for ages and tell her about everyone back home and what we've been up to. She starts to help Mrs Williams in the farmhouse, washin', cookin' meals for the workers, all those kind of things that the women do on the farm. Then she gets Eva and me peelin' potatoes for the tea that night, it feels like we're at home again together on the Mission, except the kitchen in the farmhouse is real clean and flash and there's lotsa food and only a couple of people. Not like twenty-somethin' of us squashin' together. But the farmhouse doesn't feel the same as our home. Even with Molly teasin' us and not enough food to go 'round, there's still this nice, warm, feelin', like we belong there with our family. For all its flashiness, the farmhouse doesn't have that feelin'. Aunty Mim makes it feel warm though, like we're home even though we aren't. At night, it feels so nice to be between fresh, clean sheets but still I miss my family back on the Mission so as I go to sleep I imagine they're here with me.

That Saturday night, when Uncle Ted sits at the dinner

table for tea, Eva and me thank him for lookin' after Dolly. He nods his careful, slow nod that says, 'You're welcome.' It feels weird, all of us sittin' together at the table, Old Rod, Mrs Williams, Aunty Mim and Dave, Uncle Ted and us girls, tryin' to remember to use our manners like we've been taught to do 'round walbiya mooga. But these walbiya mooga are different from most, 'cause they're our family. How strange it feels.

The next day we go with Old Rod to check the paddocks. When we drive past where we found Dolly, I think about how much she's grown since then. I'm missin' her. She really is the best friend Eva and me ever had. We even go lookin' for her together, if we get home from school and she's not there. 'Cause sometimes she'll go wanderin' round the Mission, she can be a real adventurous little girl sheep. I don't like bein' away from her and worry that we can't keep an eye on her, or Molly for that matter. So I'm glad when Old Rod drops us off at the Mission that night and we find Dolly at the back waitin' for us. It feels good to spend time on the farm, but it's good to be home too, I think, as I cuddle up between Lil-Lil and Sarah in our big old bed.

16

Goin' back to country, in heaven

One night, a scream for help jolts us out of our sleep. Ada and us kids haven't long gone to bed when Mumma starts yellin'. We can hear Papa gaspin' for breath like he sometimes does after coughin' for a long time. Ada flies outa bed, as Mumma yells for someone to get Sister, quick.

'You kids stay 'ere.'

Ada's voice sounds strange, deep and panicky, like she's talkin' in her sleep. Us kids follow her to our bedroom door and strain our necks tryin' to see what's goin' on. Next minute, Ada comes runnin' outa Mumma and Papa's room, across the kitchen and out the front door, leavin' it swingin' open for a cold gust of wind to fly in.

'Stay 'ere,' Eva repeats Ada's words to us and runs across the kitchen towards Mumma and Papa's room. All the aunties and uncles and some of the kids are rushin' over there too.

Repeatin' Eva's words to my minya sisters, I run after Eva.

We squeeze our heads into the room, past the adults crowdin' the entrance and see Mumma with the help of the others tryin' to sit Papa up in bed as he fights for breath, his chest risin' and fallin' with loud wheezin' sounds comin' from his mouth. Papa often has these coughin' fits but they're never this bad. His face is goin' real white and his eyes look like they gonna pop outa his head.

When Papa's head flops forward and the wheezin' stops, I panic and run to the front door. I know Ada has run to get Sister. Why is she takin' so long? I'm so scared, I want to scream out at the top of my lungs, 'Hurry up. Hurry up.'

Mumma starts to wail then, and as I back away from the front door, I can hear cryin' comin' from the minya back room. When I turn 'round slow-way, I see Eva lookin' back at me across the room. We both 'ave fear in our eyes. Can what we ngulu of be true? Can Papa really be in that much trouble? We dare not believe it, this thought is too frightenin'. We both walk quick-way back to our bedroom, grab our minya sisters still waitin' at the door and usher them to the bed where we all huddle together. They're askin' us questions, but I can't answer them, I can't even hear them properly, 'cause I'm too frightened. Maddy and Jane are cryin' so me and Eva pick them up to comfort them. Whenever bad things happened, it was always Papa who took control of things, who protected us, who reassured us no harm would come to us. But now that it's him needin' help there's nothin' we can do. It seems like no-one, not even my uncles, can help him now.

When Sister finally arrives it's too late. I hear her talkin' to Mumma, sayin', 'I'm sorry, Jenna. He's gone.'

I squeeze my guru mooga shut tight. Maybe he's 'gone' for a walk, I tell myself, knowing deep down inside that's not what Sister means. I don't want to believe it, Sister must be tellin' lies. I try to think of another way. But in my gut that is now churnin' I feel so angry at Sister. When walbiya mooga come into our house they usually act real boonri boonri, bossin' us around, tellin' us what to do, or what we should be doin', but this time Sister's voice is all soft and hushed as she speaks to Mumma and asks if she should get Pastor now. It's like they only act proper-way after we're dead or when someone dies. I s'pose they can't boss a dead person around any more, so there's no point in tryin'. I want to scream and tell 'er to get outa our minya cottage that our Papa built, right now.

'I'll go and get Pastor then?'

Mumma nods through her tears.

'Okay, Jenna,' Sister says as Mumma keeps noddin'.

Then Sister turns, puts her head down and walks out the front door into the windy night.

When I hear the door shut, I feel relieved. I can disappear into my numbness and pretend none of this is happenin'. I know Sister is goin' to get Pastor 'cause Papa's died. There's no hidin' from the truth now. Straight away my anger turns to fear. Somewhere in that back room lies Papa's dead body. Not the Papa that I know, full of life, but his empty shell. I shiver.

But then Mumma starts to round up us kids. I get real scared. I try to slink back off the bed to hide under it, but Mumma can see me through the door and calls me forward.

When all the kids are huddled together in the middle of the kitchen like a minya flock of sheep, Mumma clears 'er throat and dabs 'er eyes with the hankie in 'er shakin' hand. 'You kids need to show your respect to Papa and kiss 'im goodbye.'

I can't say, 'No, Mumma. I'm not gonna. I'm too scared.' That will be too disrespectful and I'll get a floggin' from Ada and maybe the other aunties. So I real nervous-way move up and stand behind Polly, who is last in the line.

I give another shudder. Why does Mumma want us to do this? Papa's dead and in heaven now, that's what Pastor says when people die, he won't want us kissin' his dead body. The line is gettin' shorter now as it moves towards the bed where Papa's body lies, covered up to his chest with a neatly smoothed out blanketie. As I get closer I can see Papa's face is the colour of ashes when the fire burns down in the mornin'. His eyes seem sunken in his head now, not poppin' out like before. I turn my head away, not wanting to remember my Papa, my dear, dear, Papa, this way. Tears start to roll down my face then, like the wanna over the boulders at Rocky Point when the waves come crashin' down, they run over my cheeks and I can't stop them from fallin'.

'Why our Papa? Why him?' I ask God, this time not in an angry demanding way, but in a sad need-to-know way, a pleadin', beggin' kind of way. I look for an answer, but can't find one to cling on to.

I'm next in line, now. I feel like I'm drownin' in my tears. It's my turn to say goodbye to Papa, to show Mumma that I'm bein' respectful. I wipe my wet face with the back of my hand and sniff back hard. Fear washes up over me again and I feel sick as I lower my head and push my lips against Papa's cheek. His skin is hard and cold and sends a shudder through my body. I don't want to remember Papa like that. I want to remember 'im as the warm, strong, caring man that protects us. I walk away from the bed and his coldness comes with me like it's sunk into me and stays there, resting.

Not long after, Sister comes back with Pastor and he calls everyone together again, 'cause some of us have gone back to our bedrooms to cry. Pastor says he is here to pray with us and to offer some words of comfort.

Comfort? That word doesn't sound right to me. How can the word 'comfort' go together in the same sentence with 'Papa dyin'? Then he tells us that Papa has gone to heaven. 'He's gone to be with Jesus and now he's safe in God's care.'

'God's care? God's care?' I shout inside my head in disbelief. 'If God cared so much how come he let our Papa die?' I'm so angry all I can do is cry in rage. 'Stuff God,' I silently scream. 'He's just out to make my life a misery by takin' Papa away from me. He wants to punish me for the sins of Ada and Old Rod, for makin' me be born a dirty, little bastard girl from breakin' his Commandment.'

In that moment I hate God as much as I hate myself. If God appeared in front of me here and now, I would scream at him.

Soon after, a truck pulls up out the front and there is a knock at the door. Then two men come in with a stretcher. Sister pulls the blanketie over Papa's cold campfire face.

I want to get as far away from that empty body as I can. 'Cause Papa wasn't in there any more and Pastor said he's in heaven. I back away towards our bedroom and once I'm through the door I run back to bed, pullin' the covers over my face. My sisters follow behind and soon we're huddlin' up close.

Then I hear the truck start up and pull away and I know where they're takin' Papa's body, to that minya room outside the Mission hospital window, right near that bed where I use to lie awake, scared-way, as a little girl. Poor Papa's spirit, I'm thinkin', if he's not in heaven yet or if he's lost his way, he'll probably be there in the Mission hospital tonight, as a guldi, breathin' in the bed next to some poor sick kid, scarin' them half to death so they're too ngulu to go to sleep.

That night, as I sleep squashed between Ada and my five sisters in our bed, I can see Papa Neddy floating through the back door and lookin' over us. I shake with terror 'cause even here in my dream, death is a fearful thing. But then I start to feel different-way 'cause Papa's guldi isn't a mean, cold, scary one like the ones that hang around the Mission hospital, it's a warm, loving one that has come back to make sure we're all right, to look after us.

I sleep real well after that and next mornin' I feel a bit better until I realise I've pissed the bed again. As I lie there, cold, wet and half asleep, I hear a strange sound like we're at Denial Bay in a storm, with the wind howlin' and waves crashin'. Am I still dreamin'? I open my eyes and sit up. Then I throw myself down again, rememberin' everythin' that happened the night before.

When I step into the kitchen, it's like a heavy thunder cloud has drifted into our minya cottage even though it's clear and sunny outside. A huge wave of misery washes around everyone with the grief-stricken hum of snifflin', sobbin' and wailin'. It's like the shore is risin' and fallin', tryin' to hold something that can't be held. Ada is already awake and sittin' next to Mumma at the kitchen table cryin', my two youngest sisters clingin' to her. My uncles and aunties all have their heads down too, and some kids are sittin' quiet-way by their parents, it's like a big wave of grief is drownin' everyone. All the feelings of last night start to swirl up in me again. I have to get out of the house, so I run outside where I find Dolly and tell her everythin' that's happened then cry into her woolly coat. She's cryin' too.

As the mornin' wears on, most of the Nyunga mooga who live on the Mission move through our cottage, past the sorrowful faces of our family, shakin' all their murra mooga as a sign of deep respect for Papa Neddy and us, his mournin' family. It's like that small motion of joinin' the murra mooga together and shakin' them says more than any amount of words can. It's always like that with us Nyunga mooga. Shakin' murra mooga somehow shares the burden or the pain of losin' a loved one and it's always appreciated by the family. Some ladies bring food and lay it on the table for our family to eat. Even Hetty Clare brings some damper. As much as she hates our family, as she so often tells us, she still walks in, quiet-way, and places the damper down. She walks up to Mumma, shakes 'er murra, then with 'er gugga down, moves around slowly and shakes every single grown-up's murra, even Ada's. There's nothin'

good about people dyin' except how the whole community pulls together and supports each other in their grief.
Seein' that makes me feel warm and proud inside.

That same mornin' Old Rod and Dave bring Aunty
Mim back to the Mission. Superintendent let us use the
phone to call them at the farm. When Aunty Mim comes
through the door she falls forward and hugs Mumma and
cries big sobs. Poor Mumma, she's so upset her whole body
shakin' in little tremors like a cold wave is washin' around
inside her, splashin' at the edge.

Old Rod and Dave give Mumma condolences and shake
'er hand, 'cause they know that Nyunga way, then they
offer to give any support that's needed. After all, Papa had
worked on Old Rod's farm for many years, fixin' fences,
buildin' sheds, shearin' sheep, helpin' with the reapin',
sewin' and lumpin' wheat bags, and many other jobs that
needed doin'. After Mumma thanks them, they shake
everyone's hand and leave to go back to the farm.

With the day of the funeral coming closer I think about
how Papa was such a special man in our lives. He was like
a father to us girls all these years even though he was our
grandfather. He was the big boonri of the family. What he
said went. He ruled the house with a big whip, but he also
made sure nothin' happened to us. He was our strength. He
cared for us in so many ways and always tried to make sure
his children and grannies were safe from harm. And now
he's dead. I can hardly believe it still but with the day of his
funeral comin' closer, it starts to sink in.

The day of Papa Neddy's funeral the old garnga mooga sit in the big tree near the church and crow loud-way like they're sayin' goodbye to Papa, too. It's a real big funeral with people from all over the district there. I can't believe how the church is full to overflowin'. Papa's so well known and respected by Nyunga mooga, and walbiya mooga too. That's 'cause he was a good man who treated people with respect and 'cause he worked real hard at his jobs on lotsa farms around the place, but mostly Old Rod's. He built houses, shops and even the Ceduna jail house. There was no hope for those poor fellas in jail if they want to escape, 'cause he built that place real strong-way.

Standin' up there, at the front of the church near Papa's coffin, Pastor again say Papa's now in heaven, and I wonder if he was on his way there when he visited me in my dream the other night. Pastor always talks about heaven being the place we go when we die but I've heard some of our Old People talk about us Nyunga mooga 'goin' back to country' when we jinga. When I hear that, I wonder if that 'country' that they talk about and 'heaven' are the same place. I reckon they must be.

Then Pastor asks everyone to stand and pray. All the jinna mooga shuffle as everyone stands up and bows their heads. Mumma Jenna and some of the aunties and uncles and us kids are real sad and cryin' and inside the church feels real heavy with sadness. It's like the tide is out now and we're all washed up and tired.

'Our Father who art in Heaven, hallowed be thy name . . .'

After the church service Pastor asks us to make our way to the cemetery and the uncles come forward to take Papa's coffin to the truck. It's a couple of miles away from the church. As the slow line of cars and trucks moves towards the cemetery a wurly wurly whips up and races across the paddock ahead of us. There goes Papa, I think, that's what the Old People say, that spirit travels in the wurly wind.

As Pastor talks at the cemetery, I hear a strange sound underneath the words of his prayer, growin' louder. First, I think the noise sounds like Papa's old car, his moodigee, or gudgud, as we call it. It's a real old-fashioned car that putts along slow as slow, but after listenin' careful-way it sounds more like the roar of big motorbikes drivin' down the road. It's like they're gettin' closer and closer 'til the sound sort of stays the same. I'm thinkin' them motorbikes should be here by now, and then I'm thinkin', who'd be drivin' that many motorbikes out this way? The sound seems like it'll drown out Pastor's words altogether, or maybe that's 'cause I listenin' so hard, tryin' to work it out myself.

I can see the grown-ups shufflin' on their feet and fidg-etin', some turning to look behind. Then in front of me I see Uncle Murdi whisper to Uncle Jerry. Uncle Jerry closes his guru mooga and nods, then a minya tear trickles down his face. I don't know what Uncle Murdi said, could be they know that whirring sound. Maybe it somethin' to do with our Nyunga way, and means that Papa has made it back to country safely. I hope so.

After Papa's funeral, night after night, Mumma Jenna lies on her bed cryin'. There isn't anything anyone can do to make her feel better but we try, anyway. Sometimes I go and curl up next to her, pullin' the covers up over us. I just lay there quiet-way. At night-time, whichever granny runs and gets in 'er bed first can sleep with her.

Mumma isn't the only one who feels real sad about Papa passin' away. All us mob feel it, we just seem to deal with it in different ways. Most of us cry like Mumma, but some are quiet and say nothin', and others want to remember all the good times we shared with Papa, so they talk all the time. Ada and us girls just sit quiet-way in our room a lot, sayin' nothin', but sometimes we cry too. It's hard to think that we'll never, ever see Papa again. He's everythin' to all us and now he's gone for good and we just 'ave to get through the best way we can.

Uncle Wadu gets real angry and yells a lot. He doesn't think it was Papa's time to go and he's sure somethin' Nyunga-way happen to Papa. He goes a bit joobardi, runnin' 'round yellin'. Polly, Sandy and Joshy come and sit in our room for a while. Later Uncle Wadu goes away to have a break from the Mission and takes Aunty Nora and the kids with him.

When Mumma stops cryin', I see her careful-way pickin' up the old tobacco tin that holds Papa's hair that she collected over the years, which she keeps in the top drawer of her bedroom cupboard, which she used to show us all the time.

'That's your Papa's hair there,' she'd say. 'I'm keepin' it in this here tin, safe-way.'

I'm standin' to the side of Mumma's bedroom door lookin' in at her and I can see her puttin' the tin in her pocket under her apron. I slip back towards the kitchen before she walks outa her room sayin' that she has some things to do and will be back later. Where's she takin' Papa's gugga uru, I wonder as I watch her from the window, hurryin' off down the road.

Not long after, one night I'm sleepin' cuddled up closeway to Mumma, when I'm woken by a strange whistlin' noise, real close by. Mumma wakes up too. I can see her outline against the moonlight comin' in from the minya window on the back wall. When she sits up the whistlin' noise gets louder. Then, from under her pillow, she picks up somethin' and unwraps it. It's a round, dark thing, like a flat disc with a hole in it, that she holds up in the moonlight. The noise is real loud now. It's comin' from that thing in 'er hand. Even though it's dark in the room I can see the round thing vibratin' by itself in Mumma's murra. I get real ngulu then. She turns 'round and sits up in bed, pullin' that thing closer to her chest, she's lookin' towards the window.

'What's that, Mumma?' I ask in a high shaky voice that doesn't even sound like mine.

She looks back down at the thing vibrating, bouncin' by itself in 'er murra. 'Shhh,' she whispers in a rough way. 'It's not safe. Someone here. Might be jinardoo.'

'Ahh.' A gasp comes outa my mouth as I grab Mumma with one murra and pull the covers up over my head with the other. I'm so scared I'm sure I'll goomboo the bed at any minute even though I'm wide awake. Jinardoo is a special Nyunga man with dangerous powers that can make people very sick or even die, and he could be outside our window. I curl up into a minya ball, my head poundin' with the sound of my thumpin' heart.

By the time I come out from under the covers, some of our mob are in Mumma's room and the minya round thing has stopped shaking and its whistle sounds like a faint wind blowin' a long way away. No-one has lit a candle 'cause they know that will allow jinardoo to see us. Whatever it is, bad spirit or jinardoo, we know if we draw light to ourselves it can see us, we know it's dangerous to us, and we know we need to keep very still and quiet.

'It's all right now,' Mumma says in a big sigh. 'Youse can go back to bed, it's gone now.'

She wraps the round thing back up in the material and puts it under her pillow again.

After everyone shuffles off to bed and a couple more kids who've joined us in Mumma's bed stop wrigglin', I whisper to her, 'Mumma, what's that wada there under your pillow?'

I know it's Papa's hair but I don't understand why it shakes and whistles by itself the way it did.

'You don't go worryin' about things like that girl,' Mumma says. 'That's for us adults to worry about. That wada there protectin' us and we safe now, that's the main thing.'

I know this is another secret but not like that shameful secret. This is a Nyunga secret, one I won't worry about findin' clues for 'cause it could make me sick or even make me jinga if I snoop around places that a young girl shouldn't be snoopin' in. I know this because Ada, Mumma and Papa taught me. But I also know that like my old Jumoo, who could look at my leg and see walbiya gu minga inside, there are special Nyunga people who can put magic into things too, good magic that can protect and heal, or bad magic, like mumoo, that can hurt.

Mumma must have taken the tin with Papa's hair in it from her cupboard that day to one of those special people who made Papa's spirit strong in that round thing so he could keep us safe even though he's gone back to country in heaven. Our Nyunga mooga are very clever how we know to do things like that. No walbiya mooga know how this kind of magic works, not even their best detectives could find the clues to solve it, and their most cleverest scientists wouldn't know how it works. Pastor would say it's of the devil but we know it's strong Kokatha ways helping to protect us.

17

Goojarb: serves yourself right

A year later, one weekend, Eva and I're over at the farm again. We've been goin' over there a lot lately, and it's startin' to feel like our second home. We're spending more time in the farmhouse with Aunty Mim and Mrs Williams, now that she's decided to come out of her room more often when we're there. We're learnin' lotsa new things, like cookin' and sewin' and how to set a table and things like that. Mrs Williams is even real keen to teach me to knit and I'm real proud-way makin' a pair of baby's booties. Some of these things we just can't learn on the Mission, like the way walbiya mooga do things, which are real strange ways sometimes. But after a while I start thinkin' that livin' like walbiya mooga might not be such a bad thing after all.

Old Rod takes us out with him checkin' the paddocks again. He tells us he's goin' to Adelaide in a couple of days to see his lawyer. Later, Eva and me both wonder if it's the same thing he's been talkin' to us about that day on the Mission, when he cried in his car.

'Promise me you'll look after my girls while I'm away?' Old Rod says to Dave and Aunty Mim before he leaves on the plane.

They nod, give their word that they will. Maybe Old Rod said that 'cause he knew God had other plans for him.

The next day us kids are playin' cricket in the backyard of our cottage when Aunty Mim comes 'round the corner, with a hankie wipin' her eyes.

'What's wrong, Aunty Mim?' I ask, Eva close behind me.

Aunty Mim puts her arms out to us and hugs us.

'It's Old Rod,' she says. 'He's passed away.'

'What? How?' Eva asks.

I back away from them, not wanting to believe what she's sayin'.

'Heart attack at his sister's place in Adelaide.'

I run into our bedroom and throw myself on the bed next to Ada who is cryin' into the blanketie.

'Why?' I ask Ada. 'Why Old Rod? He was a good man to us.'

But Ada just start cryin' more. Soon Eva and all our minya sisters cuddled 'round cryin'. Our minya bed is wet with tears again, this time for Old Rod.

After Papa died it left such an empty feelin' inside me that I think life can't get any worse. But I'm wrong, it's just the beginnin'. It starts all over again with Old Rod passin' away. And just like when Papa died, all I can see in front of me is a big, gapin' hole, but this time, it's cavin' in on top of me, just like the rabbity gudle mooga when we go to catch a feed. But now I'm the rabbity backed into the corner, suffocatin' in misery, and the only thing keepin' me from givin' in is my minya sisters.

I just can't believe Old Rod is dead. It's all wrong, nothin' makes sense. It's just before reapin' season and his crops are almost ready to harvest.

I'm sure God's still punishin' me, by takin' Old Rod away. And I feel punished all the more when Old Rod's family doesn't bring him back home to be buried. Instead, they have his funeral in Adelaide. We don't even get to say goodbye. It would've been too embarrassing for Old Rod's family and friends, for all those walbiya mooga, to have his black mudgie and gidjida mooga there at his funeral. Even if we could've gone, it would've brought too much shame on them to see us there, to remind them that a lotta their walbiya men act in these sorts of sinful ways with our Nyunga women all the time, even the married ones. Then they go to church on Sunday and pretend they're Christian. Maybe that's why Old Rod's family had his funeral in Adelaide. To hide the truth about him and Ada. Whatever the reason, it didn't matter, Old Rod was gone for good and no Nyunga magic was gonna help him look after us, protect us, ever again. From now on we're well and truly on our own. I'm almost twelve now but he'll never see me grow up. Where Old Rod went after he died I don't know. I just hope it's heaven. Maybe walbiya heaven, 'cause Old Rod wasn't Nyunga like us.

It's real confusin' for me. On one hand, walbiya mob ignore us. We aren't considered a part of Old Rod's life so we aren't included in the mournin', not able to grieve over him proper-way. We don't even have a grave to visit. Old Rod just disappears out of our lives forever. Poof! Just like that. It's like we're invisible, too, just like when Sister pulled the cover over Papa's grey face before they took him to that cold minya room 'til his funeral. We're covered the same way, blanketie pulled over, like we're empty shells of a body. My insides are cold, hollow, empty and they feel all broken up, like they fallin' to pieces. There's this really bad pain inside like when that doctor put me to sleep and cut my djuda open to take my appendix out. But this pain's worse, it's hurtin' all over inside me.

Nothin' to ease the pain either, no Nyunga mooga on the Mission shake hands with us the way they usually do to show respect when a loved one dies. At first, I can't understand it, 'cause when word comes to us that Old Rod is jinga in Adelaide, I think everyone will come over to our minya cottage and shake our murra mooga and bring food, like they always do, respectful-way, when someone jinga. But no-one comes. No-one. Not one person comes to show their respect. Are we that much of a shame job to both Nyunga mooga and walbiya mooga, Ada the adulterer and her bastard kids? My head feels mixed up and a real moogada feelin' comin' up from my djuda. I feel shame for who I am, bein' born a bastard kid. And like Papa and Old Rod now, I just want to be dead.

Later, when us kids stop cryin' 'nough to go outside, them nasty kids on the Mission spit at us and tease us.

'Goojarb, you stinkin' whitefella kids. Serve yourself right,' they say.

As if it's our fault that Old Rod died and that we were born bastard kids, like we had some choice in it. They just seem real happy that Old Rod's dead, like it's somethin' they looked forward to and now it's time to celebrate, like Christmas or holidays at Denial Bay.

'You a proper bastard kid now that you got no father. Ha, ha,' 'Arold and some other kids laugh.

I just stare back at them, like I'm lookin' outa dead guru mooga. The taunts feel like they'll never stop until I'm numb all over. After a while they're all I think about. I want to lash out but my shame holds me back. I hate myself for who I am, some dirty, not quite Nyunga not quite walaba girl who doesn't fit in anywhere. And now that Old Rod, the fella who looks out for us, has gone, I don't feel safe. Sometimes I'm so numb inside I feel like I'm fadin' into nothin', almost invisible. Other times it feels like I'm the animals that the butchers hang upside down, my insides hangin' loose. Maybe this is what I deserve.

Ada is too sad from Old Rod's dyin' to help us kids. She hears what the mean kids are sayin', but she doesn't say nothin' to stick up for us. She stands there with her mouth shut tight, just lookin' straight ahead, like she got no voice.

Of course Mumma is there but now it's a real struggle for all of us without the extra food that Old Rod use to provide.

'Hey! Williams' pigs, who's gonna feed you now?' the kids call out, and other nasty things like that.

I feel too gutted to fight with them like I would've when I was younger. I hate them as much as I hate myself, for being who I am, for being who Old Rod and Ada made me. Every nasty word that is thrown just pulls me down further. I feel like I'm fallin' into a place inside myself that I keep from everyone around me. It's no longer a hidden treasure chest of secret-pretty-things that makes me feel nice, it's now cold, damp and hollow, and sickness seeps out of me. The weepin' sores on my wrist are proof of this. As the scabs grow bigger and weep more, I feel like they're draining out from my insides, that the brown crusty skin and pussy, weepin' stuff that oozes out is 'cause I can't keep it from festerin' inside me any longer.

Stabbin' hunger pains now come as often as a feed used to, 'cause soon after Old Rod dies, his son Dave takes over the farm, and the five pounds a week goin' into the Mission shop that Old Rod paid for Ada and us girls to eat, stops too. Dave says he has to cancel it 'cause the farm is in debt. But I know it's always that way before the harvest, 'cause that's what Old Rod always told us. All the farmers have to borrow money from the bank for seed and petrol and other stuff, and then he pays them back after the reapin', with plenty to spare to keep the farm goin' for the rest of the year. And Old Rod said that with a big farm like his he had to borrow more money, but that meant he could make more money too.

With that extra money he would let Ada buy us pretty minya dresses with matching shoes from Mona Tareen's Frock Salon, too. I remember when I asked him why he bought us these nice things, he threw his head back, laughed and said he'd reaped one of the biggest crops in the district and could afford to buy us somethin' a little bit special.

The way he said it was like he could have bought us a million dresses if he wanted to, but I was so happy just to have one. It was so pretty and I felt like the most special minya girl in the whole world.

After Old Rod dies, there are no more trips to the frock salon, no more food freely flowin' from the store. Ada seems too sad to notice or care. When she stops cryin' enough to leave the house she's never home. She just takes off and only comes home sometimes. It's like, after all these years of telling us kids, 'If it wasn't for you girls, I'd have my freedom,' now she has it, not because she doesn't have us girls to look after, but because Old Rod is no longer 'round to keep her close to us and him.

Soon after, Eva's getting ready to leave for Adelaide to go to a Lutheran college for high school, like some kids who do well enough at the Mission school. Eva's packin' her bags in the bedroom, our minya sisters all 'round her askin' questions.

'Where you goin', Sissy,' Lil-Lil's askin' for the fourth time.

'I told you, Lil-Lil, I'm goin' to the big city to go to college.'

'Can I come?'

'Me too,' says Sarah quiet-way, crawlin' over the bed to get closer, not wantin' to miss out.

Jane and Maddy are playin' on the floor near the door.

'No, you can't, you gotta wait 'til you're older.'

'But I'm gonna miss you, Sissy,' Sarah starts to cry.

Eva reaches over and gives her a big hug. Lil-Lil leans over and snuggles into Eva. 'You wait and see. Before you know it I'll be back for 'olidays.'

Mumma calls from the kitchen, 'Eva, your lift's 'ere.'

'Well, I'll see you then, Grace,' Eva says.

I stay sittin' at the end of the bed with my back to her, lookin' at the wall.

'See you,' I say moogada-way, lookin' over my shoulder.

I'm so jealous of Eva gettin' to leave this hole of a place. I want to go with her, but I have to stay and go through another year of hell.

She shrugs, picks up her bag and walks into the kitchen, our minya sisters tag behind grabbin' onto her dress. I stretch out and kick the bedroom door hard, then throw myself on our bed and cry. I hear the car drive away and my minya sisters are cryin' too. I already hate my life and now Eva who helps with lookin' after our minya sisters is gone. I'll have to look out for them by myself while I'm still goin' to school to make sure I get good enough marks to join Eva when my time comes.

As the school year starts, Ada comes home for a while and I'm real pleased to see her.

'Look, Grace,' she says smilin', 'I've brought fruit and some meat 'ere for you to eat.'

I smile back, it's so good to fill my djuda and see my minya sisters eatin'.

'Mumma, Mumma. This real nice mai,' they say, cuddlin' into Ada.

'Yeah, it's nice,' I say grateful, but I wonder where she got the food from this time, and how long 'til she's gone again.

After about a week the food runs out and Ada's off again and I have to decide what to do, stay home to look after my minya sisters or go to school. It's hard to stay away from school 'cause I'd get in the biggest trouble from Teacher and Headmaster, and even from Granny Alfie, Mumma Jenna's brother, 'cause if he sees us kids runnin' 'round the Mission, he'll growl us too and send us to school. And it's hard to stay home, even though I worry about my minya sisters the whole time I'm at school.

Some days I sit in the classroom and strain my neck lookin' out the window for Jane and Maddy. Are they all right, I'm always thinkin' when I can't see them, instead of doin' my schoolwork.

'Grace, will you keep to the task at hand.'

Teacher's screechy voice pulls me back to the schoolwork on my desk. I go back to my arithmetic, sly-way peekin' a look every now and then 'til I see my minya sisters playin' with each other, safe, and I sigh with relief and go back to my work. But in the back of my head I'm always thinkin' what will happen to them after I leave? Will they be safe?

Some days, I feel too shame to go to school 'cause the sores on my wrists are gettin' worse. They've got so bad that I always accidentally knock them and the pain is awful. I can't even hold my pencil to write, so I just nurse my hands in my lap and my dress gets all sticky with blood and weepy pus. I'm moogada with Ada for leavin' us all the time, with my minya sisters screamin' in hunger and me not bein' able to do nothin' about it. I know she goes to get food for us and when she comes back we have a good feed, and even though it's so good to see my little sisters eatin' 'til their minya djuda mooga are full I know Ada will be gone again when we run outa food. I just wish she could stay.

One evenin', when Ada has been away for a few days, she turns up with a Nyunga man and brings him into our room. I'm so moogada. How dare she bring this stranger into our bedroom with my minya sisters. This is our special place. How can she do that?

Ada tries to push us over to make room for her and this man to lie down next to us in our bed. As my minya sisters wriggle over, I jump outa bed and start yellin' at that fella. Doesn't she know this bed is our bed, always has been. Nobody but me, Ada and my little sisters sleep in this bed. She must've forgotten. This is my safe place and no-one but us is supposed to sleep in it.

'No friggin' way. You get outa here, now. This not your place.'

Ada's so angry she tells me to shut up and tries to hit me. But I dodge her. The man puts his hands in the air, tryin' to calm me down.

'Hey,' he says over the top of our screamin' voices. 'I don't mean no harm.' The whites of his eyes are flashin' in the dim light.

Ada and me stop arguin' then.

The man carefully lowers his hands, picks up his suitcase in one, and a blanketie in the other. 'You can have these, if you like.' He looks down at his hands and pushes his gifts towards me. 'It's a real deadly suitcase, this one.'

'I don't want your stupid case, I want you to get outa here,' I yell. 'This here bed's for me and my sisters, not some ugly idiot like you.'

Ada goes for me again. 'Why, you cheeky minya . . .'

But before she gets to me I run over to the corner of the room, pick up a brick that we use to keep the door open, and throw it real hard-way at the man, hittin' him in the arm.

'Ahh,' he yells and falls back, droppin' his suitcase. Then scurryin' like a crab to his feet, he grabs his case, throws his blanketie over his shoulder and runs out the front door of our cottage. Ada flies at me again but Aunty Dorrie runs in and stops her by grabbin' hold of me. She tells her sister, 'Don't you hit her, Ada.'

Ada runs out after her mudgie, cursin' me at the top of her voice, but she doesn't come back that night. I won't let her, not with him anyway.

My little sisters are cryin' when I climb back into bed to comfort them, tellin' them, 'There's no way I'm gonna let anythin' happen to you girls. I'll keep you safe, no matter what, even if it means throwin' a big brick at ugly Nyunga mooga tryin' to climb into our bed with us.'

Jane laughs then. 'You got 'im a good one too, Grace.'

'Yeah, I did, indie,' I say with a big smile on my face.

We all giggle then and snuggle up together under our blanketie to go back to sleep. I don't know where Ada is that night but for the first time I don't care. As long as my sisters are safe that's all that matters. But what if Ada brings him back again? I feel like I want to run away. The only place I can think of that's safe is the farm. I'm big enough to run there by myself in the dark too, like we did lots of times before with Ada. But I can't go without my minya sisters and I can't drag them all that way. I lie in bed cryin' quiet-way under my breath so my minya sisters won't hear. I've won the fight with Ada, but our bed feels empty without her. I stay awake into the early hours of the mornin', lyin' there listenin', scared that Ada might bring that stranger back. There's no way I'm gonna let that happen. No bloody way.

Some days that follow, especially Christmas and Easter, are like our water tanks in summer: low, hollow, almost empty. Old Rod never comes to visit to give us food or presents or to pick us up to take us to town or home to his farm for chicory and toast and to play us music while we snuggle in between comfy clean sheets. Now, with only the Mission rations to feed us, and child endowment once a month, and an occasional feed from Ada when she decides to come 'ome, which isn't very often, we're close to starvin' all the time. In the past, at different times we went hungry, but now it's a way of life. I feel like my djuda will ache a gudle into itself and I'll be walkin' round the Mission with the wind blowin' through it. But my hunger I can cope with. It's hearin' my minya sisters cryin' out for food that guts me.

One day it gets really bad because food's short for everybody for days and there's no spare food in the house to go 'round. I just snap. I start yellin' and goin' off my head at Ada even though she isn't even there.

My aunties try to calm me down but I'm goin' crazy. I just wish Mumma was here. She's gone to stay somewhere else for a while but I'm not sure where. I come home one day from school and she was gone.

I run outside yellin'. Then I stop. At the end of the street I see a walbiya car droppin' someone off at the Mission.

Runnin' down the road as fast as I can to catch them before they leave, I wave my arms in the air.

'Hey. Hey. Hey, Mister,' I yell, surprised at my lack of shame.

'Hello. You're Ada's young girl, aren't you?'

'Yes, Mister.' I nod. He looks familiar, but I don't know his name.

'What can I do for you, young lady?'

'If you're on the way to town can you please give me and my sisters a lift to 18 Mile Tank? I need to take my sisters to my mumma.' I try to sound official, not too desperate, so the man will agree.

'Is that right?' he asks with one of his eyebrows right up high on his ngulya.

'Yeah,' I say, not wanting to say any more 'cause I don't want to lie.

'Okay, I'll wait here,' he says. 'But don't take too long now, because I have other business to do.'

I run as fast as I can to get my minya sisters. Aunty Dorrie tries to argue with me that I can't go takin' them away like that, but there's no stoppin' me. Soon we're in the back of the walbiya man's car and on the way to 18 Mile Tank, a place I know Ada will be 'cause I hear the grown-ups talkin' 'bout it all the time.

When the man pulls up to drop us off and I see Ada sittin' on the other side of the campfire drinkin', I thank him and help my sisters outa the car.

I've put on a polite, calm face to get there, but now my rage starts to fester up again, when I look at Ada drinkin' away and laughin' with Nyunga and walbiya mooga near the campfire. I storm over to her with my little sisters in tow.

When she sees me, the smile on her face turns to moogada.

'How dare you do this to us,' I scream with such force my throat feels raw.

Ada staggers to her feet and I can hear my minya sisters callin' out for her and cryin' behind me.

'Just look at us, Ada. We're bloody starvin' and you're here drinkin' with these arse'oles. You should be fuckin' ashamed of yourself.'

I know I've over-stepped the mark talkin' to Ada like this, and she'll give me a good floggin' now but my rage is beyond control. It's like the weepin' pus inside me is burstin' out, like a big festerin' boil that's reached its limit and is now explodin' all over Ada.

'You filthy mouthed little cow,' is all Ada can manage as she runs towards me like a mad woman. 'How dare you come here and talk to me like that.' Her face has now gone a deeper shade and the veins in her neck are showin'. 'How dare you come here and bring your minya sisters to this place.'

Next thing, we're hittin' at each other. I've never hit Ada before but my rage pushes me forward.

'We're starvin', fuck you. We're starvin', Ada,' I scream between mouthfuls of spit and hair pullin'. 'What kind of a mother are you, lettin' your little girls starve like this?'

Someone comes to pull us apart, and next thing I know we're all bein' driven back to the Mission, Ada as angry as hell and me with the devil in my guru mooga.

Goojarb, I think as we head home. Ada wanna leave us home starvin' like that. I'm glad I shamed her there in front of all them drunken idiots. My minya sisters need her home, I need her home, with us.

18

Growing changes

It's like our big family's slowly breakin' up into minya pieces and driftin' away. First was Papa Neddy, then Old Rod. Mumma's been away, and come back again but I know she'll be goin' soon too. All the aunties have got mudgie mooga now and even Molly's found a mudgie, from Point Pearce, and will probably be marryin' him soon and Mumma will most likely go and live with them. Since Papa died Mumma seems to have got old real quick-way and just isn't up to lookin' after us grannies like she used too. She's more absent-minded, lost in her own thoughts all the time.

With less people in the house workin' there's less food, so we're hungry more often. Although my Uncle Jerry and Uncle Wadu and their wives, Aunty Ruth and Aunty Nora, are real good to us and help to feed us kids, sometimes I feel shame when we eat their food. I'm thinkin' it should be Ada here feedin' us kids, not them, they got their own kids to feed.

Durin' this time, I start to think about food all the time. Is there gonna be enough food to go 'round? Will Ada be home soon with a good feed for us? What am I gonna do if my minya sisters start cryin' hungry-way again? How can I get more food into their little djuda mooga? It was easier when I was younger 'cause I was real clever at survivin' and gettin' food but now there seems to be less options and I have my minya sisters to think about now, too. I remember when I was little goin' over to old Jack and Jude Clare's place and workin' real hard-way, washin' dishes and doin' their floors and hangin' 'round until they'd give me a plate of food. Jack Clare always had work, so his family nearly always had food at their house. Then there used to be old Mr Dempsey who I'd help to do the weedin' and he'd give me money to buy my sultana cake at the Mission shop and if I had enough left over, pineapple juice, bush biscuits and Iced Vovo biscuits. But now Mr Dempsey too old to do his weedin' job on the Mission footpaths and no-one needs me to help them with their work any more, so I can't earn any bunda to buy food.

I try to look after my minya sisters now that Ada isn't home very often. Other than endowment from the government, when Ada's home to buy food with it, and the Mission rations of tea, sugar and flour, we have no food of our own to contribute to our household. We're all that sick of eatin' boonu, a pasty mixture of flour, water and sometimes sugar. Boonu clogs us up and at times we get

so sick of it that we don't even wanna eat it at all. Drippin'
on bread is even a luxury now. And when we get real desperate we go out and chew on sour sobs for a feed when
they're in season but when we eat too many we get djuda
minga. Sometimes I take my sisters out in the scrub to try
to find a feed of Nyunga mai like Mumma, Ada and the
aunties taught me, but it seems to be hard to find 'cause
everyone's cleaned it out close to the Mission, unless we
walk a long way away, and that isn't always safe, 'specially
for the little girls.

I remember when I was Jane and Maddy's age, Mumma
takin' us kids down to the caves along the beach between
Ceduna and Thevenard in the hot weather and gettin' us to
lick the salt off the cave walls. Normally, salt is imin, tabu,
bad or evil, something that might make us sick Nyunga-
way, and we never put it on our meat, but takin' it like
this was all right, it must have been good for our minya
bodies. Mumma knows so much about how to keep us
strong Nyunga-way but now she's growin' old and weak
and everything's changin', even those cliffs near the beach
where Mumma took us when we were younger are startin'
to be washed away by the tides.

Sometimes Dave and Aunty Mim pick us up and take
us to the farm, then we can have a good feed. Durin' these
times, once every now and again, Dave will complain, in
a round-about way, about us girls. It's in the way he says
things and how he acts, and sometimes it makes me feel
a bit shame. But Aunty Mim always reminds him of their
promise to Old Rod before he left for Adelaide and I'm
always real thankful that she and Dave look after us real well

when we spend time with them. Mrs Williams has asked us to call her Grandma now. I think she must know about Old Rod's promise too 'cause she treats us real nice-way.

When Eva comes back for holidays, sometimes Dave and Aunty Mim pick up just the two of us. If Ada's home, she'll look after the minya ones and if not, the aunties and Mumma will, or sometimes we all go together. Other times, they take Eva and me to the football at Charra, a dance, or some walbiya place for a supper. Occasionally, we go to the Children's 'Ome and pick out some second-hand clothes and other times Aunty Mim makes clothes for us to wear. Then she helps us dress up at the farm beforehand.

My most favourite time is when we go to the Charra Hall for tea and a dance after the football 'cause they serve the biggest feed of roast meats, salads and desserts on big trestles. When everyone finishes eatin' they clear the tables and move them and the stools back to the side walls to make space for the dance floor. Then the music starts up and everyone dances away. And even though we don't mix with people much 'cause we're real shy, usually standin' back in the shadows in the corner, we see how them white-fellas behave among themselves and how we're expected to behave when we're 'round them. And even though the whisperin' behind people's murra about us still happens, I don't feel as shame as I usually do. Maybe it's because I'm there with Dave and Aunty Mim and they're married, not like Ada and Old Rod, 'cause he already had a wife.

One day, Dave and Aunty Mim come to pick me up to take me to supper at another farmhouse and lots of other farmers will be there too. I haven't got any clean clothes to wear, only my dirty, old, stained dress and my wrists still have those sores on them.

'We can't take her like that,' Dave says, lookin' me up and down.

I feel real shame. I can't help it if my sores won't go away and that we don't have any money to buy Velvet soap to wash the stains outa my clothes.

'Let her come,' Aunty Mim pleads. Then she turns to me and says, 'Grace, do you wanna come and you can wait in the car for us?'

I nod my head, real pleased. That way I can still go with them to the farm after, for the weekend. I'm glad 'cause I'd rather sit in a car in the dark than stay on the Mission.

Later one of the older walaba girls comes out to the car and gives me a plate of food. I thank her, we talk for a while, and then she goes back inside. It feels strange that a walaba girl is treatin' me nice like that but it makes me feel good inside, too.

As I sit in the car and wait for the supper to finish that night, I think about Ada, how she's changed since Old Rod's died. I wonder what it's like for her now. Did she feel like she was sittin' outside in the dark too, now that the money going into the Mission shop has stopped and her sister, Aunty Mim, was now in charge of the farmhouse? After Old Rod died, Dave and Aunty Mim moved into Old Rod and Grandma Williams' bedroom and Grandma Williams moved into the front room. She kind of disappears into the background after that 'cause she's no longer the main woman runnin' the house, although she's always there supportin' Aunty Mim and helpin' her with the cookin' and housework. But this must be hard for her.

It must be hard for Ada too, to cope with lookin' after us kids by herself, she must be real sad missing Old Rod but it doesn't excuse her for runnin' 'round like she does. I promise myself that when I'm old enough and find a mudgie, I'll get married and not have kids like her and Old Rod. No way will I marry any of those ugly Nyunga boys on the Mission, especially not the ones that call us names. I'll marry a handsome man like the movie stars I've seen in the magazines at the hospital and the films they sometimes show in the Mission hall. And when I have kids, I'll work hard to support my family, and make sure my kids are well fed and looked after. No kids deserve to go through what my sisters and me have been through, and if I have my way my kids never will. But Ada seems to have settled down more now, getting work as a milkmaid on the Mission and so we've got more food and us kids are eatin' better now.

There's a lot of changes for everyone at this time. Everythin' seems to be changin', includin' me. My minya wunyi body's growin' into a woman's and there are things happenin' that I feel shame about. There's no hidin' my mimmi mooga that are growin' out in front of me that I can't cover up even if I stoop forward and put on layers of clothes. The Mission boys seem to be noticin' my changes too. They look me up and down real slow-way, like they're studying me real hard with their goola goola guru mooga, which makes me feel shame and moogada with them too. I want to throw bunda mooga at them and hit them in their stupid heads to stop them starin' at me like that. I don't know what they see in me anyway.

Sometimes I try to see what they see, strainin' my guru mooga in Mumma's little sliver of a mirror near the bowl of water where we cook and sometimes wash our hands, but it's too small to look properly. I can only see one minya part of me at a time: an eye, a nose, part of my mouth. I can't see the full picture of what other people see.

Then one day, on a rare occasion that the Mission bus takes us into town, I stand in front of a shop with my minya sisters pretending to look at the display. Instead I look at my reflection in the window. My hair is shoulder length, thick and wavy, and my figure, slim. As my sisters happily chat away about a dolly they can see, I turn sideways. My mimmi mooga are gettin' bigger, pushin' out from the front of my dress, and my hips more curvy than I remember. But look at those skinny legs. They're just as skinny as when I last looked at them in the mirror at Mona Tareen's, but now they are real long. I look quite tall standin' next to my minya sisters. I can't believe how much I've changed. Is that what them boys see? But true to God, I wish they wouldn't stare the way they do.

Even my smell starts to change, especially under my armpits, my nguggil smell is more like a big woman's now, more like Ada's or Mumma Jenna's. I remember Mumma Jenna smiling at me with her loving eyes as she wipes her murra mooga under her armpits and tells me how her nguggil, when wiped over my minga leg, will make it strong. I know that's not the way whitefellas look at it; they turn their noses up at nguggil, screw up their faces, tell us to go wash ourselves, or just walk away. I think of Old Rod telling us to keep clean and wash ourselves regularly, wash away any trace of those strong powerful smells from our bodies. We're comfortable with our own smell, but walbiya want us to wash it away, want us to smell like them.

With them Mission boys starin' at me, and goin' out with Dave and Aunty Mim, I'm noticing the stains on my dresses now, my dirty legs and my knotted hair, and now I'm always trying to keep clean and tidy. And 'cause we can't get clothes from Mona Tareen's any more, my clothes aren't flash either. Feelin' shame, I often stay at home instead of runnin' 'round and playin' with the other kids on the Mission like I used to.

When I do go out, or to school, the teasing starts again. But now it's about boys. This time it's about a boy called Bradley Winterman. 'Grace loves Bradley Winterman. He's your mudgie, ah, ah, ah.'

'Shut up. He is not,' is all I can manage in my defence.

I'm so moogada with their stupidity. I know Bradley Winterman quite well, he is a quiet boy who lives in the Children's 'Ome and goes to the Mission school but I have no intention of making him my mudgie.

Next it is another boy. 'Grace loves Arnold Clare.'

In the end I just ignore them. I have nothin' but contempt for these boys on the Mission and there is no way I am going to marry any one of them. For starters they're black and all my life they've teased me that I'm a 'whitefella kid' so it seems to me that we don't belong together. And I think all them boys are ugly anyway. Although I have a rough idea that Nyunga-way some of these boys might be the right skin for me to marry. The old Kokatha people on the Mission would know this, if I cared to ask. But I have no intention of listenin' to anybody, 'cause I know they'll want me to stay on the Mission and marry one of those miserable, nasty boys.

Besides, I'm headin' to Adelaide to go to high school soon, and I know from my time in hospital that life in the city is very different from life on the Mission. When I come back I'll see the world differently, just like those other girls who've gone to Adelaide, including Eva. They always seem more confident and use their manners when they come back for holidays. Anyway, I want to be more like them pretty actresses I see in the movies. Then I can find myself a handsome walbiya man to marry like those lady actresses do. They're always so confident and comfortable with their selves too, and wear beautiful clothes and drive in nice big cars like Old Rod's. And I'm always so impressed how they know exactly what to say at the right time and always end up with the most handsome man in the movie.

That's how I wanna be and those ugly boys on the Mission aren't gonna be my boyfriend. With all their teasin' over the years I just don't feel like I belong there anyway. Leavin' is what I really want to do.

19

Wash me away

The following month, as I stand at the back door of our minya cottage, I know the time's comin' soon for me to leave my minya sisters and go to Adelaide to high school. As I watch them playin' out in the backyard sadness sweeps over me and fills my guru mooga with tears. I really don't want to leave them alone but I have no choice. The Superintendent has already made the arrangements for me and Neta Bales to travel on the bus together.

On the other side of the yard, I can see my uncles cleanin' a biggy ngunchu in the metal tub in the shade from the side of the house. This tub is more often used to clean wadu mooga before they get cooked but they've somehow got hold of a biggy ngunchu and are now shaving its dead body with a sharp knife. Uncle Jerry is holding the stiff front legs while Uncle Wadu shaves the back of its fat pink body. Every now and again they wave their hands over their faces to shoo away the yumbra mooga that buzz around.

I want a bath but I'll have to wait 'til they finish cleanin' the biggy ngunchu. The grown-ups mostly use the tub to have baths but sometimes it's used like it is now, for cleanin' dead animals before they're cooked. It's usually left outside 'cause it takes up too much room inside.

A gust of wind whips up around the back of the house. I think of Papa, his spirit movin' through the wurly wurly at his funeral, then me kissing his cold cheek and the blanketie bein' pulled over his face. I shudder. I miss the warm, livin' Papa. He was like the mortar that held our minya cottage together and now it seems that we are slowly crumblin' and tumblin' down. I walk over to the old copper boiler to refill it and heat up the water for my bath.

When my uncles have finished I go over to empty out the tub. There're yumbra mooga floating on the surface of the stinkin' water. Attracted by the smell, they have now drowned. When I empty the tub, they skid over the ground and come to a sticky halt in mud. Then, using all my strength, I drag the tub back towards the front door. As I heave, I can see the tub gougin' a deep line in the dirt behind me. In the past when I decided to have a bath, I'd usually bitten off more than I could chew. The tub was so heavy that nearly always I had to get an adult to help me lift it into our room. And after my bath, it was always too heavy to drag it out again and Ada would growl me for being such a nuisance 'cause she'd have to drag it out herself.

Now that I'm bigger and stronger I can just manage by myself to pull the tub across the yard, through the front door of our cottage and into our bedroom. Nudgin' it into the corner means no-one can see me through the gaps in the door. The hinges are loose so even when the door's closed, if you look real hard, you can see through into the bedroom.

After the copper boiler heats up, I pop a bar of Velvet soap into the tub, then cart bucket after bucket into the bedroom, pourin' the steamin' water into the tub until it's deep enough for a nice bath. I slip off my clothes and step into the tub with one leg. The water's hot. I pull my leg straight back out and I can see my skin is red. Grabbin' at the edges of the metal tub, I lower my leg back in a little longer until my skin adjusts to the heat, then I step into the tub with the other leg. As I gently lower myself into the hot soapy bath the smoky blue metal sides of the tub feel hot in the palms of my hands.

My knees are drawn up close to my body because the tub's small, round shape doesn't allow me to stretch out. I can only roll my body sideways. There's no chance of being completely submerged, but the water that laps at my shoulders and the top of my knees feels relaxin'. I grab my ankles and squeeze the tension out of my body. Closin' my eyes, it feels good to let go of all the stresses I've been carryin' around inside me for so long, just lettin' them wash into the water. My breath begins to deepen and slow down as I melt into the warmth. Openin' my eyes, I can see dirt streakin' down my legs from the layers of mud on my knees so I feel for the Velvet soap on the bottom of the tub. It slips from my fingers a couple of times until I grab it with two hands and bring it to the surface. I turn the soap in an old cloth until it's slimy with suds, then let it slip back into the depths below. I move the cloth over my knees and legs, around the back of my neck and over my shoulders and under my armpits, washin' my body in all the places that are in need of washin', washin' away all my stinkin' smells. It feels so deadly to be sittin' in the water and cleanin' myself like this.

In front of me, above the water line, I can see small biggy ngunchu hairs stuck to the inside of the tub. Or is it wombat hair? I try not to think about the things I've seen being cleaned in this tub. Kicking my foot through the water at the end of the tub I wash the hairs away and still my mind, trying to wipe it clear too. I tap my foot in the bath and the water turns into a chant.

'Williams' Pigs, Williams' Pigs, Williams' Pigs. You're nothin' but Williams' Pigs.'

A sickenin' understandin' washes over me with the lappin' of the water. They called us Williams' Pigs because we're Old Rod's stock, sloppin' in his pig troughs, bein' thrown his scraps. I shudder again. Although I feel clean on the outside, and even though the sores on my wrist have now cleared up, the festerin' filth is still inside me. Out of the blue this feeling comes up and falls, appears and disappears again. Sometimes it lies quiet, forgotten. That's how I like it, hidden and invisible, but here it is again rearin' its ugly head as I wash myself clean in a bath. Will I ever feel clean?

Lyin' back in the bath I think about how things have been for me and what it might be like for me headin' over to live in Adelaide with Eva and the other girls from the Mission. I'm scared for myself and for my minya sisters but

I can't wait to get off the Mission away from all those rotten, mean kids who've made my life a misery as far back as I can remember. And I'm nervous too, I know how walbiya mooga have funny ways, how they can cut you down with a nasty word or even with just a glance, ignore you, pretend you're not there and treat you like dirt. Goin' to Adelaide means I'll be at their mercy. But at least I'll be with Eva and the other girls and we can stick together, look out for each other, like Mission mob do when they leave town.

In more recent times, Eva and me have learnt a lot about how walbiya mooga live from our trips to the farm and outings with Dave and Aunty Mim and maybe this will help us cope better. Eva and me have learnt to clean. And we've learnt a lot when we help with the cookin', what the different frypans, saucepans, and kitchen pots and pans are used for, and how spices and herbs are used in the mai. And makin' the beds that have sheets on them, and showerin', brushin' our teeth, and washin' our face every morning with a flannel and towel, and usin' a brush or comb, not a fork, to do our hair. We've learnt how to set the table with all the forks, knives and spoons, how the plates and glasses are set out, and how everyone sits around the table at breakfast, dinner and tea time, what they eat and how they act by using walbiya manners. We've learnt so much in just a short space of time. I'm sure knowin' all these things will help us when we're goin' into the walbiya world. Sometimes Dave and Aunty Mim even take us into Ceduna with them for shoppin' and other times down the beach. Sometimes it's hard to go back to the Mission after the luxuries and comforts of the farmhouse.

The bath water has soaked my fingers 'til they're all wrinkly like a gubarlie or tjilbi. I think about Old Rod again, and how I tried to work out the riddle of who he was, and how even when I did, it didn't solve anything for me 'cause I still felt I didn't belong anywhere. And nothin's changed. I'm still a blackfella who's a whitefella's kid, a big shame job to Nyunga and walbiya mooga on the Mission, and to walbiya mooga in town. It's like they've thrown a blanketie over us, the children of a black woman and a white man. We're hated on one side for bein' whitefella kids, and on the other side for bein' Old Rod Williams' bastard kids. Us girls don't fit in anywhere, just one big shame job place set aside just for us to live, like a sty for pigs.

I realise that Old Rod wasn't just cryin' about his sins that day in his car, he was cryin' about what he'd done to us. He'd brought us into the world to be hated by everyone. Sometimes, I even feel like Ada hates us too. Maybe she hates herself for what she's done.

I slide forward and dunk my head under the water, lettin' the air in my lungs bubble to the top. I hate myself too, I think, as the last of the bubbles pop on the surface. I hate myself for bein' here in this place and for being despised by everyone. I break the surface of the water and gasp for air. Maybe, I'm already in hell with fire and brimstone and that's God's way of punishin' me for who I am.

The water in the tub laps in big waves, some splashin' over the edge of the tub. Maybe things'll change when I go to school in the city. Other girls that come back from there seem different, know more, are sure of themselves. Maybe that will happen to me too.

My thoughts swirl around with the suds. Tiltin' my head back I stare at the wall, all the stains and marks from me and my sisters over the years. The kitchen walls and floors are like that too. No matter how hard Mumma, Ada and the aunties have scrubbed our cottage over the years it is still caked with dirt. But somehow it doesn't matter, the main thing for Mumma, for all of us, is that we're with Mumma and we're safe and together. Mumma must be feelin' sad with her family goin' away, makin' their own lives. I look up and see a loose spiderweb floatin' in the corner of the ceilin'. All her family have just drifted away.

I think back to when I lay on the bed with my jinna minga and how the old fellas growled me for runnin' 'round dangerous places, dangerous campsites to step on mumoo. How shame I felt when they accused me of that. I feel that shame now, but for different reasons. I remember the relief I felt when my old Jumoo told me I didn't have a mumoo inside my leg. I let go of that shame, only for it to jump back into me again when he told me I had walbiya gu minga inside my leg.

I shudder. I was so scared, wonderin', 'What is this walbiya gu minga? How did it get there?' Then, I was sent away for all that time, not bein' able to see my family for so long. Somethin' started to die inside me then, somethin' that connected me strong-way to my family, somethin' that guided me, Nyunga-way, right-way. After that it was like I was sittin' back and lookin' at everyone 'round me in a different way. Sure I came back ahead with my studies but somethin' had shifted inside me. That walbiya gu minga in my leg was like a poison, makin' me sick from deep inside.

Not knowin' who I was, was eatin' away at me too. When they cut me open and scraped the white man's sickness outa me, only then could I get better. But I can't scrape the whiteness outa me. I can't scrape out that shame of who I am.

Lookin' at the sun stream into the minya dusty window on the side wall, I think that knowin' who my father was made me feel good but when he left it felt like a part of me died too. Maybe not knowin' made me sick in the first place. Anyway, I'm still a bastard, a child born from my parents breakin' the fourth Commandment. God wouldn't want me this way so I might as well curl up and die.

I close my guru mooga shut tight-way again and lean forward, my head between my legs, try to think of some good things, nice things, things that make me feel better. I see Ada dressed in deadly white clothes goin' to a tennis match at Charra, to play against walaba weena mooga. She looks real graceful as she throws the tennis ball high in the air and slams it into the court on the other side of the net. The walaba weena jumps out the way to stop the ball hittin' her and Ada wins the point. I feel real proud of her, she's a deadly player always thrashin' those other weena mooga and she looks real yudoo in her white tennis bultha. I always wanna touch her clothes 'cause they look so pretty, so fresh and clean. I reach my murra up, wanting to stroke the nice fabric.

'Get your bugadee murra off my bultha,' I hear her growl me, slappin' my hand away.

I look up at her sad-way. 'It's real pretty, Ada,' I say, but she pushes me away.

I step back and look at my hands. They have dirt all over them. I look down at my dress, it's streaked with dirt, so are my legs and my feet.

I cover my face now with my clean hands and start cryin'. 'I'm lookin' forward to this big adventure to the city, away from everythin' that I hate so much,' I tell myself. 'Everythin' will get better once I'm there and my sisters will be safe.'

The water is gettin' cold so I get out of the tub and dry myself with some old clothes, then put on a dress that I've picked out from the Children's 'Ome. I haven't realised that I'm still cryin' until my tears drip onto my clean dress. The hidden wave washes up again and I throw myself on our bed, breathin' out deep loud sobs.

'Grace?' Mumma's old voice is close to my yuree. She cups her wrinkled hands under my chin and turns my face to look at hers. 'Why you look so sad, girl? It's not the end of the world, you know.'

I grab her hand and squeeze it, holdin' tight as I can.

'Oh, Mumma.' Tears runnin' down my face. 'I hate my life so much. I hate this Mission and the nasty kids here. I hate how Ada leaves us kids the way she does, I just hate who I am and I just wanna die.'

Mumma sits down next to me then and puts her hand over my shoulder and pulls me into her mimmi like she use to when I was little. 'You listen here now, girl,' she says. 'You gotta stop this feelin' sorry for yourself. You're special young woman and those kids see that in you so they wanna pull you down but you'll only be pulled down if you let it happen. You just gotta walk with your head high like our Old People and stop feelin' so sorry for yourself.'

Mumma's dress is wet from my sobbin'.

'I'm not special. I'm whitefella bastard kid,' I blubber.

Mumma sighs. 'You remember that story I told you 'bout your Granny Charlie that time at Denial Bay?'

I nod. I can recall what she said about Granny being strong and standin' for things that are wrong, and how sometimes, when you're beaten and put down all the time, you start believin' you're low and you look 'round at your own mob and start thinkin' the same about them too. So you start actin' that way towards yourself with no respect, and towards your own mob disrespectful-way, too. Mumma was right, but hell it isn't easy to look at things that way, 'specially when what people say hurts so much.

'You be proud of who you are, Kokatha and walaba. There's no shame in that. The Good Lord made you that way, girl.'

'But I've been born from breaking his Commandment.'

'Now don't you go talkin' like that, Grace. We've all been born into sin, that's what Pastor always says. God loves each and every one of his children and through his Son Jesus dyin' on the cross, all our sins are washed away and don't you forget that.'

I sit up and wipe my face on my dress. Mumma pulls me into her again.

'What about my minya sisters when I go to Adelaide? What if you go, Mumma, who will look after them?'

Mumma gives a big sigh and rubs my arm.

'Ada's just goin' through a bit of a hard time, tryin' to cope with Old Rod's passin'. She'll settle down properly again soon, and I won't be goin' anywhere until she does.'

We sit down on the bed together and Mumma continues. 'Everyone has their own way of copin' when a loved one dies.' Mumma's voice sounds sad and distant. She pushes my wet hair away from my face. 'She might even find a husband now, nice fella to look after her and them minya ones properly.'

I turn towards her and think of Papa.

'As you grow older, Grace,' Mumma goes on, 'you'll find the wisdom to know what you can change and what you can't. The Good Lord will give you that wisdom if you pray and ask 'im for it.'

I nod again, to her familiar words.

'You must never lose faith in God, and never forget who you are. Will you promise me that?' She looks at me with old knowin' eyes.

Somethin' happened then, I sat up and wiped my eyes. Mumma always has a way of making you feel better about yourself but this was different. It was as if suddenly I knew what I had to do and where I was goin'. I was leavin' the Mission and makin' a new life for myself. In my mind I was already there. I was free at last. Soon my bag was packed. I was saying my goodbyes, I was ready to go.

Author's note

My mother and I are Kokatha women. We are of the south-eastern group of the Western Desert peoples who, by traditional Aboriginal lore and Kokatha custom, are inseparably connected to and with the areas in and around the Yellabinna Regional Reserve and Wilderness Protection Area, Yumbarra Conservation Park, Pureba Conservation Park, extending just west of Fowlers Bay, to the east of Elliston following our Dreaming tracks towards Port Augusta, where our country takes in sections of the Gawler Ranges in South Australia.

The Kokatha language place names along these Dreaming tracks are evidence of our connection to country. My mother, her mother and grandmothers all lived on the Koonibba Lutheran Mission on the far west coast of South Australia, and always travelled beyond the Mission to maintain our country. Although today my family, my mother and I still hold strong to our Kokatha culture and language, we have had to fight colonial forces ploughing through the landscape of our Aboriginal identity from frontier times to the present. Over the years, government bodies, policies and institutions have all had a massive impact on our Aboriginal country, culture and sense of self.

The storytelling process is important to us because of its capacity to tell truths overlooked by history as a Western discipline, and to challenge non-Aboriginal historical and current accounts, and acts of colonisation. Hearing a story in our own voice, in our own language, in our own way of speaking – and from our own perspectives as Aboriginal people – can be empowering. But it can potentially also bring about understanding and healing. This has been my mother's experience in telling her story, and it has been my experience too.

'You're Aboriginal. Always be proud of that.'

My mother's words are etched in my mind. As a child I saw my world in two parts: me as an Aboriginal person, and everything and everyone outside of that as separate. At a very young age, growing up in Ceduna in the 1970s, I realised that Aboriginal people were treated differently by others, spoken about negatively: we were perceived as being 'less' than everyone else. I also saw the distress this caused my mother and other Aboriginal family and community members.

Yet I knew, from what my mother had taught me, that being who I was, an Aboriginal person, was a good thing: everyone who treated us differently from that belief was wrong in their negative actions towards us, and should be questioned or challenged. It was very complex, often distressing and even traumatising (and at times it still is), especially given that we lived in a small rural town with many people who had openly racist attitudes. Sometimes it was very confusing: we grew up under the assimilation policy that encouraged Aboriginal people to marry into and blend with the white community, but my siblings and I didn't look all that dissimilar to others in the community. Yet there were always times when we were set apart for who we were as Aboriginal people, sometimes in the most painful, discriminating, and humiliating ways.

My mother wanted her story to be told. She wanted:

> to describe what it's like for me and other Aboriginal people living in this area between black and white, it will help people to understand our situation. We were Aboriginal children who were basically powerless, and had no recognition of our paternity. We were denied our rights on our white side, who considered us nobodies. And those same people stole our Aboriginal land, our hunting grounds, to build their wealth while we remained in poverty struggling to survive.

Mum often describes herself as being 'caught between two worlds', a place that marks her as different and sets her apart. As a child her worldview was that of an

Aboriginal person, but she says her illegitimate status and being fathered by a white man sometimes separated her from other Aboriginal people on the Mission.

In the early stages of writing Mum's story, I spent a lot of time undertaking archival research in the State Library of South Australia, the Family History Unit of the South Australian Museum, State Records, Special Collections in the Barr Smith Library and Lutheran Archives, looking at documents and photos relating to our Kokatha ancestry. Many hours were spent in reading rooms, searching catalogues, taking notes and connecting hundreds of pieces of information. To make sense of all this data I created a massive timeline on butcher's paper. It spanned several metres – from invasion to the mission era – listing all the government policies through to the present. I also included family members: births, deaths, marriages, dwellings, photographs, maps of grave sites, and leases of land, dating back to the 1800s, belonging to Mum's white ancestors. Almost every detail that I uncovered and collected was recorded on this one big sheet: a visual document of the existence of both our Aboriginal and white lineage.

During this time I often broke down and cried at the reality, so clear in my visual representation, of colonial destruction and what it revealed: plummeting Aboriginal population numbers through disease; frontier conflict; diminishing Aboriginal hunting grounds and food; starvation; rape of our Aboriginal girls and women; the Elliston massacre that involved our people being rounded up and pushed off a cliff to their deaths (Aboriginal oral history places one of our grandmothers several generations ago as a child survivor of this massacre). Our people were corralled onto missions like cattle and dispossessed of our traditional territories. And, although denied our right to practise our culture and language, we continued to, out of the authorities' sights.

There is a point, a 'fissure', in this timeline, where the lineages of black and white meet. It occurs when my grandmother, a twenty-two-year-old Kokatha woman meets my mother's father, a forty-three-year-old white man. It is near this point in the timeline that *Mazin Grace* is set.

Some of the field notes that I read – as a Kokatha descendant three and four generations on from the Kokatha 'subjects' that were researched by non-Aboriginal so-called experts – include obvious inaccuracies in language and cultural data. I recognised the inaccuracies because of my family's oral traditions, which were passed down to me from my mother, aunties and grandmothers, through ancestors, and through countless generations. It was obvious that these non-Aboriginal people had little understanding of how Kokatha culture and lore worked, and that vital information would not have been shared with or open to them – because it was closed knowledge. These same people also informed racist government policies and legislation, such as the assimilation policy that has caused much destruction in Aboriginal communities. Further damage continues to occur when inaccurate information is used to support native title claims over wrong sections of country, as we Kokatha people are currently experiencing, with others claiming areas of our country where we still perform our cultural obligations to keep country alive and strong.

Despite the restrictions that came with the government policies of the day and the strict Mission rules that limited cultural activities, some cultural knowledge was still passed on to the younger generations. Mum often speaks of the strength and resilience of the Aboriginal people she grew up with on the Mission, and much of this has been documented in *Mazin Grace*.

Sometimes during the research and writing of this book, I felt extremely uncomfortable that my mother had asked me to seek out her father's story. But I honored her request, and in so doing found rich material in the archives and elsewhere. One of the main sources was a book by members of his family titled *Pioneers in South Australia*, published in 1988 by the Oliver and Sara Haseldine and Descendants Association. The genealogy that unfolds in this book omits my Aboriginal grandmother, and my mother and her siblings, despite the fact that other children born out of wedlock are listed in other sections of the family ancestry. I also discovered there was another daughter fathered by my grandfather, and born to an Aboriginal woman before his relationship with my grandmother, who was not included in the genealogy either. It would appear that people in this branch of the family did not want to share these 'shameful secrets' with their white relatives.

To me, and to Mum, it was just another cover-up of the facts of family history, another example of colonial blanketing of the truth.

★

From the beginning, my mother was very clear about how she wanted the story of her early years told. She did not want me to scribe her memoir. She was adamant that her life be written in a way that invited the reader into her life experiences as a child. Mum wanted readers to be able to exist in *her* space: to be immersed in the emotions she felt as a illegitimate Aboriginal child of mixed ancestry growing up on a Lutheran mission in South Australia in the 1940s and 1950s, but with strong links to her Aboriginal family and country.

We both faced many challenges during the writing of Mum's story. When she spoke through the perspective of her child-self from the past, she carried the same emotional experience to the present time. In listening to her story and discerning the emerging themes of her life, I recognised feelings from my own childhood: shame, guilt, self-hate. Sometimes Mum's story took both of us to deeply traumatic places. And at these times there did not seem to be a clear or safe way forward.

Deciding on a writing style also took some time. Mum wanted her voice to be as authentic as possible. Finally, after exploring many techniques, we decided on a first-person narrative using my mother's voice as a child, expressed in Aboriginal English and Kokatha language.

Mum and I spoke at length to various family members about the writing of her story and these discussions helped shape this book. But Mum decided that people's names should be changed to fictional ones. It was one thing to try to tell a story as close to the truth of her life as possible, but quite another thing to be held to each individual's account of that reality.

I understood that even though much of Western story-telling was essentially linear in structure, Aboriginal stories were often cyclic in their telling. Although it was important for me to see this book as a work of fiction, it was also critical that, as faithfully as possible, it followed the shape, form and sequence of Mum's narrative. I listened carefully to Mum's stories and their patterns and recorded them as accurately as I could, following the natural flow of the Aboriginal English and Kokatha language, and the movements and perceptions of the book's narrator – Grace.

So while the Kokatha cultural memory might be strongly represented in the story, my freedom in the writing process was somewhat limited. In this sense I was bound by my cultural responsibility to tell a communal story, not one that I myself might choose to write, drawing on techniques learnt and crafted over the years.

Mum's academic background was an immense advantage to me when it came to unpacking her story, exploring narrative approaches and finally writing the book. My mother had studied for her honors degree in anthropology at the University of Adelaide, and therefore had knowledge of the history and dominant white discourses of that discipline. But at the same time she also had an insider's view of her Aboriginal community and cultural experience. What a powerful position.

Many complex issues arose as Mum's story touched on the white privilege of the workers on the Mission and the broader white community of the rural west coast districts, of which her father was a part. More complex was the white privilege that existed within the Aboriginal community and was played out between family groups and individuals, and racist government policies like assimilation were at the core of it: if Aboriginal people 'acted' white, they were rewarded. If they had a fairer complexion, they were seen by white society in both a positive and negative light. A common Western belief at the time, stemming from Social Darwinism, held that the more white blood an Aboriginal person had running through their veins, the more intelligent they were, and thus the greater likelihood of successful assimilation.

But lightness could also mean that a child was at greater risk of being taken away from their family by state welfare bodies. Moreover, according to Western social mores in the 1940s and 1950s, whiteness within an Aboriginal person signified 'shame'; it represented the 'unholy', 'unnatural' union of black and white, in most cases white men and black women who were not married but produced mixed-race children, who were often denied by their white fathers.

All of these factors would have impacted heavily on the sense of self of Aboriginal people on the Mission. What took place was an internalisation of Western value systems, which, in more recent times, has come to be called 'lateral violence' in the Aboriginal community.

When the assimilation policy was officially introduced by government in the 1950s, Aboriginal people were suddenly expected to act white despite the fact that racism marked them as black with all the associated stereotypes and deficit representations. The intention of the assimilationist policy was to cancel out black identity and fully immerse Aboriginal people in white Australian society. The level of confusion this created for Aboriginal people at the time was enormous, and the impacts are still felt today.

In more recent years our Kokatha family and people have faced the intellectual property theft of our Aboriginal culture, knowledge and language by what we term 'Aboriginal cultural piracy'. This situation has largely been brought about by the ignorance of non-Aboriginal so-called experts. In our case, anthropologists and linguists have taken our Kokatha knowledges and language and have misrepresented both, and us – in some instances reframing our Kokatha culture as the lost knowledges and language of an allegedly other cultural group: Wirangu. Our strong oral traditions tell us otherwise.

In the 1990s, an academic linguist came into our Kokatha community and used my grandmother Pearl, her sister Millie and other fluent Kokatha speakers as Aboriginal informants. Nana and the others believed that the linguist was recording their language in order to produce a Kokatha dictionary, and so were happy to contribute to this research. Only later did the linguist tell them they were speaking Wirangu. Nana Pearl refuted this claim. As far as she was concerned, it was ridiculous. She and the other nanas knew their Kokatha language and culture. It had been taught to them by their Kokatha elders for many generations. Nonetheless, the linguist went away and produced a Wirangu Aboriginal dictionary on the basis of that research, which was later published.

My nana Pearl went to her grave with the belief that

her Kokatha language had been stolen and 'reclaimed' as Wirangu. Now in their seventies and eighties, the other nanas never once heard the word Wirangu when they were growing up on the west coast of South Australia – not once. I am just grateful that Nana Pearl did not live to see the ongoing Wirangu language programs that continue to perpetuate this act of Aboriginal cultural piracy.

For me, writing Mum's story has been an enormous privilege, an act of social justice and cultural survival, and, importantly, a journey of healing. But I'll let Mum have the last word:

> What's important here is that I have been able to heal from this process. I have been able to reclaim a little bit of my past that has been denied me – to partially fill the emptiness. And yes, understanding is important here too. It's always been an important reason why I've wanted my story told, so others, whether they be black, white, or in that space between, can better understand.

Author Dylan Coleman (*left*) with her mother, Mercy Glastonbury,
after her PhD graduation ceremony in 2011.
(Photograph courtesy of Janette Milera)

Acknowledgments

I acknowledge my Kokatha ancestors, who are ever-present and guiding me through life.

I would like to thank my mum, Mercy Glastonbury, for sharing the laughter and tears of your childhood and for trusting me to write your story. This journey with you has been both a privilege and a wonderful gift. Also to my many family members and friends (too numerous to mention individually, but you all know who you are), especially my nanas, aunties and sisters – especially to my sister Tammy Edwardson for her support throughout my life and her encouragement in the writing of our Mum's story – thank you for your input and shared ongoing support. Over the years it has kept me going. Thanks to my dad, George Mastrosavas, for encouraging me to document your story, which set me on the path to writing.

This journey would not have possible without the understanding, patience and support of Aaron Williams, and my son, Wunna Coleman-Goddard. Sometimes words like 'deep feelings of gratitude' fall short of conveying meaning. All I can offer are the two humble words 'thank you', then expand them to infinity.

Thank you to the Creative Writing Program at the University of Adelaide, in particular my PhD supervisor, Dr Sue Hosking, for your exceptional academic support, and for your sensitivity and understanding during the difficult times of writing *Mazin Grace*. Thank you to my co-supervisors, Dr Jan Harrow, Dr Nicholas Jose and Dr Mandy Treagus. Also, thank you to Professor Thomas Shapcott and my fellow creative writing students at the University of Adelaide.

To Marg Bowman, for mentoring me during my PhD, and for your exceptional editorial support over the years, which has helped me in the development of my writing craft – a big thank you. Also thanks to ArtsSA, for the editorial mentorship funding to work with Marg to complete my first manuscript, my father's story, which was later shortlisted for the 2011 David Unaipon Award. This mentorship helped to set the foundation for *Mazin Grace*.

Thank you also to staff and students within the University of Adelaide's School of Population Health and Clinical Practice, especially Associate Professor Jenny Baker and Professor Annette Braunack-Mayer, for the time you afforded me in the last stages of my PhD, as well as the Yaitya Purruna Indigenous Health Unit, Wiltu Yarlu Aboriginal Education, and the Barr Smith Library. Over the years I have received a lot of support from within the university environment, for which I am extremely grateful. A very special thank you to dearest friends Dr Olga Gostin and Susan Cole, for your support over the years within (and outside) the university and in my personal life, and most of all for believing in me from the beginning.

To my dear friends of the South Australian Indigenous Storytellers and Writers Group, who have provided fantastic support and encouragement over the years – a heartfelt thank you.

Thank you to my dear friends and colleagues in the Aboriginal Political Party Movement, who have been a lifeline and who have sustained my belief that social justice and change is possible through persistence.

Thank you to Ali Abdullah-Highfold, Aboriginal Family History Officer at the South Australian Museum, and to the Lutheran Church of Australia Archives in Adelaide, for permission to reprint our family photograph on the back cover of *Mazin Grace*.

And, importantly, thank you to Dr Janet Hutchinson, for your exceptional editorial support for *Mazin Grace*, and to UQP publishers Madonna Duffy and John Hunter, senior editor Rebecca Roberts, editorial assistant Ella Jeffery, marketing and publicity manager Meredene Hill, and rights assistant Simon Stack, who have made this experience an enjoyable and enlightening one.

Lastly, thank you to all of those who made the Queensland Premier's Literary Awards possible. Such initiatives are enormously important in growing and maintaining authentic and vital Australian literature and should be supported. Without this award, Grace's voice may not have been heard.

About the David Unaipon Award

Established in 1988, the David Unaipon Award is an annual literary competition for unpublished manuscripts in any writing genre or Indigenous language by an Aboriginal or Torres Strait Islander writer.

The award is named after David Unaipon (1872–1967), who, in 1929, was the first Indigenous author to be published in Australia. He was also a political activist, a scientist, a preacher and an inventor. David Unaipon was born in Point McLeay in South Australia and is commemorated on the $50 note.

This prize is judged and chosen by a panel of established Indigenous authors and a representative of University of Queensland Press. The author of the winning manuscript is mentored and the work published by University of Queensland Press.

Previous winners of the award include Tara June Winch, Gayle Kennedy, Sam Wagan Watson, Larissa Behrendt, and Nicole Watson. Jeanine Leane's *Purple Threads*, which won the 2010 David Unaipon Award, was shortlisted for the Commonwealth Book Prize in 2012.